When the hur--- form of the Eye had gone, Nanos looked into th— —————————— Eye was still there – still cl—

Nanos per—  ned a waterproof —————————————— —un- dred discs, ea—————————————— that had been m—————————————— and instruction —————————————— Very carefully, as if he were ———————— osive, Nanos manipulated, with the aid of forceps, one of the discs into the pupil of his own right eye.

Within seconds, he was writhing in agony. It was as if a hot pin had pierced his retina. Terrible shapes swam before him. He experienced all the pain of the centuries. It was as if the Four Horsemen of the Apocalypse were galloping through his brain. Nanos screamed a scream of such terror that the Innuendo guards outside feared to enter the laboratory. By the time they summed up sufficient courage, it was too late.

Nanos the dwarf lay in a crumpled, disfigured heap upon the ground. His fingers had plucked out his own eyes. His skin was marred by deep scratches. His brain was pulp.

One of the guards vomited. The other assisted him outside. They stumbled towards their barracks and their commander. The Eye strolled into the laboratory unobserved. He leaned over the dwarf's hideous corpse. "Thou shalt not steal," he said icily. He snatched up the box containing his precious, tiny personality memory discs.

The Eye exited the building like a wisp of smoke escaping a fire, like a passing shadow in the dusk.

But this shadow would not pass. It would darken the Earth.

THE NOVEL OF QUEEN THE eYe

BOXTREE

"For Janet – always"

First published 1997 by Boxtree,
an imprint of Macmillan Publishers Ltd
25 Eccleston Place, London, SW1W 9NF
and Basingstoke

Associated companies throughout the world

ISBN 0 7522 0371 1

Copyright © 1996 Queen Productions Limited

All rights reserved. No part of this publication may be reproduced, stored in or introduced into a retrieval system, or transmitted, in any form, or by any means (electronic, mechanical, photocopying, recording or otherwise) without the prior written permission of the publisher. Any person who does any unauthorized act in relation to this publication may be liable to criminal prosecution and civil claims for damages.

9 8 7 6 5 4 3 2 1

A CIP catalogue record for this book is available
from the British Library

Typeset by SX Composing DTP, Rayleigh, Essex
Printed and bound in Great Britain by
Mackays of Chatham PLC

Prologue

*"Cast a cold eye
On life, on death"*
W. B. Yeats

In the beginning of the end there was, "The Eye". From whence It came, by whom or by what It was made, is not known. It is because It is there. Here, there and everywhere, It is unconquered. No one and nothing has succeeded in closing the Eye. From the beginning of time to time's end, the Eye will have seen, will see, forever.

The Eye may never die, but It should. Be in no doubt, this is an evil Eye and It will triumph over all the Earth and beyond until and unless It is destroyed.

Why destroy It? Because It is there.

The Eye opened and did what any eye would do. He watched. He watched centuries roll by. He watched every living thing on Earth. He saw wars and pestilences, famines and deaths and he learned, by such observation, almost all there is to know. The Eye never closed and missed nothing. There was a Universe, a million unseen stars, but the Eye saw only the Earth. It held his complete, malicious attention.

In a world of humans, who close their two eyes in sleep and in ignorance, the ever-open Eye would surely be a king.

One of the lessons he learned, and would never forget, was that the most dangerous animal on Earth and beyond was the human. Each human being represented death – on two legs.

The Eye recorded the ways of humans so that, when the time came, as it surely would, he could copy them. It would not be the flattery of imitation, but a means by which he could better know his enemy in order to destroy it.

The Eye had decided, godlike, but not entirely upon a whim, that most of the human race would be annihilated. It was logic that dictated this course of action. If humans were permitted to continue in the style of their ancestors, their greed, arrogance and selfishness would lead to inevitable conflagration and the annihilation of the Earth itself. This could not be allowed to happen. The Earth was far too beautiful and the Eye had an eye for beauty.

The human race conspired in ignorance to despoil the Earth. The globe warmed, the forests were felled, the seas became cesspits of human detritus, the rivers were fouled with waste. The human race danced the dance of oblivion.

This was fine by the Eye, except that the humans, in a rage of self destruction, would take the Earth with them and where would the Eye hide then? The mountains of the Moon were inhospitable, the Sun too hot, and none of the other planets could offer anything to compare with this world, the jewel of the Universe. Though he knew a lot, the Eye was not omnipotent. He had seen the past, watched anxiously over the present, but could not imagine the future.

He needed to exert his influence over the Earth and the only way he could do so was by assuming human shape or, better still, many human shapes. Could it be done?

If he was anything, the Eye was patient. He had no other choice. But his patience had an incomparable ally – Time. Time that, while it permitted the Eye to accumulate knowledge, permitted the human race to do the same. If not on the same scale.

The Eye had to admit that humans could be resourceful and, like himself, were not averse to the learning process. They had conquered the air, captured fire, controlled water and cultivated the earth. They could, and would, go further.

They did. After slow centuries of progress, the human race exploded into action. In one century, the twentieth, they developed their resources beyond the wildest dreams of their ancestors. The automobile, the airplane, nuclear fission, jet propulsion, an army of medicines, the microchip, the holograph, the list was endless and the Eye was very impressed. Sooner than he had anticipated, it was his guess that his time was at hand. He knew that, however advanced humans became, there was an atavistic pitilessness within them that would seek, at whatever cost, to continue that advance. The weak would go to the wall and the poor would become slaves. Only the ruthless would survive. There would be nothing more ruthless than the Eye itself.

Father Time nudged Mother Nature and the Earth's sleeping tigress awakened in a fury.

The Eye was alarmed. Nature had the power to do what he himself intended. Such a pre-emptive strike would ruin all of his plans. If it had been possible, the Eye would have held its breath.

Nature erupted. She conjured up earthquakes and attendant tidal waves of epic proportions. She caused the islands known as Japan to disintegrate and eliminated the western seaboard of the Americas by drowning it in the now less-than-Pacific Ocean. Simultaneously, she melted Arctic and Antarctic icecaps and caused hot winds to surge north and south and collide at the Equator. Electrical storms pranced over the

Earth and satellites fell from the skies. Rivers dried up and the heat of the Sun fired the grasslands. Not since Noah's flood had the Earth seen such devastation. The Eye had witnessed that flood. It was the only time in history that it had blinked.

But Nature was kinder than the Eye. Destruction was not completed and the resourcefulness of the human race was allowed to flourish once more, albeit, on a lesser scale. The Earth's Southern Hemisphere was a desert inhabited by vicious or terrified sub-humans. In the East there were several millions desperate for water and for food. The West was wild and desolately beautiful. Only the strong would survive there.

The Eye looked North. The industrialised North had remained relatively intact. Its canyoned cities had withstood the tempest. Its resources of fuel and food were well saved. Its always arrogant inhabitants imagined they could rule the world. Well, now they did.

Nature had withheld her Armageddon, but the Eye would not be so generous. If only he could manifest himself. He chuckled. Of course. Mankind itself must assist the Eye in his imitation. Thus it could be said that humans, as ever, would be responsible for their own fate. A fate they would inadvertently gift to the Eye.

*

Half a century passed. This was but a twinkling for the Eye.

A new kind of world order had been established by, inevitably, the powerful forces of the industrialised North. The South was a target for rehabilitation and the North's new army prepared to invade it. This same army held at bay the sick Eastern hordes. It marauded in the West. It was an army the like of which the world had never seen. Well trained, well equipped, highly intelligent, highly motivated, its soldiers considered themselves as strong as prides of lions and strutted about like peacocks. It was assisted by the very latest technology, meaning that which had survived Nature's holocaust. This army was under the nominal control of The Leader, a far from benevolent character who indulged himself in all the vices of humankind and, because he was who he was, could not be denied. His titular superior, known as The President – found it hard to keep the Leader in check. He managed to do so simply because he and his like-minded Committee controlled the means by which the army functioned.

The President's Committee ruled the world. Or thought it did. Apart from the President himself and the Leader, there were two others – The Mother and The Notary. The Mother supervised the needs of the people by managing the supply of foodstuffs, water, medicines and the like. The

Notary was a scientist, forever seeking new means of creation and destruction. Of course, there were subordinates. Well fed and well flattered, they were unlikely to bite the hands of their benefactors, or close their ears to fawning words.

Nonetheless, a section of the army was deployed to ensure loyalty. Each member of the Committee was attended by his, or her, own troop. The President's troop was titled, The Arena; the Leader's was called, The Works; the Mother's, The Theatre; the Notary's, Innuendo.

The Eye saw all this come about and was impressed. His mind attuned to humanity, he decided, for the moment, to concentrate his gaze upon the Notary, the scientist. He it would be who would initially assist the Eye's ambitions. But this Notary would require some encouragement.

The Eye saw where it was. Somewhere that, inexplicably, had never been discovered by any Human. Humans had passed close by, but there are none so blind as those that cannot see. The Eye existed at the undiscovered source of the world's greatest river – the Amazon.

For centuries mankind had sought out this source. Some claimed to have found it, but they were always wrong, always a kilometre or two astray. But, history was about to be made because Nature, too sentimental for the Eye's liking, rested on her laurels and, whilst eliminating many other waters, permitted the Amazon and its source to survive in all its former glory. A glory that the Eye would share with mankind, his chosen ally for the present, his certain enemy of the future. He remained patient as a small group of explorers, scientists supported by troops from Innuendo challenged the mighty river and traversed its length from the Atlantic Ocean to the dense inland forests of the southern Americas.

The Eye watched them all the way.

The leading explorer was a dwarf – Nanos – an expert in what his name implied, nanotechnology, the science of the miniature. Nanos, like Pandora before him, would unleash all evils, leaving nothing but hope. Hope versus the Eye would be a no-contest.

When Nanos discovered – stumbled over – the Amazon's source, the Committee was mightily pleased. None more so than the Notary. Nanos himself was close to ecstatic. The dwarf received orders to conquer and keep The Source in the name, and for the benefit, of the North. Whatever that was supposed to mean, thought the Eye.

Because he was so small, Nanos was the only member of the expedition who could enter the narrow river channel that, at the time, led into the cave that held the slowly melting mountain of ice feeding the Amazon. Preserved in the ice was the Eye. Seemingly for eternity.

The dwarf gasped when he caught sight of the cave's magnificence. He stood in wonder. Then, using a miniature radio, he described his findings to his colleagues at the mouth of the channel. He was almost breathless with excitement. The Eye willed him on.

The dwarf stepped onto the ice and, inevitably, slipped to the base of the mountain. He struggled mightily to extricate himself from a pile of slush. He lost his radio and most of the rest of his equipment.

The Eye sighed. On the very edge of achievement, the human race could almost always be trusted to make a mess of it. For only the third time in his history, the Eye "blinked" – and the dwarf saw him. Come closer, thought the Eye, like a spider thinking of a fly.

Nanos took a small pick and attacked the glacier until a tiny section of it crumbled away. The dwarf, half excited, half terrified, could see the Eye behind a thin skin of ice. He broke through it.

For the first time in the history of the Universe, the Eye spoke. He couldn't think of anything earth shattering to say. The shattering of the Earth would come later. "Welcome," he muttered hoarsely.

The dwarf clung to shards of ice as if his life depended on it. Which, of course, it did. Not surprisingly, Nanos was momentarily stunned and unable to respond. Equally unsurprisingly, there wasn't much the Eye could do about it.

The Eye remained patient.

The dwarf was transfixed.

The Eye spoke again, this time quite clearly.

"Congratulations. Not only have you discovered the source of the Amazon, but you have also discovered what might be described as the very Source of Life itself. Now you have to decide whether you will keep me for yourself and use me for your own ends, or share me among your fellows. The choice is yours."

Nanos regained some composure. "Instruct me," he said.

The Eye's chuckle was not like that of any human, but a quivering of his lashes. The movement fascinated the dwarf. The Eye asked the question most humans longed to hear.

"Would you like to rule the World?" He didn't really require any answer, having already guessed the dwarf's reaction. Greed is invariably number one on the hit parade of sins.

"Instruct me," said Nanos, yet again.

This could become monotonous. "Very well," said the Eye and instruct him he did.

*

A decade died.

The army of the North had re-conquered part of southern Europe and was advancing into the African wastes. A small expedition wiped out a ragtag army threatening from the East. "They cannot drink water, so let them drink blood," said the Leader. The Committee turned a blind eye to banditry in the West. Just as long as it did not encroach on the boundaries of the North.

Nanos, the dwarf, was promoted to the Notary's staff. He was put in charge of developing the resources at the source of the Amazon and, in ten years, had wasted little time. Apart from being a means of transportation, the edges of the great river were cultivated for fruits, vegetables and narcotics. The ice mountain within the Source's giant cave provided a never ending supply of fresh water. Water concentrated in such strength it could lubricate the cores of nuclear power sources. Sources that would produce weapons of mass destruction to serve, in time, to increase the power of the North. Rather, the power of those few who ruled in the North.

The Eye was eager to join the few.

As he had anticipated, Nanos had kept the Eye to himself. He had removed him, encased in a block of ice, to a laboratory that he, Nanos, had caused to be built as close as possible to the mining and other activities conducted at the Amazon's source. The laboratory was guarded by troops from Innuendo. Inside, there had been accumulated, on the Eye's instruction, a mass of technological aids and, again on the Eye's instruction, Nanos had manufactured a series of miniature computer discs. Not in themselves unusual in the twenty-first century, Nanos's discs were different in that they contained the details of personality or of personalities. Personalities devised by the Eye. The discs – lenses – were no larger than the pupil of a human's eye. Any one of them could be secreted in the Eye himself, thus permitting him to assume the personality encoded on the disc and project itself in human form.

On the first day of the beginning of the end, Nanos approached the Eye, a tiny disc held by forceps in his hand.

"Instruct me," he said. Nanos had a very limited vocabulary.

The Eye watered. "Place the disc in my tears," he said.

Nanos approached and obeyed, releasing the disc from the forceps with great delicacy. The Eye assimilated the disc.

"What now?" asked Nanos.

The Eye closed.

Nanos swore an oath. He heard a sound behind him and whirled round. Before him stood a man, much like himself, but taller.

"Who the hell are you?" Nanos whispered.

The Eye smiled. "Call me what you will."

It was Nanos's turn to smile. "I've done it," he said, not caring to hide a note of triumph.

"We've done it," admonished the Eye.

"What now?" exclaimed Nanos.

"Why now, we'll rule the World." said the Eye.

"We?"

The Eye smiled a secret smile. "Don't tell me you're not prepared to share our success?"

"Do I have a choice?" asked Nanos.

The Eye did not deign to reply.

"What shall I call you?" Nanos asked, almost of himself.

The Eye said, "You already have The President, The Leader and The Notary. I'm not cut out to be The Mother – so think of something as grand, if you will."

"How about 'The Eye'?"

The Eye blinked his first human blink. "Not very original, but I suppose it'll do," he said rather huffily.

Nanos crossed to a window and glanced out. "I must smuggle you out of here. If you are seen, you are likely to be exterminated. The human race fears nothing worse than the unknown."

The Eye too crossed to the window. He could see that there were two Innuendo guards in attendance. "Draw them away from the laboratory," he instructed. "I'll make my own escape."

"What about me?" asked Nanos, somewhat alarmed.

"What about you? You don't have to pass by unnoticed."

"When shall we meet again? How shall we meet again?"

"Oh, we shall. You must trust me on that."

"Why should I?" Nanos was scowling.

"Because you have all the other discs. All the other facets of my multiple personality. Without them, I am nothing. Or very little, at any rate."

Nanos seemed mollified.

"Do as I say," said the Eye.

Nanos, looking once more at the guards, bit his lip. "Very well," he said at length.

The Eye smiled.

"If you can't trust me, Nanos, you can't trust anybody," he said. "Don't try to get in touch with me. I'll be the one to get in touch with you."

"When?"

"When you least expect it."

When the human form of the Eye had gone, Nanos looked into the ice container. The original Eye was still there – still closed.

Nanos permitted himself a secret smile as he opened a waterproof container. Within it lay the several hundred discs, each no larger than a small contact lens, that had been manufactured according to the design and instruction of the now manifestly human Eye. Very carefully, as if he were handling a miniature explosive, Nanos manipulated, with the aid of forceps, one of the discs into the pupil of his own right eye.

Within seconds, he was writhing in agony. It was as if a hot pin had pierced his retina. Terrible shapes swam before him. He experienced all the pain of the centuries. It was as if the Four Horsemen of the Apocalypse were galloping through his brain. Nanos screamed a scream of such terror that the Innuendo guards outside feared to enter the laboratory. By the time they summoned up sufficient courage, it was too late.

Nanos the dwarf lay in a crumpled, disfigured heap upon the ground. His fingers had plucked out his own eyes. His skin was marred by deep scratches. His brain was pulp.

One of the guards vomited. The other assisted him outside. They stumbled towards their barracks and their commander. The Eye strolled into the laboratory unobserved. He leaned over the dwarf's hideous corpse. "Thou shalt not steal," he said icily. He snatched up the box containing his precious, tiny personality memory discs.

The Eye exited the building like a wisp of smoke escaping a fire, like a passing shadow in the dusk.

But this shadow would not pass. It would darken the Earth.

Innuendo

"Affection beaming in one eye, calculation shining out the other"
                                    Charles Dickens

The Notary was not amused. His finest micro-engineer had come to dust. The two guards at the Amazon source laboratory had been executed, but that wasn't going to bring Nanos back. True, the North would still benefit from the dwarf's discovery of the river's source. But what had he been doing in the laboratory that the Notary hadn't been informed of? What was the dwarf's extracurricular activity in aid of? The Notary determined to see for himself.

He journeyed to the southern Americas aware that, in his absence, there might be staged some kind of coup intended to remove him from the North's Committee. The Notary, unloved, was not popular. His scientific experiments, on humans as well as other animals, chilled the populace and, though few in number, there were those with the ambition to replace him. His arrogance denied their talent to do so, but talentless ambition, if it is made of stern stuff, can create catastrophe.

The Notary did not trust every member of his hundred-strong Innuendo guards, but kept a few close to him. These chosen few were chained to him by vices that he was able to indulge. Wine, women and song – with additional narcotics – are sure addictions.

Seeing it for the first time, the Notary was as awed by the ice mountain within the glittering cave as Nanos and his cohorts had been. Of course, he knew nothing of the Eye. He entered the laboratory and scanned its contents. Expert that he was, it did not take him long to grasp the fact that the dwarf had been experimenting with miniature computer technology. But why and for what purpose? And why in such secrecy? None of Nanos's Innuendo guards knew anything of his activities. The dwarf had worked alone.

The Notary had the laboratory stripped to its bare walls. Any piece of equipment, however minute and apparently inconsequential, had to be brought to him for his study. There was nothing of interest until, on the third day, a guard brought him a tiny, charred disc, no bigger than the nail of the little finger of a dwarf.

Using modern magnetic equipment, he was able to see that the miniature disc, though misshapen and fired as if in a furnace, had been programmed. The Notary thought of the Lord's

Prayer inscribed on the head of a pin. He assumed, for no other reason than that his educated instinct told him so, that he had found the key to Nanos's experiment. He had to return to the North, where his own greater resources would allow him to study the disc more closely and cause it to yield up its secrets.

A jet-foil carried the Notary and his closest guards to the mouth of the Amazon, where an aircraft would transport him to the North in less than four hours. There were only four of these craft – one for each member of the Committee.

He looked to the South. In time, the North's army, using the edges of the Amazon as a base, would invade the jungles and spill over into what had become a vast desert. The discovery of the river's source would assist that enterprise. Nanos, then, would have died a hero. Not bad for a malignant, greedy dwarf – useful though he had been to the Notary's designs. He would have to be replaced by someone of equal talent in miniaturism.

Beyond the far side of the Amazon was the realm of the West: bandit country. The Notary made a mental note to have that bank of the river reinforced. It wouldn't do for mere bandits to overrun the Source.

The aircraft circled the only landing ground in the North. Nature having destroyed most fossil fuels in her fury of six decades past, only one was required. Fuel had to be conserved to meet the needs of four Committee aircraft and four hundred helicopters assigned to the guards of Innuendo, Theatre, Arena and Works. Naval craft received very little to assist their propulsion, except the few jet-foils that were also attendant upon the whim of the Committee. The Notary was not averse to the new era of sail. Otherwise, the populace moved about on foot or, if privileged, on electrically charged bicycles. Though few in number, horses were often put to good use. Essential goods were transported by coal-driven trains. But coal was king no longer and, in short supply, was used sparingly. Water and heat drove the North's economy. Water came from the newly formed icecaps of Scandinavia and the Russias and now from the ice mountain at the source of the Amazon. Heat was generated by solar power. Together, water and heat, controlled by the Notary and his fellow scientists, had all but recreated and regenerated technology available prior to Nature's ruinous outburst. Those of the human race in the North could produce electricity, mine various metals, conserve coal and natural gas, manufacture a few weapons of mass destruction. Above all, the North's reduced population could be fed. What the North didn't have, it would take – from the South, the undernourished East and the potentially rich West. That the denizens of the North paid little attention to their souls or to their consciences was nothing new and was of no interest to the Notary and his close comrades.

The Notary was met and greeted by the Leader, his closest ally on the Committee.

The Leader smiled lazily. The Notary raised an enquiring eyebrow.

"You haven't returned a minute too early," the Leader said. "There's some unrest among the lower orders."

The Notary shrugged. "There's always unrest among the lower orders. It's because they want to join the higher order."

"Yes, but their dissatisfaction is directed at you. At you and no other."

"So, the President, the Mother and you are safe? How convenient for you. How inconvenient for me?" The last sentence was an enquiry.

The Leader looked about, as if afraid he might be overheard.

"Come on, come on," the Notary hissed impatiently.

"The camp where you keep your special subjects has been discovered."

The Notary scowled. His "special subjects" were degenerates, prostitutes and such, captured in raids on the South, East and West, used as human toys for the pleasures of his elite

Innuendo guards. "Discovered by whom?" he asked through gritted teeth.

The Leader seemed to be enjoying his role as Messenger of Doom. "The Mother, not your closest ally at the best of times, launched a Seek and Locate operation. She seized the opportunity of your absence in South America to organise a raid. All items of evidence have been made available to the President. He is not pleased and you are summoned before the Committee to answer for your, shall we say, misdeeds."

"Does anyone outside the Committee know of this?"

The Leader snorted, a mixture of surprise and disgust. "Of course. The soldiers who carried out the raid, the Mother's supporters among those you coyly refer to as the lower orders, the President's immediate staff. Need I go on?"

"What shall I do?"

"Face the music. Brazen it out. You're not ashamed, are you? Well, not too much."

"Bitch."

The Leader bridled. "I hope you're not referring to me?"

The Notary laughed a humourless laugh. "The Mother's piety is sickening," he said.

"Oh, I couldn't agree more. But the Committee, the World, must have some conscience, mustn't it? Sin isn't any fun if doing good isn't an alternative." The Leader smiled.

"Who led the raid on the camp?"

"One moment." The Leader turned to one of his aides who whispered in his ear. "A young officer who has taken the Mother's fancy. His name's Dubroc."

"Any mileage there?"

"How do you mean?"

"My dear Leader, try not to be so obtuse."

"Ah. Possibly. He's a handsome young man and she, the Mother, is not yet past her prime."

The Notary grunted approvingly. "All right. Let's get it over with. Take me to our leader."

The Leader stiffened. "*I* am our leader. I'll take you to our President."

The Mother was a strikingly beautiful woman, just over forty years of age. Born in the Americas, she had Native American pueblo blood which revealed itself in her fine cheekbones, hawk nose and piercing black eyes. The President, a native Middle European confined to a wheelchair, was approaching his seventieth year and becoming increasingly bitter about his deteriorating condition.

The Notary, an Anglo Saxon, was tall, handsome and austere. The Leader almost matched his good looks, but these were marred by the fleshiness of indulgence. The Leader was a Russian.

The Committee met in a large, airy room furnished with antiques salvaged after Nature's rampage. The room was one of several used for conference purposes in a castle built by Ludwig, the mad king of Bavaria. The Notary always considered this an apt venue.

The President looked aggrieved, the Mother indifferent as the Notary and the Leader were ushered in by guards representing all four arms – Works, Theatre, Arena, and Innuendo. Heavy oak doors closed behind them.

"This is a sorry business," said the President.

"I'm not sorry," the Notary retorted. "How else am I supposed to keep my Innuendo guards satisfied, cosseted and, above all, loyal?"

The Mother smiled icily. "What ever happened to honour, decency, patriotism, *esprit de corps*?"

"Oh, don't be so naive," the Notary half laughed. "We rule through fear. Anyone who steps out of line risks being crushed by our system."

The Leader coughed. "I deal with such matters," he said ominously.

The Mother glanced at him contemptuously. "In the end, we must answer to the people," she said.

"Only if the people ask a question," interjected the Notary. "I don't hear any cries for my resignation. Mobs are not storming the barricades outside my home. By whom am I accused of wrongdoing? You and you alone."

The President spoke quietly. "No one is accusing you of anything, Notary." He wheeled himself to a picture window and gazed out at snow-capped mountains. "But we in the North have a civilising mission. We must repair the ravages of the past, spiritual as well as physical, and create a world fit for heroes, not degenerates. I was disgusted by what was found on your estates, your encampment of whores."

The Notary shrugged. "All right, I'll abandon it. Then what? How else do I keep my troops loyal? Troops that stand between me – and you, for that matter – and the mob? And what am I supposed to do with the inmates, my prisoners?"

"Well, we could put them to work in the uranium mines," suggested the Leader.

There was a sharp intake of breath from the Mother.

"I don't think that will be necessary," said the President, as quietly and reasonably as before. "They must be released into the community and become workers in our normal leisure activities."

The Leader burst out laughing.

The Notary shook his head ruefully. "What do you think constitutes 'leisure activities'?" he asked with interest. The Mother tried hard to conceal a smile.

"What goes on between humans in private is a matter of conscience," said the President. "As long as such activities do not undermine the basic honour of the state, they do not concern us."

"What about the privacy of my estates?" asked the Notary. "A privacy so rudely invaded by the Mother's troops?"

"That's different," said the President wearily. "There you reduced people to slaves. Reached the depths of depravity."

"All against the law," said the Mother quietly.

"You mean, getting found out is against the law?"

The President smiled ruefully. "What the eye doesn't see, the heart doesn't grieve over."

The Notary picked up on his cue. "Am I to assume that, though reprimanded, I may carry on much as before, just so long as I'm not, how shall I put it, exposed?"

"Well, not quite." The President assumed a degree of solemnity. "Discretion should be your byword. I appreciate that our troops must be, shall we say, entertained and that the populace must be allowed pleasures, both private and public."

"Otherwise, they'll rise up and destroy us," said the Leader airily.

The President did not appreciate the interruption. "But these must be reasoned and civilised," he continued, "otherwise we are no better than beasts. Where is the future of the North, let alone the whole world, in that?"

The Notary looked suitably shamefaced. The Leader followed his example. The Mother was not taken in. The President was.

The Notary smiled. "I shall go forth and sin no more," he said.

Once outside the room the Notary said, "What was all that supposed to be about?"

The Leader sighed. "He's senile. He'll be dead before very long."

"I wish I could believe that, but science has made great advances and there are all sorts of techniques and medicines that could keep him alive."

"Ah, yes. But who controls those resources?" asked the Leader.

The Notary stopped in his tracks. "What are you suggesting?"

"I'm suggesting nothing. I think it will suffice if we allow Nature to take her course. She's been fairly devastating in the past. It doesn't look to me as if the President is long for this world. It probably won't be necessary to assist his passage into the next."

"What if it is?" enquired the Notary anxiously.

The Leader's eyes narrowed. "Oh, you can rely on me."

The Notary nodded understandingly. "Just as long as you are the next President," he said. "Is that right?"

"Mum's the word," said the Leader.

"Yes. We'll have to do something about her," replied the Notary, thinking of home.

Dubroc had searched and located the Notary's camp. It hadn't been too difficult. The Notary was a believer in the "place your secrets beneath the noses of those searching them out and they'll be readily overlooked" school of intrigue. Stupid, maybe? Dubroc didn't underestimate the Notary. It wasn't stupidity, it was arrogance. The Notary felt secure in his depravity. Well, perhaps the Mother might have a say in that.

For the moment, though, she was silent. There had been the order to Seek and Locate, but not to Destroy. Dubroc was impatient. He wanted to finish the job and wound some of the Notary's pride. Though by no means possessed of messianic fervour against the "sins" that human beings had always been heirs to, Dubroc believed in an ordered, decent and just society. The games of life were hard enough without the Notary, or the Leader, trying to bend the rules.

He cast his eye over his eight support soldiers from the Mother's Theatre troop. None of them admired that title. It suggested pretence. Whereas, these troops were primed and ready for decisive action. For the moment, however, with no word from their command structure, they were inactive. Leashed in like hounds ready for the chase. Patience being one of Dubroc's lesser virtues, such inaction was hard to endure.

"He's somewhat headstrong," said the secretary, an attractive woman who, from time to time, enjoyed a role as one of the Notary's occasional mistresses.

"He's quick to anger. If he suspects an affront to his honour, he's capable of reacting with considerable violence." The secretary punched some buttons and a photograph of Dubroc was projected onto a screen. The Notary studied the young man's face.

"A little gung ho, would you say?" The Notary was sincerely interested.

"All men are the same," the secretary replied wearily.

"Not quite all." The Notary preened. "Tell me more."

The secretary studied her computer console. "What do you want to know?"

"Everything."

"We can never know everything about anybody."

"Do your best," the Notary hissed.

"He was born in the Americas, but raised here in the North. We're not certain of his age. Late twenties, perhaps. Educated at the Theatre school, so he's one of the Mother's protégés.

Then, having passed the test, he moved into the Theatre section of the army."

"His teacher and superior?" The Notary enquired.

"General Lamar."

"That old fool."

"He has a fine record."

"The record is a little scratched. Go on."

"Dubroc is a small arms expert. He favours the five seveN."

"How many has he killed?"

"It's hard to say. He's campaigned in the West and in the East."

"Perhaps we can lose him in the deserts of the South?"

The secretary smiled thinly. "That's up to you."

The Notary, not for the first time, checked that the door to the computer office was locked.

The secretary raised an eyebrow. "A little jumpy, aren't we? Or do you have something else in mind?"

The Notary smiled slyly. "I'm prepared to put that 'something else' to the back of my mind for the moment."

The secretary returned her gaze to her console. It was hard to tell if she was disappointed. She continued her recitation.

"Dubroc's immediate family remained in the Americas. It's thought that, when he campaigned there, he may have contacted them. Assuming they're still alive. But there's no hint of disloyalty."

"Perhaps I can do something about that. Spread a few rumours of discontent. My section of the Committee is not called Innuendo for nothing."

"He speaks nine languages and is computer literate. He's fit, very strong and well liked. His subordinates would follow him anywhere," continued the secretary.

The Notary scowled. "He sounds too good to be true. Has he any vices?"

"The usual."

"What's that supposed to mean?"

"He drinks – in moderation. He had one woman for a short while."

"Had?"

"She died. Renal failure due to contaminated water."

"Who was she?"

"The Mother's daughter."

The Notary clapped his hands with glee. "Then I've got her exactly where I want her."

"How do you work that out? The daughter's dead. If you're thinking of going against the Mother, you'll have Dubroc to deal with. He looks like tough opposition."

The Notary snorted. "Looks can be deceptive. He doesn't impress me that much."

The secretary smiled. "Well, he impresses me."

The Notary took advantage of the locked door. At first, the secretary objected but, aware of the power of the man who tore her clothes off her as if she were a slave on sale in a market, she reluctantly succumbed to his slavering kisses, his awful sexual demands. One day, she thought, the tables might turn. Then again, they might not.

Dubroc was finding it hard to keep his troops occupied. He ordered them, not for the first time, to check all of their weapons. He handled his own five seveN lovingly. In his opinion, it was the best weapon produced at the conclusion of the twentieth century by the Czech gunmasters. Based on the .357 Magnum, it was forty percent more accurate, sixty percent lighter, chambered sixteen high-velocity, metal-jacketed projectiles with rapid reload facility, possessed little or no kick and was capable of stopping a rhino in its tracks. Because of limited production, it was issued solely to Committee-approved troops.

The communications officer leaned towards him and whispered in his ear. The order had come through: destroy.

The nine men were well prepared and this was by no means a difficult assignment. There were few Innuendo sentries and these were swiftly and silently disposed of.

The Notary's "pleasure" compound consisted of half a dozen prefabricated buildings, each one projecting a certain sensuous theme. Dubroc and one other burst into Building One, which celebrated the decadence of Ancient Rome. A few more than twenty young women and men were sprawled on soft pallets scattered about the room. Some were sleeping, some drinking various exotic liqueurs, some indulging in various forms of intercourse. All were surprised by Dubroc's sudden intrusion. One man, recovering quickly, hurled himself at the intruder. Dubroc's five seveN cut him in half. The dead man's companions froze.

"End of the line," said Dubroc. "All Innuendo troops will form up outside. You're now under the command of the Theatre section. Anyone who steps out of that line will be eliminated." He gestured at the fallen man. "If any of you are tired of this world and anxious to enter the next, we'll be happy to assist you on your way." Most of the men grabbed articles of clothing and, muttering darkly, left the building.

Dubroc spoke to the mostly young and frightened women who remained. "You are under the protection of the Mother. This compound is about to be destroyed. You will all be taken to the capital. There you'll be found alternative employment." He turned on his heel and stepped outside.

One of his subordinates approached him. "We have thirty Innuendo guards enjoying, 'rest and recreation'. It's an interesting set up. Each building has an historical theme. I've just raided the Middle Ages. What did you get?"

Dubroc smiled. "Ancient Rome."

"Any good?"

"About the same as the Middle Ages, I'd say."

"There are five casualties, all on their side. That includes the guard you killed."

Dubroc frowned. "He was foolish. There was no reason for him to die."

"What do we do now?"

"Make sure everybody's out and burn it down."

The subordinate hesitated. "The Notary's house is just a mile away. What if the wind's in that direction?"

"It wouldn't bother me a bit," said Dubroc.

Within minutes, savage flames leaped into the sky and clouds of dense smoke blotted out a sickle Moon and all the stars. The subordinate wiped his brow. "It's hot," he said.

Dubroc smiled slightly. "When the Notary finds out about this, it's going to get a lot hotter."

The Notary was interviewing General Lamar.

Lamar, in his sixties, was a rugged warrior of the old school. Though his body bore the marks of many wounds, sustained on and off the battlefield, he was handsome enough. While campaigning in the East, a hooked spear had buried itself in his left leg and he now walked with a pronounced limp. By no means incorruptible, he held the grudging respect of his peers and of the Mother. He was the kind of man with whom it would be wise to deal cautiously.

The Notary had approached his quarry warily.

"Good of you to come," he said politely. They were meeting in a small, well-furnished room in Ludwig's castle which was set aside for the Notary's occasional use.

"I didn't think I had much choice," growled Lamar. "Your request of my presence was somewhat peremptory."

The Notary ignored the jibe and offered the General a glass of fine wine. Lamar accepted it.

The Notary smiled a predatory smile. "Dubroc. Tell me about him."

Lamar eyed him over the rim of his glass. "Good soldier," he said.

"Oh, I've no doubts on that score. After all, didn't you train him?"

Lamar chuckled. "You know I did. Why not dispense with the preliminaries and cut to the chase?"

"Dubroc led a raid on my estates. At the instigation of the Mother. It's not entirely unknown that my estates house a pleasure compound for Innuendo troops. I've been suitably admonished by the Committee. So that's that." The Notary stretched like a contented cat. "Did you know of this?"

Lamar smiled. "Of course. I'm Chief Officer of the Theatre section."

"What were Dubroc's orders?"

"Seek and locate."

"Ah, well he's done that. I shall have to discipline some of my guards. It seems they made Dubroc's task a little too easy."

Lamar had paused for effect. "And destroy," he added.

The Notary was shocked. "What?"

"I think you heard me."

Hot anger flushed the Notary's face. He had difficulty keeping his rage under control. "Who gave that order?"

"I did," said Lamar lightly, "just before I came along here to meet you."

The pupils of the Notary's eyes dilated. "And the Mother instructed you?"

"Of course. We waited until you returned from the Amazon. You can't say we got up to anything behind your back."

The Notary offered more wine as if presenting Lamar with a poisoned chalice. Lamar shook his head and covered his glass with his hand.

"How do you think Dubroc will have gone about things?" the Notary asked.

"Thoroughly."

The Notary raised an eyebrow.

Lamar smiled broadly. "He'll have taken out your guards and burned your pleasure dome to the ground."

The Notary gripped his own wine glass so tightly it shattered in his hand.

The Mother smiled at Dubroc. "Well done."

Dubroc half-smiled back. "I had five men killed."

"That's your job."

"I know, but it doesn't come any easier."

The Mother was seated behind a desk. She stood up, walked round it and perched on its edge. She studied Dubroc carefully. "It's good that you take no pleasure in killing."

Dubroc pondered for a moment. Then he smiled at her. "Well, we all die. It's just a question of when."

The Mother did not smile. "If the Notary has his way, it'll be sooner rather than later for you and me."

"How can you know that? It would seem that the Notary and the Leader are toeing the Committee's line. What makes you imagine you're in danger?"

"A woman's intuition."

Dubroc looked at her seriously. "I respect that. But I can't help feeling you've provoked the Notary by ordering the destruction of his – what shall we call it? – recreation centre."

"I intended to provoke him."

"Why?"

"A pre-emptive strike."

"I have respect for that too."

The Mother stood and approached him. "Do unto others as they would do unto you. But do it first."

They both laughed.

"My daughter loved you," the Mother said.

"And I her."

"I know. It's because of that I place my trust in you. Together, maybe we can reduce the Notary's ambitions."

"What about the President?"

The Mother bit her lip. "He's dying. It won't be long. Then there'll be a power vacuum."

"And you want to fill it?"

The Mother sighed. "Not at all. But there must be someone out there capable of leading us."

"Where to – the promised land? There's no such place."

"But there's a better place than this. We must help to forge it. Otherwise, I fear the Notary and the Leader are capable of causing far greater damage than Nature has so far managed."

Dubroc looked nonplussed. The Mother smiled at him benevolently. "At least, time is on your side," she said.

"They're bad enough, but I'm sure we could do a lot worse than have to combat the Notary and the Leader."

"I doubt it," said the Mother grimly.

The Eye was tired. In his human form, that is. In himself he was restless and eager to progress with his plans for world dominion, oppression and eventual destruction. He wouldn't destroy everybody and everything, of course. What would be the point in that? He would preserve the world's natural wonders for his pleasure and allow some humans to survive so that they might attend his needs. The humans would have to be carefully selected. How to do that? He paused to consider the matter. He would come to a conclusion in due course. For the moment, he was anxious to remove himself from the Amazon's immediate vicinity.

He regretted Nanos's death. He had liked the little man. Nanos had worshipped all human vices and the Eye could understand that. The false and the sensually frail are easily manipulable. Not that the Eye would be averse to taking on a moral opponent. Just so he, or she, proved worthy. No one could hope to win the Eye's game of life and death. Or could they? The Eye chuckled. Well, they could hope. All in all, though, any human who could give the Eye a run for his money, as it were, might be worth saving. The Eye shuddered with self disgust. What was he thinking about? The only humans worth saving would be the beautiful and the pliable. He would ensure that glamorous servitude wouldn't be entirely unbearable.

To the matter at hand.

The Eye was sore. Too much tropical sun. Upon leaving the Amazon's source with Nanos's discs he had killed a trader who supplied victuals to Innuendo troops, stolen his longboat and sailed towards the Amazon's estuary. Once there, he'd been challenged by an armed officer of the port and he too had had to be killed. The Eye didn't object to killing, but it became tedious after a while. Because, of course, the Eye was forever undead. But where is the fun in indulging in a conflict one couldn't lose? Still, needs must when the devil drives. The Eye found that amusing, for he considered himself to be the ultimate in devilry.

The Eye transported himself on horseback (his horse stolen from a poorly watched corral) into the part of the world known as the West. If you were from the North, this was bandit country. As far as the Eye was concerned, it was the land of opportunity.

The first humans he encountered termed

themselves Dog Soldiers and he treated them accordingly. There were five men with one woman. The woman was very attractive. Quite a compliment from the Eye. After all, he had seen many beautiful women through the centuries. It was clear they intended to steal his horse and anything else they could lay their hands on. The leader of the group aimed an old-fashioned pistol that the Eye recognised as a Colt .44. The Eye spat on the ground. The Colt fired. The Eye didn't move a muscle.

The group's leader swore an oath. The rest backed away apprehensively. All save the woman, who eyed the Eye curiously.

The head bandit licked dry lips. "You going to fight, or what?"

The Eye smiled condescendingly. "I am unarmed."

"But still dangerous," said the young woman.

The Eye's human arm flicked out like the tongue of a snake and his hand gripped the bandit by the throat. Within seconds he was choked to death. The Eye let the surprised corpse drop to the ground. The four male bandits fired a fusillade of shots. They passed through and around the Eye, ricochets kicking up spurts of dust, snapping twigs off scrub and water-deprived trees. When their ammunition was exhausted, the bandits turned and ran. Only the woman remained.

When the echoes of gunfire and the noise of human flight had subsided, she smiled at the Eye. "I'm impressed," she said.

"So you should be," he responded.

"What are you called?"

The Eye shrugged.

The woman persisted. "You must have a name."

"An amiable dwarf once called me the Eye."

"Ah. Single descriptive names are all the rage nowadays. Like the Mother, the Notary, the Leader and the President. They rule the North, by the way."

"Who rules the West?"

The woman smiled again. "Seems like you do."

The Eye, who already knew it, asked her name.

"I'm called Kazan," she said.

"What were you doing with those sorry specimens?"

The woman shrugged. "The usual."

"What's 'the usual'?"

"Larceny. On a petty scale, I must admit. Some thuggery."

"Kill anyone?"

"Only in self defence."

The Eye looked at her searchingly. "What else did you get up to with these men?"

Kazan laughed. "Not what you're thinking.

Oh, I've waltzed around the park a few times, but none of those boys was ever my dancing partner."

"What are you looking for?"

"The usual."

The Eye was becoming exasperated. "What's that?"

"A way out of here. So I can go to the North."

"What's wrong with the West?"

"There's nothing exactly wrong with it, but there's nothing entirely right. Since the earth shook, the West's pretty much reverted to where it was maybe two hundred years back. It's become a little wild all over again."

"So, you crave civilisation?"

"Hey, you're not as dumb as you look."

"How do you know you'll find it in the North?"

"I don't. But I'll take my chances. I can always come back here if it doesn't work out. From what I hear, there's lots of opportunities for a girl with ambition. Particularly one who's addicted to room service."

The Eye laughed. "I too intend to visit the North. Actually, I intend to rule it."

The woman's eyes widened. "Do you know, I almost believe you?"

"Shall we travel together?"

The woman's eyes widened still further. "You sure make your mind up quickly. A few minutes ago I was trying to kill you."

The Eye's human eyes narrowed. "No. Your friends wanted to kill me. Something tells me you didn't."

"Who or what is that something? You place a lot of faith in it."

"Well, I'm a little older than I look and, therefore, that much wiser. What do you say?"

The woman thought for a moment. "Doesn't seem to be a bad idea," she said at length. "But what happens if we should fall out?"

"That won't be a problem," said the Eye casually. "I'd kill you. That's what would happen."

"Unless I got to you first."

"Your friends tried and failed. What makes you think you could do any better?"

"You must have a weakness," Kazan said coyly.

The Eye said, "Have you ever heard of Samson and Delilah?"

"Sure. His strength was in his hair. She barbered him."

"Quite. Assuming I do have a weakness, I'll keep it to myself for the moment."

Kazan nodded approvingly. "Seems reasonable." She eyed the Eye's horse. "Where have you come from?"

"The source of the Amazon."

"My. That animal brought you all this way?"

"Hardly. I also took a boat."

"Just kidding."

"I prefer horses to humans," the Eye said. "Where is here, by the way?

"Kind of Central America."

"I can tell geography isn't your strong suit."

The Eye picked up the bandit leader's abandoned gun. "Do you want this?"

"I doubt it'll do me much good."

"Yes, well you're not going up against me, are you?"

Kazan accepted the weapon and tucked it into her belt. She looked at the Eye curiously. "What now?"

"We must head for the nearest city."

Kazan snorted. "There aren't any cities in the West. This is wild bandit country, remember? Best we can offer are a few townships. Best we can do is stay away from them."

"Then what do you suggest?"

"Head for the coast? Snatch a ride across the ocean?"

The Eye brightened. "Seems reasonable. We'll ride double for a while."

Kazan looked dubious.

The Eye said, "Don't worry, I'm perfectly harmless."

Kazan smiled grimly. "That wouldn't exactly be my description of you."

The Eye chuckled. "Come along. Time waits for no man. But of course, it will wait for me."

Kazan thought that was funny.

The President died. Of natural causes. Given his fears with regard to the new ways of the world and his suspicion of the Notary and the Leader, together with, unbeknown to him, the advent of the Eye, he couldn't have chosen a better time. *Après le President, le Déluge.*

The funeral was impressive. All the inhabitants of the capital, all fourteen thousand of them, lined the streets to show their respect. The Mother recited a eulogy. The Notary and the Leader traded conspiratorial smiles and the elite troops provided an honour guard. On the one side were troops from Theatre and Arena; on the other, those from Innuendo and Works. There was little love lost between them.

Afterwards, the remaining members of the Committee, attended by representatives of the populace, assembled in the great hall of Ludwig's castle.

The Notary wanted to stage a coup, but the Leader, ever the practical military man, dissuaded him. He indicated that neither of them could guarantee the loyalty of their own troops, and they certainly could not depend on the Mother's Theatre squad and the late President's Arena section.

The Notary was irritated by the fact that the Mother, an admittedly attractive and persuasive woman, was so popular. She it was who addressed the assembled throng, informing it that an election would take place to fill the vacancy on the Committee and that a new President would be chosen.

"Why?" muttered the Notary.

"It's called democracy," said the Leader.

"Well, I don't like it."

The Leader was amused. "Very few potential dictators do."

The Mother reiterated her praise for the dead President and urged the people – not only the people of the capital, but the inhabitants of all of the North – to assist their leaders in every way. There was a power vacuum and enemies to the East, South and West could take advantage. She called for an election within one month. The Leader, smiling benignly, gave her his support and assured everyone that the army would be vigilant on their behalf. The Notary, finding it difficult to smile, merely nodded his assent.

The assembled company dispersed and the remaining three members met in Committee.

The Mother was conciliatory. "I suggest we lay aside all our differences," she said, "and try to work together for the general good of the North and, eventually, the world. What's left of it."

The Notary looked to the Leader. Neither spoke.

"Let's face facts," the Mother continued. "I'm well aware of your ambitions. But, in order to achieve them, you'll have to resort to civil war and, you have my assurance, you won't win it easily."

The Notary looked embarrassed. The Leader frowned in seeming concentration.

The Mother spoke again. "Do we really want a pitched battle between Works and Innuendo – Theatre and Arena? Whatever the result, the world will lose."

The Leader stood. Smiling like the Pope about to bless his congregation, he spoke quietly and sincerely. "The Mother is quite right," he said. "There is no mileage in self destruction. We must await our new Committee member – whoever he or she may be – and then decide how and to what end we shall go forward. In the mean time, we must be on our guard against our enemies, particularly our enemies within."

The Notary seemed ready to explode with indignation. The Leader took a firm hold of him. "Are you about to protest?" he asked.

The Notary hesitated.

"If you are," continued the Leader, "then you're about to protest too much and too soon."

For a moment, there was palpable tension in the air. The Notary, shaking his head in resignation, withdrew into unguent politeness. "Forgive me," he said, "I'm a little headstrong. Under the circumstances, that's unforgivable."

The Leader released his grip. "Doubtless, grief over our President's death has adversely affected you," he said, with apparent sincerity.

The Mother winced. The Notary looked suitably chastened.

The Leader became businesslike. "The army will protect our State," he said firmly. "The Notary will continue his admirable work in the field of science and technology and you," he nodded and smiled at the Mother, "must continue to serve the people with your usual compassion."

The Mother wasn't taken in for a moment, but she smiled back at him. The Notary appeared shell shocked.

"In a month," said the Leader, "we shall be in a better position to decide our and everyone's future. If you'll excuse me, I have business to deal with. Our frontiers must be guarded properly. I'm sure the Notary, his latest misdemeanour behind him, will wish to return to his estates and his important work at the earliest."

The Notary, not a good actor, reluctantly agreed.

The Mother shook each of them by the hand and looked into their eyes. She didn't like what she saw there.

When the two had gone, she said, "You can come out now."

Dubroc stepped out from behind a hidden panel. "I don't think they intended to kill you," he said.

The Mother grimaced. "Not today. They're just biding their time. We need a new Committee member. They'll try to ensure one of their puppets is elected. Then they might not have to kill me. I'll just die of neglect."

Dubroc said, "We'll have to wait and see."

"Yes, but I can't afford to be idle. There aren't many candidates suitable for the Committee, so I'll have to be sure they're all properly vetted."

"Do you have anyone in particular in mind?"

The Mother shrugged. "No."

Dubroc tried to be encouraging. "It's for sure, someone will turn up."

The Eye hadn't wasted any time. Kazan was impressed by his energy and expertise. Also, she was not averse to his charm.

They reached what had been the Panama Canal. Once a great water conduit for commerce and trade expansion, it was now dried up and desolate, its many water locks crumbling to dust, the land seceding to creeping vegetation. "What a dump," said Kazan with feeling.

"I remember it in better times," said the Eye.

"You do? How old are you?"

"Oh, I've been around for several thousand years."

Kazan appeared stupefied. "Give me a break. You're kidding me."

"Why would I do that?"

"I don't know. You've got a weird sense of humour?"

"You don't have to believe me," said the Eye.

"Prove it," Kazan said.

"All right. Ask me anything you like."

"Is there a God?"

"Ah, you've got me there." The Eye looked pensive for a moment. "In all honesty, I'm not certain. I would guess that's up to the individual. There is something that comes pretty close to being godlike. You're looking at it."

Kazan took an involuntary step backward. "Good God," she whispered.

The Eye laughed. "Not necessarily."

"What's the world been like over thousands of years?" Kazan asked tentatively.

The Eye shrugged. "The world's been doing fine. It's its inhabitants who seem to have been doing their best to destroy it."

"And you intend to do something about that?"

"You can bet your life," said the Eye forcefully.

"Will I have to?" Kazan asked quietly.

"Maybe. Life and Death. That's the name of the game."

Kazan sighed. "Well, we'll all die one day."

The Eye smiled. "I won't."

The Notary met with the Leader.

"We had an opportunity to kill her. Why didn't we take it?" he asked.

"There'll be plenty of other opportunities," the Leader replied. "Chances are, we won't have to kill her. She'll just fade away. Of course, that depends on who the new Committee member turns out to be. He'd better be on our side, rather than on hers."

"I still think we should have killed her."

"There'd have been war between her troops and ours. Who knows which way the people would have leaned."

"The people can be subdued. Crushed, if necessary. My Innuendo troops would see to that. And with you controlling the Works, I don't see how we could lose."

The Leader grew impatient. "We could have lost in the first round. Don't think the Mother was alone at our conference. There was a gunman concealed close by. We were well covered."

The Notary was incredulous. "Who?"

"Dubroc," came the reply.

The Notary snarled, "He keeps turning up, like a bad penny."

The Leader smiled. "Some people might describe him as a good penny."

"Well, the sooner that currency goes out of

circulation the better," the Notary said tersely.

"For the time being," the Leader suggested, "we must go our separate ways. We will, of course, continue to work together for our mutual benefit."

"Who do you have in mind as the new Committee member?"

"General Lamar."

The Notary snorted his disapproval. "You're out of your mind. He's the Mother's closest ally."

"Only while she retains the power to indulge his vices."

"What vices?"

"Oh, we all have them, Notary, you should know that. Every man has his price."

"And what's his?"

"The Presidency. Lamar will like the idea of everyone kowtowing to him and, as President, he can indulge himself to his heart's content without fear of retribution. We'll see to that. The Mother will think there's a fair balance of power. By the time she finds out otherwise, it will be too late."

The Notary shook his head. "I have my doubts."

The Leader became irritable. "Yes, well you're not exactly action man, are you? Leave everything to me."

The Notary started to protest, but was interrupted.

"Oh, you'll have your part to play, be in no doubt of that," said the Leader consolingly. "But, just for the moment, actions speak louder than words and, remember, I control the army."

"Not all of it."

The Leader scowled. "You'd better hope I control enough of it, or we'll be the ones in fear of our lives, not the Mother."

Kazan, at the instigation of the Eye, stole a helicopter from a Works troop based in what was left of Panama City.

"You're very good at this," complimented the Eye.

"At what?"

"Theft. Do you know how to fly this thing?"

"Don't you?"

"I could learn, but we don't have the time."

"Oh, then I'm useful for something?" said Kazan teasingly.

"I'm sure you're useful for a lot of things. But again, we don't have the time."

"This crate won't take us far. In case you didn't know, the world's short of fuel and this is a short-range craft."

The helicopter flew east, then north. It wasn't very long before Kazan pointed out that the craft was taking a buffeting from contrary winds and, flying over a sea that stretched from horizon to horizon, there was nowhere left for them to go.

The Eye seemed uninterested.

Kazan shook her head resignedly and, with one eye on the fuel gauge and altimeter, continued piloting the aircraft.

The Notary returned to his estates. Not best pleased by the destruction of his pleasure facilities, he treated his staff vilely. They avoided him as best they could and he withdrew to his private research facility situated in the basement of the Georgian mansion that was his home.

For the moment, he was prepared to go along with the Leader's plans, such as they were. He knew that there was a tide in the affairs of a man that would surely rise at some point. Taken at the flood, that tide would carry him to fortune and success. Nothing short of absolute power. He wasn't worried about absolute corruption.

In the mean time, he turned his attention to the charred disc he had recovered from Nanos's laboratory at the Amazon source. It didn't take him long to realise that it had been electronically coded. Breaking the code would not be a problem, but would use up precious time. The Notary set about it, utilising the state-of-the-art equipment at his disposal.

"Stop," said the Eye.

"What do you mean, stop?" shrieked Kazan. "I do that and we end up in the Ocean." She looked down at the swirling waters some thousand feet below the aircraft.

"I mean, hover," said the Eye apologetically.

"I've said it before and I'm saying it again. We're about to run out of fuel."

"Don't worry about that. We can settle on the surface of the water."

Again Kazan gazed at the Ocean beneath. "That'll be one hell of a bumpy ride."

The Eye sighed. "Trust me."

"Why should I? You're not a doctor, a lawyer, or a priest, are you?"

"In a sense, I am all of those things."

"You've lost me."

"More importantly, we'll both be lost if you don't do as I say."

Kazan shrugged. "I'm listening."

"Switch on the communication equipment."

As she obeyed, Kazan said, "It doesn't have a long range."

"Don't worry, the receiver will pick up the signal."

"And who, or what, might that be?"

"The Notary's private airplane."

Kazan snorted in disbelief. "You contact them and they'll come and blow us out of the sky."

The Eye smiled. "On the contrary, they'll greet us with open arms."

A red light glowed on the communication console. The Eye began to speak into its microphone. Kazan listened in amazement as the pilot of the Notary's jet aircraft, flying an exercise over the now barren Azores, agreed to alter course and rendezvous with the helicopter at the co-ordinates dictated by the Eye.

"How the hell did you manage that?"

The Eye looked smug. "The Notary's plane will be with us in two hours. I've ordered the pilot to waste no time. He obeyed my instructions because his security system links his orders of the day to a voice identification code. My voice pattern is identical to that of the Notary."

"I say again, how the hell did you manage that?"

"I merely learned the Notary's voice rhythms. I'm a quick learner."

"Who was your teacher?" Kazan asked archly.

"Oh, a little dwarf told me."

"We're about to go down," Kazan said, pointing to the helicopter's fuel indicator which was hovering just above zero.

"Take her down gently and settle on the sea. This craft is very solid. We'll be shaken up a little bit, but we'll be quite safe."

"I get seasick."

The Eye grimaced. "Yes, well don't throw up all over me."

*

The Notary's computers cracked the code on Nanos's disc.

Because it had been damaged, the information it contained was far from clear, but clear enough for the Notary to realise that a human psyche had been edited into it. He marvelled. Nanos had been far cleverer than he had thought. He understood that the disc, once inserted into a living being, could alter that being's personality to match that of the disc itself. Inserted where? There weren't too many alternatives – ear, eye, nose or throat. It didn't take a genius to figure out that it had to be the eye.

The Notary remembered where the damaged disc had been found. Amidst the mess that had once been Nanos's face. Again, it didn't take a genius to figure out that the dwarf must have inserted the disc in his own eye and that it had killed him. So, what was on the disc, in its pure form, that could be so devastating? Whatever it was, the Notary intended to have it.

The jet aircraft scooped the helicopter and its passengers from the surface of the sea in the area known as the Bermuda Triangle. Once on board, the Eye and Kazan, carefully watched by an armed guard, were presented to the officer commanding.

"Who are you?" the officer asked, clearly puzzled by the circumstances in which he found himself.

The Eye did the talking. "You received the Notary's message?"

The officer nodded.

"It was security cleared?"

"Impeccably."

"Well then?"

The officer, whilst realising he needed to remain polite just in case his instincts were wrong, was still suspicious. "What am I to do with you?" he asked.

"Take us to the North," said the Eye airily, "and set us down near the Notary's estate."

"There's no landing ground there, save for helicopters."

"Quite. You will refuel our helicopter and lower us onto an expanse of ground neighbouring the Notary's home. Then you will leave as quietly as you will have arrived. You must switch to Stealth approach."

The officer looked startled. "I am not authorised."

"I'm authorising you." The Eye stared long and hard at the officer. The officer looked away, then nodded to the guard.

Kazan smiled seductively and the guard's attention was momentarily distracted. One moment was enough for the Eye. He caught the officer by the throat and in much the same way he had treated Kazan's bandit leader in the West, crushed his larynx in seconds.

The guard hesitated. His last mistake. Kazan felled him with a brutal kick. "What now?" she asked breathlessly.

The Eye cast her an admiring glance. "There are two other members of crew. One of them is expendable."

Within five minutes, the Eye and Kazan had disposed of the other crew member. Only the pilot remained.

With Kazan's pistol jammed into his left ear, the pilot was terrified, but co-operative.

"What is your name?" asked the Eye, not unkindly.

"Parrish."

"Well, Parrish, I feel sure you are prepared to obey my every instruction. Am I right?"

Parrish swallowed hard. "I'll do whatever you say."

The Eye smiled broadly. "You'll go far, Parrish. Well, at the very least, you'll go as far as the North and put this aircraft down close to the Notary's estates. You will do that, won't you?"

"Absolutely."

Kazan said, "I thought we were going to use the helicopter?"

"You don't think, do you? We've eliminated the crew. Who would lower the helicopter to the ground?"

Kazan bit her lip. "Guess I'm a lot dumber than you."

"That's not a guess, that's a certainty." The Eye did not smile.

"All right, Parrish. Switch the craft into Stealth mode."

Parrish looked aghast. "How did you know about that?"

"Oh, I know a lot of things."

"I don't," said Kazan. "What's Stealth mode?"

She exerted pressure on the pilot's ear with her pistol.

"It's a mode whereby the plane slips under detection devices. It means that we can fly into any region unnoticed, as if we are invisible. We'll use up a lot of precious fuel doing it."

"Never mind about that," said the Eye. "Once we're in the North and I've achieved my ends, I'll promote you to Fleet Commander and you'll have first call on any available resources."

For a moment, Parrish looked excited by the prospect. "How will you gain the power to do that?" he enquired.

"Oh, didn't I mention it? I'm taking over from the Notary."

Parrish spluttered in disbelief. Kazan laughed.

"Don't forget the Stealth mode, will you?" said the Eye menacingly.

Parrish threw a few switches and the aircraft became strangely silent.

"You can jettison our helicopter," The Eye said.

"But we're flying over land," protested Parrish, "there could be people down there."

"Well, it'll give them something to talk about, won't it? Please do as I say."

Parrish threw another switch and there was a great rumbling sound from the rear of the aircraft where the helicopter had been stored, followed by a rush of air as the unloading bays opened. There was a silence. Kazan imagined the helicopter plunging earthwards. The unloading bays crashed shut.

"If you were to shoot me, " Parrish said to Kazan, "you'd interfere with the craft's air pressure and we'd crash."

"Well, you'd better not give me any excuse to shoot you, had you?" replied Kazan tersely.

The Eye laughed and Parrish managed a weak impersonation of a smile.

The Notary was alarmed. He had played what remained of Nanos's disc through a visual aid programme and almost suffered the same fate as the dwarf. The visual aid was aborted just in time.

For a moment, the Notary was in a quandary. What he had seen was dazzling. Should he share his discovery? With some reluctance, he admitted to himself that he had no choice. He called on a pilot. "Prepare for take off," he ordered, "you're flying me to the capital." He switched to another communication channel. "Where is the

Leader?" he enquired. It was the secretary who had revealed Dubroc's history to him who replied, "The Leader is at present in the East. There have been rumours of insurgency."

The Notary swore and broke the connection.

He swept out of his mansion and sprinted to a waiting helicopter. As he climbed aboard, he issued rapid instructions to the pilot. "Radio ahead and tell the mechanics to have my jet ready."

"It's on an exercise in the mid Atlantic," said the pilot.

The Notary snarled. "Have it recalled immediately."

The jet plane cruised unnoticed into Northern airspace. Parrish altered direction co-ordinates and the craft headed towards the centre of the North, once middle Europe, and the Notary's estates in what had once been Austria. Kazan had fallen asleep. The Eye had lain her gently on a bunk bed towards the centre of the airplane. The centre had been converted into luxurious living and sleeping quarters. Parrish was very afraid of the Eye and was not prepared to jeopardise his future by doing anything foolish.

Meanwhile, the Eye opened the case containing Nanos's assorted personality discs, all programmed according to various aspects of the Eye's vast experience and knowledge.

It was pointless the Eye looking at himself in a mirror as he cast no reflection. He didn't exist other than in the eyes of beholders. The Eye Itself existed, but was entombed in ice close to the Amazon's source and, for the time being, was closed in a deep sleep.

The Eye removed Nanos's disc and, in nanoseconds, replaced it with another.

Kazan awakened. She yawned and stretched expansively. The Eye admired her naked figure.

"I'm nude," said Kazan, apparently not in the least put out. "What have you been up to?"

"I regret to say I haven't been up to anything. Later perhaps?"

Kazan looked petulant. "You want to take a rain check?"

The Eye was puzzled. "I suppose so," he said hesitantly.

Kazan smiled, then frowned. "There's something different about you."

The Eye feigned innocence. "Is there?"

"I can't put my finger on it," said Kazan, "but there's definitely something."

"How can you tell?"

"Woman's intuition?"

"Ah. We mere men cannot legislate for that."

"You look the same," Kazan said slowly, "but you're more muscular. Like you've been working out, or something. But you haven't had time for that."

"Why don't you get dressed?"

"Why don't I stay as I am? You're very attractive."

"So are you," sighed the Eye, "but we'll be landing soon."

Kazan leapt off the bed and flounced towards a washroom. "Who seeks and does not take when once 'tis offered shall never find it more," she said on exit.

The Eye ventured to the cockpit and sat beside the pilot.

"How long?" he asked.

"Ten minutes."

"Good. Very good." The Eye gave Parrish a sideways glance. "You will work for me, won't you?"

Parrish smiled insincerely. "Of course."

"The alternative," hissed the Eye, "is death. You'd better believe that."

Any hint of a smile disappeared from Parrish's lips. He attempted humour, as those who are afraid often do. "I feel as if I'm being tempted by the Devil," he said lightly.

"Not a bad analogy," responded the Eye. "You'd do well to yield to temptation. The Devil can offer a lot."

"He has the best tunes," said Parrish.

The Eye's face became a mask of fury. "I'm not a lover of music," he said with a ferocity that caused Parrish to break into a sweat of fear.

"You seem a little different," the pilot said at length and very tentatively.

"What big eyes you have," said the Eye. "I suggest you look the other way. Then, like a wise monkey, you will see no evil."

Parrish thought it best to say nothing.

Kazan, fully clothed, joined them. "OK, Red Baron," she said, "when are we landing?"

"Right now," said Parrish and the airplane's nose dipped groundwards.

The Notary was furious. "What do you mean, you have no idea where my aircraft is?" he demanded of an Innuendo officer, a good and loyal soldier upon whom he could generally rely. The officer had a taste for young girls from the East and the Notary had been able to supply them. His name was Venom.

Venom was not to be intimidated. "It was on a brief exercise over the Azores. A reconnaissance of the South in preparation for the invasion. It headed west for no reason anyone can come up with, hovered over the Triangle, then disappeared from our screens. We're checking security procedures and codes right now."

The Notary calmed somewhat. "When I find out who was responsible, he'll wish he'd never been born."

A junior handed Venom a note. He smiled thinly as he read it.

"What does it say?" demanded the Notary.

"According to this," answered Venom, "you ordered the craft to leave the Azores and head west."

"I did? Impossible."

"Voice identification was precise. If you didn't give that order, someone who can perfectly replicate your voice did. I didn't think that could be done."

It came to the Notary in a flash of inspiration. Nanos's disc. If it could be programmed for personality, that personality would have a voice. It was too damaged for a pattern of speech to be recognised, but there had been a pattern and that pattern could have reproduced the Notary's voice. Not possible. The disc was in the Notary's possession. Therefore, there must be others.

"Track the airplane," He ordered.

Venom said, "With what? It's obviously in Stealth mode."

"Commandeer the Mother's craft."

"She won't like it, or allow it."

"Then take the President's. He's dead and won't be needing it."

Venom laughed. "Your wish is my command." He bowed mockingly.

Parrish put the jet down on a series of cultivated fields. It devastated many crops. "The farmers in the hills won't be too pleased," he said regretfully.

"That's the least of our worries," said the Eye. "News of our arrival is sure to spread quickly. We mustn't lose any time. Point us in the direction of the Notary's estate."

Parrish hesitated.

"Remember," went on the Eye, "if you are not with me, you are against me. Your fellow crew members were against me."

"And me," interjected Kazan. "And you know what happened to them."

"It's a couple of clicks in that direction." Parrish pointed straight ahead.

The Eye frowned. "Clicks?"

"Kilometres."

"How many Innuendo guards are there?"

"Very few. I'd say four at the most. The Mother ordered a raid and closed down some of the Notary's – er – activities. There'll be a few house staff – unarmed."

"How convenient," said the Eye.

"We'd better get a move on," Kazan said.

"What about me?" asked Parrish.

"Leave here in Stealth mode. Fly south to the deserts of Spain and land near Cadiz."

"It's desolate. It was destroyed years ago."

"That's why nobody will look for you there. Await my instructions. I'll communicate with you from the Notary's radio room. Stay tuned to that waveband."

"What about refuelling."

"You have enough to get to Spain and back and you can refuel once I've taken control of the North's airfield."

"You're going to do that?"

"Believe me, I will."

Parrish looked to Kazan. She merely smiled.

"Very well." The pilot nodded assent.

"I'm so glad you're on my side," said the Eye. "Should you think of turning your coat once again, you should consider how severe my vengeance might be." With that, the Eye descended from the plane, closely followed by Kazan. Neither of them bothered to watch the craft take off, but moved swiftly towards their target – the Notary's estate.

Parrish had been accurate. There were only four armed Innuendo guards. Unlike the Eye and Kazan, they paid a good deal of attention to the departing jet plane. This was their undoing. While they were distracted, Kazan shot two of them and the Eye, swifter than the flicking tongue of a snake, strangled the others. Within a few seconds the Eye entered the Notary's house. Kazan, concealed by the front entrance, covered the grounds.

A worried servant approached the Eye and was felled by a karate blow to the side of the neck. The Eye's new persona, extracted from Nanos's second disc, had improved his physical strength and martial arts ability. Kazan's kung fu elimination of the jet plane guard had persuaded the Eye that he'd better be ready for anything.

The Eye had no difficulty in finding the Notary's basement research facility and was impressed by its contents. The equipment was as good as, if not better than, that accumulated by Nanos at the Amazon's source.

The Eye searched various computer consoles. Nothing of interest, until he switched on the visual aid computer. Although Nanos's charred disc had been removed, the visual aid's automatic memory was still capable of playing its content.

Unlike the Notary, or Nanos, the Eye was unaffected by the dazzling display before him. After all, he'd seen it all before. He questioned another computer. "Where is the Notary?"

The computer indicated the North's capital.

The Eye could hardly contain himself. He felt he was about to burst into uncontrollable laughter. But the Eye possessed admirable self-control. It took him but a few seconds to programme the computers to self-destruct in one hour and take the Notary's estates with them.

He returned to Kazan at the house's entrance. "We can leave now," he said quietly, but authoratively.

"You're all action, aren't you?" Kazan commented.

The Eye led the way to a garage adjoining the house.

Kazan said, "You sure know your way around. How do you do it?"

"*Déjà vu*," came the reply.

In the garage were several electrically powered cycles. Kazan and the Eye selected two that were fully charged and raced out of the building.

"We in a hurry?" Kazan shouted.

"Sort of," the Eye shouted back. "This place blows apart in an hour."

Kazan accelerated her cycle. Laughing, the Eye followed suit.

The dead President's jet, piloted by Venom, with the Notary breathing hard on his neck, scoured the skies for Parrish and the missing craft.

"Well?" demanded the Notary.

"You'll need to be a little patient," said Venom. "Parrish has only just re-entered Stealth mode and it'll take a couple of minutes to make contact. You understand that's only possible if we're both in Stealth operation?"

"Yes, of course. What was he doing out of Stealth mode?"

"Landing and pausing a while and taking off. I'm searching for co-ordinates now." A light glowed on the pilot console. "Ah, there he is," Venom said.

"Where's he going?"

"South."

"Order him back."

Venom sighed exaggeratedly. "He's flying an armed fighter bomber with high destructive capability. I can ask him to come back."

The Notary was becoming agitated. "Talk to him."

Venom spoke into the communication transmitter. "Parrish, this is Venom. Do you read?"

No response.

"Try again."

Venom tried several times to contact Parrish, but to no avail. "I don't think he wants to talk to us," said the Innuendo officer, not without good humour.

"Run him down. Blow him out of the sky," said the Notary.

Venom gave him a long, hard look. "Take it easy, Mr Notary. We'll track him for the moment. Later on we'll decide whether or not to eliminate him."

The Notary looked suitably shamefaced. He knew Venom was right. "Very well. Track him."

Dubroc said, "I can't make any sense of it."

The Mother nodded agreement. "It doesn't make any sense, that's why. Half our jet airforce running around the skies, one apparently in pursuit of the other. What to do?"

"Nothing?" Dubroc suggested. "Wait and see

what happens."

"You're sure the Notary is on the President's plane?"

"Yes."

"And on the other?"

"The Notary's pilot – Parrish."

The Mother shook her head wonderingly. "Curiouser and curiouser."

Dubroc smiled. "It's quite funny, if you think about it."

"I've got something that'll wipe that smile off your face," said the Mother. "I've just heard the Leader's on his way back."

Dubroc frowned. "Maybe we should launch your plane? We could be in at the start of an air war."

The Mother thought for a moment. "There's more to this than meets the eye. We'll do as you suggest. We'll do nothing. For the moment."

The Eye and Kazan reached the capital as a red sky pushed aside a black night.

"There's a castle on the outskirts." Kazan said.

"I know," said the Eye.

"Is that where we're heading?"

"Clever girl." The Eye accelerated his machine.

After fumbling at her controls, Kazan followed on.

They swung their machines into the courtyard of Ludwig's castle, to be greeted by Theatre guards.

"Dismount!" ordered a sergeant.

Having obeyed, the Eye looked around him as dawn lightened the sky. "Just as I imagined it," he said. "You could say I've been here before, but not quite in the way you think."

The sergeant disarmed Kazan. "You have no weapon?" he enquired of the Eye.

The Eye smiled. "I don't feel I need one."

"Who are you and what do you want?" asked the sergeant brusquely.

"I am the Eye. This is my associate – Kazan. And I'd like to meet the Mother."

"No chance," said the sergeant. "You'll have to apply through the proper channels."

"There's no time for that. Kindly inform the Mother that we're on the brink of civil war. Not that she doesn't know that already. Tell her I've wiped out the Notary's base and that I fully anticipate one of your aircraft will go missing any time now. If she won't see me after that, I'll just sit back until the war's over. Then, if you're still alive, which I doubt, I can say I told you so." The Eye spoke quickly and was running out of breath.

The sergeant eyed him warily. "Wait here," he said and signalled that the other guards should watch the two visitors. Three five seveNs were trained on the Eye and Kazan as the sergeant left them to enter the castle proper.

"I've just thought of something," Kazan whispered to the Eye.

"Better late than never."

"The Notary's estate has been destroyed. How can we communicate with Parrish?"

"We can't. I'm afraid I've sent him off on a wild goose chase. The Notary was sure to notice the disappearance of his jet and to set off in pursuit. I don't hold out too much hope for Mr Parrish, or his aircraft."

Kazan was stunned. "Why?"

"The North's airforce is small, but very powerful. If I am to assume authority here, it must be destroyed. Along with the Notary and, when he comes back from the East, the Leader."

"How do you know the Leader's in the East?"

"Oh, I'm not omnipotent, but I know a lot."

"You're quite something, aren't you?"

The Eye smiled modestly. "Yes I am."

The sergeant beckoned to him from the castle door.

Kazan stepped forward with the Eye. There were ominous clicking sounds as five seveNs were locked and loaded. "Not you," barked the sergeant, "just him."

"Wait for me," said the Eye.

"Don't worry. I'm not going anywhere," Kazan said.

As the Eye strode towards the Sergeant waiting at the castle door, he heard her say, "Well boys, what nice big guns you've got. Mind if I take a closer look?"

The sergeant led the Eye through many corridors, some wide and well furnished, others narrow and secretive. At length, he was ushered into the Mother's private quarters. She turned from gazing out of a window to greet him. "I'm sorry about the detour," she said. "I wanted to be as certain as possible that you weren't seen by all and sundry." She indicated to the sergeant that he should leave. "Take care of this gentleman's companion," she instructed.

"In what way?" asked the sergeant.

The Mother smiled, as did the Eye.

"Treat her gently."

Once the sergeant had left the room, the Mother looked enquiringly at the Eye.

The Eye's smile broadened. "Perhaps you wouldn't mind asking your other guest to leave? I get a little fidgety when I know I have a weapon as powerful as the five seveN pointed at me."

The Mother perched on the end of her desk, a curious smile playing around her lips.

Dubroc stepped out from his place of concealment. He looked apprehensively towards the Mother.

"You can go," she said, "but leave the gun."

Dubroc placed his five seveN on her desk. He looked at the Eye, his gaze never wavering. "I'll be just outside the door," he said. "Just call, and I'll come running."

"Thank you."

The Eye observed that the Mother looked at Dubroc with affection, as well as respect.

Dubroc left the room. The Eye watched him go.

"I understand you imagine the North is on the brink of civil war?" the Mother said.

The Eye chuckled. "It's not just my imagination, it happens to be a fact. You believe it too, or you wouldn't have so readily agreed to see me."

The Mother nodded approvingly. "Go on."

"You are surely aware that the Notary and the Leader have plans to remove you from office at the earliest? How they do it does not touch their consciences. All depends on who becomes the fourth member of your Committee. If it is their candidate, you are lost. On the other hand . . ." The Eye's voice trailed away.

"You're suggesting my candidate would be a better bet?"

"For you, the North and the rest of the world. Do you have anyone in mind?"

The Mother shook her head.

The Eye smiled a dazzling smile. "Well, now you do."

"You?"

"Why not?"

"Why?"

The Eye began to pace about the room like a restless tiger. "We don't have time for me to explain in detail," he said. "All you really need to know for the moment is that, with me on your side, you can defeat the Notary and regain the loyalty of most of his Innuendo troops. You may also defeat the Leader, who has recently implemented his own plan of mayhem and murder. Again, the loyalty of most of his Works troops can be redirected."

The Mother had a hard time concealing shock and surprise.

The Eye continued before she could summon the breath to interject. "I have already destroyed the Notary's estates, his base of operations. He is at present pursuing his own jet aircraft which was, shall we say, borrowed for a while. By me, as it happens." He paused.

"Who are you?" enquired the Mother, an incredulous note in her usually velvet voice.

"I am the Eye. The saviour of the North. Check your communication traffic. You will discover that what I have told you is true. You can leave the Notary to me. It's the Leader you need to watch closely."

"He's just returned from the East."

"Then arrest him at once. If he should escape

our clutches, there'll be hell to pay. Instruct your best man. The one who just left the room."

"Dubroc."

The Eye stood stock still. "Ah. I'll remember that name."

The Mother faced the Eye. "I'll need time to think over what you've said."

The Eye snorted in anger. "You don't have any time. Time's on the run and we must catch up with it."

For what seemed like an eternity, the Mother stared at the Eye. Unblinking, the Eye stared back. The Mother reached a decision. "Very well. Let me check up on the condition of the Notary's estates. I'll instruct Dubroc to locate and detain the Leader. You will stay here. Then we shall see what we shall see."

Venom was chuckling.

"What's so funny?" asked the Notary.

"I have good news and bad news."

"Well?"

"The good news is that Parrish is within our sights and I can force him out of the sky. The bad news is that I've just heard your estates have been demolished."

The Notary looked fit to vomit.

Venom said, "Maybe the Leader has double-crossed you?"

The Notary regained a little, not much, of his

composure. "Maybe. More likely it's the Mother's work. Executed by Dubroc."

"Ah, Dubroc. I have a feeling he and I may face each other one day," said Venom. "That feeling tells me Mr Dubroc may not be too long for this world."

"You can take care of Dubroc later. Right now, I want Parrish dead and my jet retrieved in one piece."

"The first I can guarantee. The second is a little more difficult."

The Notary had almost recovered from the shock of the loss of his base. "One thing at a time, Venom," he said icily. "Parrish, the plane, the Mother and Dubroc. In that order."

"And the Leader?"

"Try to contact him. We'll find out where he stands."

"First things first," Venom said, as he put the ex-President's plane into a dive.

He fired two rockets that straddled the aircraft ahead of him.

Parrish swore and executed evasive tactics. The two rockets collided and exploded on his starboard side. He checked his computer: the jet piloted by Venom was sixteen miles astern. Too close for comfort. He checked his fuel gauge and swore again.

*

"All right," said Venom. "He knows we're on his tail. Now he'll turn it."

"Turn what?"

"Tail. He'll turn tail and run north. He has no alternative because he's about to run out of fuel. Flying over the Azores, a return trip west and now this run south, most of it in Stealth mode, leaves him very little leeway. My guess is he'll head for Sicily. There's a fuelling station there. He could head for Provence, but that would be touch and go."

"Make your mind up," the Notary snapped.

Venom remained calm. "Sicily it is."

The ex-President's jet altered course.

Parrish knew he had to act and act quickly. Sicily or Provence? They housed the nearest fuel dumps. Sicily was nearest, but his pursuers, knowing he must need fuelling at the earliest, would guess Sicily would be his likely destination. He put the jet on a reverse course, Stealth mode, while he thought things over. It had to be Provence or he'd see Palermo and die. He might die anyway, but flying further into the North could give him an outside chance of staying alive. Parrish decided to take that chance, programmed the aircraft to overfly Sicily and headed for southern France.

The Mother stared at the Eye in a kind of wonder.

"Everything you have told me is confirmed," she said. "I must apologise for doubting you."

The Eye assumed a suitably modest expression. "Now is the time to act," he said.

The Mother activated a televisual link with the command structure of her Theatre troops. She issued her instructions clearly and rapidly. All Innuendo troops were to be arrested and disarmed. Arena forces, pending the next President's election, were to come under her immediate command. Works soldiers not accompanying the Leader must be placed under observation and, at the first hint of dissidence or rebellion, should be treated as enemies and arrested and disarmed, or shot.

The Eye marvelled. The Mother was almost as ruthless as he was. He'd have to bear that in mind. She might prove more difficult to remove from the scene than he had previously thought. Still, that would come later. There remained the problem of the Notary, not to mention the Leader.

"Dubroc is waiting for the Leader at the airport," the Mother said, "He hasn't landed yet. Another half hour and we'll have him."

The Eye swore. "Too late," he cried. "The Leader's no fool. He'll smell a rat and run back East."

"Even if he does, there's not much hospitality for him there."

"On the contrary. Check his visits over the past year or so. You'll find he's been East more often than you thought. Building up an alliance, if I'm not mistaken. Remember, the Leader is an Easterner – a Russian."

The Mother smiled tolerantly. "You're expecting him to descend on the North with an army?"

"It's happened before. Genghis Khan made a fair job of ripping Europe apart. I know – I saw it."

The Mother's eyes dilated.

The Eye smiled. "There's more to me than meets the eye."

The Notary was linked in communication with the Leader. He informed him of all that had happened. There was a pause on the other end of the line. "Are you still there?" asked the Notary.

"Oh yes," responded the Leader tersely, "but not for much longer. I'm returning to the East. Thanks to your ineptitude, two jets are out of circulation, your troops are probably running about like headless chickens and the Mother is waiting in the wings to have me arrested or worse."

"What about me?" whined the Notary.

"It's every man for himself. I'm sure you'll come out of this smelling of roses. If not, well, good luck and goodbye."

The communication link was broken.

The Notary howled with indignation.

"There's no honour among thieves," remarked Venom.

"I'll have him tortured before I kill him," snarled the Notary.

Venom laughed. "We'll add him to our list, but first things first. We're about to land in Sicily."

Having doubled back on his flight path, in Stealth mode, Parrish was closer to Venom and the Notary than they had anticipated. The ex-President's aircraft had just settled on the fuel base's runway when, Parrish having switched to Open mode, his jet screamed out of the sky. The Notary, Venom and their crew raced for shelter.

Parrish smiled grimly as he unleashed all his homing rockets in tumbling mode. This meant that they would revolve out of the sky and bounce like bowling balls so that they would strike the jet on the ground from underneath and make certain of its total destruction. The President's plane became a fireball visible from miles around.

The Notary stood and stared in stunned silence.

Venom nodded approvingly. "Smart move," he muttered to himself. "I should have thought of that."

The Notary's sharp ears overhead the private comment. "Yes, but you didn't, did you?" he said, his words dripping sarcasm.

Venom shrugged. "We all make mistakes." He looked directly at the Notary. "You've been known to make a few in your time."

The Notary backed off. "What will Parrish do now?"

"Oh, he'll head for Provence. There's nowhere else to go."

"You said he couldn't make it."

"I said he might not make it, but Parrish seems to be ahead of us on that one. He's prepared to take his chances."

The Notary spoke with regained authority. "Radio Provence. Have him executed as soon as he lands."

Venom replied contemptuously. "Provence comes under the authority of Theatre troops, blindly loyal to the Mother. The last thing she'll do is kill him. He'll probably get a medal."

"What do you suggest we do?"

"Top up with fuel, weapons and every technological device we can find and head east. We can join up with the Leader."

"But he's run out on us. He's my enemy. I want him dead."

"You seem to want everybody dead. The dead can't help you. Alive, the Leader just might. You lost your temper earlier on. Bring it under control. Be more practical. Fly to the east."

The Notary thought for a moment. "You're right," he said at length. "There's nothing for us here. The Mother has clearly decided to eliminate us. Who put her up to it, that's what I want to know."

The Eye listened as Dubroc reported in from the North's airport. "The Leader has retraced his course," said Dubroc. "He's heading east. Shall I pursue?"

"That would leave no jet defence," said the Mother. She looked to the Eye for help. He frowned as he considered the position.

"No jet pursuit for the time being," said the Eye. "Prepare for a helicopter advance east – some helicopters to be fuel carriers. Dubroc can lead the expedition. In the mean time, where's the Notary?"

The Mother checked the information computer. She gasped.

"He's just landed the President's plane in Sicily and it's been destroyed on the ground."

The Eye pranced with delight. "One down, three to go."

"What?" asked the Mother.

The Eye ignored the question, realising he had been caught temporarily off guard. "Where are Parrish and the Notary's jet?" he asked.

"Out of Stealth mode, heading for our fuel

base in Provence," the Mother replied, having once again consulted the computer. "His getting there in one piece will be touch and go after all the flying he's done."

"Once he lands," said the Eye, "have your troops detain him and service the aircraft. We must get down there right away."

"What if he doesn't make it?"

"Then we'll turn round and come back."

Venom commandeered all the vehicles at the Palermo fuel base. Electric powered cycles weren't going to get them far, but there was a petrol-driven armoured troop carrier available.

"I thought these were obsolete," said the Notary.

"They are," responded Venom, "but somebody forgot to tell the Sicilians. Lucky for us."

"How far will it carry us?"

"Loaded with extra fuel, which will slow us down, we should make the helicopter base at Cassino in a couple of days."

"We may be too late," said the Notary anxiously. "What if Theatre or Arena troops are waiting for us?"

Venom smiled grimly. "We'll face that problem should it arise. For the moment, I happen to know there are only Works troops there. Lower grade, not the Leader's personal force. They'll obey my orders. They'll even obey your orders."

"We'd better get moving, hadn't we?"

"More haste, less speed," said Venom. "We need fuel and we need weapons. Let's go to work."

The Leader was going to have to put his jet down somewhere in what had once been the Ukraine. His pilot, a trusted aide called Scarab, had indicated that that was as far as they could go.

"Order the fuel base in the Urals to fly some out to us," said the Leader.

"It'll take time," said Scarab. "They'll have to overload and that's risky."

"Just tell them to do whatever they have to do. Tell them to do it quickly. The Mother is certain to order them to stand down. I can only depend on their loyalty for a short time."

"Very well." Scarab whispered instructions into his communicator.

When he had finished, the Leader issued further orders. "Tell Goran to meet us at the Black Sea. Tell him to mobilise his army. Tell him he's in for a fight."

Scarab stared coldly at his master. "Goran is a barbarian."

The Leader chuckled. "We're all barbarians at heart. You have to admit, he's treated us well up to now. You've enjoyed some of the Eastern girls he's provided. You've drunk his wine and you sang his songs. With his help, we'll conquer the world."

"It'll be a very different world," said Scarab cautiously.

"Indeed it will. I admit, I've lost a certain amount of control. I blame the Notary. Bloated with ambition, he hasn't the strength of character to achieve it."

"Whereas you have?"

The Leader patted Scarab on the shoulder. "Fear not, my friend. Once Goran and his mongrel hordes have placed me in power, I'll use that power to bring him and his followers to heel. It'll be a hell of a world in which to live."

"I think I might prefer Heaven," said Scarab ironically.

"Very tiresome," said the Leader. "The Devil has the best of everything. At a price, of course."

Parrish ran out of fuel over Corsica. He did everything he could to keep the jet airborne, but to no avail. It crashed into the muddy ditch that had once been the Mediterranean. Parrish parachuted clear and was picked up by a Theatre troop patrol. He was bloodied, but unbowed.

The Eye and the Mother had not yet left the North's capital. When the news of the ditched aircraft came in the Eye managed to conceal his delight. "Parrish deserves promotion," he said, remembering his promise to the pilot – a promise he had been quite prepared to break when it suited him. "He's a brave man. It's men like him and – er – Dubroc who promise well for our future," he added with fake sincerity. He was well aware that sincerity appealed greatly to humans. Fake that and they'd believe anything.

The Mother said, "I doubt we'll be able to salvage the plane."

The Eye shrugged. "If you play the game, you must expect to have to sacrifice a few of your pieces."

A young Theatre officer burst into the room. "The Leader has landed in the Ukraine," he said, "due to lack of fuel. He's ordered our base in the Urals to re-supply him."

The Mother winced. "Can we stop that?"

The Theatre officer shook his head. "We're too late."

The Eye said, "Never mind. We'll deal with the Leader in due course. Or rather, Dubroc will. What's become of our friend the Notary?"

"He's transporting towards Cassino. He and his group are crossing to mainland Italy as we speak. They're probably bogged down in the mud that was the Mediterranean."

The Eye thought for a moment. "What's at Cassino?" he asked.

"A dozen helicopters and forty Works troops – second grade."

"But still deadly," interjected the Mother.

"Will they obey you?" the Eye asked.

"No."

"Then they must be taught that there is a price for disobedience." He stared at the young officer. "Can you fly the Mother's jet?"

The young man hesitated, but only for a second. "Yes," he said firmly. "But I'm only trained for short flights."

"Good enough. Fly me to Provence. Parrish can take over from you."

The Mother was alarmed. "What do you intend to do?"

"Eliminate the Notary. With your permission, of course."

"And if I don't give it?"

"Then live to regret your decision."

The Eye waited impatiently until the Mother made up her mind. She looked at the officer. "Obey the Eye," she said quietly.

Kazan was seething with boredom when she saw the Eye and the young officer racing towards electric cycles for their journey to the airport. "Hey, what's going on?" she cried out.

The Eye glanced in her direction. "Come along and find out." He indicated to the Theatre sergeant that he should release his "guest".

The young pilot officer eyed Kazan appreciatively.

"Keep your eyes on the road, Sugar," she said.

"There'll be time to get acquainted later on."

The Eye, in high good humour, laughed.

The Leader stood close to his landed plane in a wheatfield in the Ukraine. "How long before the helicopters get here?" he asked Scarab.

"Soon."

"How soon is soon?"

"Soon enough."

The conversation that was going round in circles was interrupted by the roar of rotor blades as four helicopters raced overhead. Scarab and the Leader watched them come down.

Two of the helicopters were laden with spare fuel, weapons and supplies. The other two were for transporting the Leader and his small group to the Black Sea. Having identified the commander of the flight, the Leader asked after the fuel for the jet.

The Commander looked shamefaced. "There's a severe shortage of jet fuel," he said apologetically. "The jet will have to remain here until we can service it."

The Leader cursed. "The locals will rip it apart," he said with feeling. "Put a guard on it."

"Apart from pilots, I only have five men."

"They'll have to do."

The Commander was reluctant, but obliged to obey.

The Leader's helicopter piloted by Scarab, the

flight took off. They were waved away by the Commander and his apprehensive quintet.

"The locals aren't very friendly," observed Scarab. "I doubt those troops will survive."

"I'm more concerned about the plane," snapped the Leader.

"Pieces of it will turn up for sale in the Middle East."

The Leader sighed. "I'm afraid you could be right."

Parrish was astonished to be reunited with Kazan and the Eye. Delighted with Kazan, he was tentative in his relations with the Eye. "I had to overfly Cadiz," he said. "I was being chased south."

"You did very well," said the Eye benevolently. "You can take over from this officer and fly us to Cassino."

"Cassino? Why?"

"Yours not to reason why."

The young officer from Theatre took reluctant leave of Kazan.

"Catch you later," she said warmly.

The officer disappeared through the plane's entry hatch.

"Time to go," said the Eye. "Time is not on our side."

The Mother's jet took off and headed east towards Italy, a country only partially, and painfully, reclaimed from the desert legacy of Nature's fury.

Parrish recounted what had happened since he had last met with the Eye and Kazan. Kazan was impressed, the Eye less so, but he was encouraging all the same. "You've done well," he praised. "Now get us to Cassino as fast as you can."

"Stealth mode?"

"That won't be necessary. We're the only jet in the air." The Eye chuckled mischievously.

"No sooner said than done," said Parrish enthusiastically.

The jet sprinted across the sky.

Venom, the Notary and three Innuendo troopers chugged towards the Cassino fuel base.

"Can't this thing go any faster?" the Notary enquired petulantly.

Venom smiled sadly. "To travel hopefully is sometimes better than to arrive," he said quietly.

"What's that supposed to mean?"

"Whatever you like."

"Just get a move on."

Venom pressed hard on the armoured carrier's accelerator. Clouds of exhaust fumes followed it along the dirt road. The Notary coughed, his eyes streaming. The three troopers looked distinctly uncomfortable. Venom's smile seemed fixed.

They came in sight of a bare mountain.

"The dump's up there," Venom informed the Notary. "We'll have to take it slowly or this crate might topple over."

"Can't you call them up on the radio?"

Venom was not inclined to be indulgent. "Discretion being the better part of valour, I favour surprising everybody up there. Otherwise, we might not get too pleasant a welcome."

"You're right," said the Notary.

"I usually am," said Venom.

Parrish banked the Mother's jet so that it circled the mountain.

"Blast the helicopter base," ordered the Eye.

Parrish hesitated. "There are men down there."

"That didn't seem to bother you over Sicily. They're Works guards, am I right?"

"Right."

"If we land, they'll kill us. If we don't blow them off the mountain, the Notary will requisition every helicopter they have."

"Right."

"Then do as I say."

Parrish flew directly towards the mountain top and unleashed two rockets. As the jet banked away, the mountain of Cassino erupted like a volcano. The blast shook the jet plane.

Kazan said, "I think I'm going to throw up."

"Not again," said the Eye. "Remember, don't do it over me."

"Or me," added Parrish quickly. "Or over the instruments."

Kazan snorted derisively. "OK, OK, you've made your point."

"Where to now?" asked Parrish.

"Home sweet home."

"What about the Notary?"

"Let him stew. Wherever he's going – it'll take an eternity to get there."

The force of the blast at the top of the mountain had rocked the armoured personnel carrier so violently it had overturned. A trooper of Innuendo had his neck broken. The others scrambled out of the wreckage of the vehicle. Unusually for the Notary, it was he who remained calm in the face of Venom's fury.

When he had calmed down and checked that the other two troopers were suffering nothing worse than cuts or bruises, he turned his attention to the Notary. "What now?"

"I thought you'd never ask. What do you think? We move on."

"How and where?"

"As best we can and as far east as possible." He glanced up at the sky. "They may be back."

The four men salvaged as much equipment as they could and trudged eastwards, towards the Aegean Sea. As an adjunct to the Mediterranean, this was no more than a vast gully of mud. Only when heavy rains fell could it really lay claim to being anything resembling a sea.

"We'll never cross it," said Venom. "Not on foot."

"Do we have any choice?"

"There are villages around here. We'll raid one and steal some horses."

The Notary looked disgusted. "Is that all you can come up with? I haven't ridden a horse in my life. I wouldn't know how to."

Venom smiled. "Now might be a good time to learn."

Parrish landed the jet at the North's airport. As the Eye and Kazan disembarked, the Mother was there to greet them.

"The Cassino helicopter base has gone off the air," she said, a hint of anticipation in her tone.

Kazan said, "Yeah. And it sure as hell won't be coming back on."

"It's been destroyed," said the Eye quietly. "I assure you it was necessary. The Notary is temporarily stranded."

"What about him?" asked Kazan before the Mother could ask the same question. "What will he do?"

"Go east, young lady. He has no other choice. He'll have to trust that the Leader hasn't turned against him. He is, as it were, between the Devil and the deep blue sea."

"Yeah, well we're all on good terms with the Devil."

"May I enquire as to the whereabouts of Dubroc?" the Eye asked civilly.

"He's mobilised and is moving east," said the Mother.

"Good. Then he'll catch our tiger by its tail. We, on the other hand, must be prepared to go head to head with the Leader."

"How're you going to manage that?" Kazan asked.

"What happens when you take hold of a tiger's tail?"

"It turns to attack you," said Kazan.

Once their spare fuel tanks were empty, the Leader ordered two helicopters to be ditched. The other two approached the Black Sea. Like the Mediterranean and the Aegean, this was little more than a mud basin, a reservoir of very little water. But the rains were due at any time.

The Leader spoke to one of the pilots who had flown out from the Urals. "Was my message transmitted to Goran?"

The pilot nodded. "We all hope your negotiations with him will bring peace to the frontier," he said feelingly.

Scarab turned away so the other pilot could not see him smile. The Leader remained stone faced.

"I'll do my best."

The helicopters swooped low over Odessa. Once a thriving town and seaside resort, apart from witnessing the start of the Russian Revolution, it was now little more than a pleasant village of no strategic value to East, North or South. As such, it was the perfect location for clandestine meetings of foes who would be friends.

The helicopters landed on a beach, their rotors swiftly falling silent. The Leader, Scarab and the rest stepped on to the sand.

Suddenly, there was a sound like rolling thunder as close to a hundred horsemen galloped out of Odessa to meet them. At their head rode a fierce, ugly Tartar. The men from the Urals wanted to break and run. The Leader and Scarab forced them to stand still.

The horsemen swirled around the small group and the downed helicopters. There was much whooping and wailing and shots fired into the air from old carbines, shotguns and the like. As suddenly as they had appeared, a majority of the horsemen reined in, turned their mounts and raced back to Odessa. Only the fierce Tartar and two sturdy companions remained. The Tartar dismounted and approached the Leader. He smiled an evil smile that revealed stained teeth. "Leader. How good of you to come," he growled in a voice like sandpaper.

The Leader stepped forward. "It's good to see you, Goran."

The Tartar grunted. "I don't see you for months and here we are meeting again in the space of a few days. Do you have a problem, or do I?"

The Leader smiled reassuringly. "I have the more pressing problem. But it's nothing that can't be resolved with a little help from a friend."

Goran smiled in return. "A friend with an army to back him, you mean?"

"I can see we understand each other perfectly," said the Leader.

Goran glanced at Scarab. He took a step towards him and the two men shook hands. "Scarab is a good man to have on our side, don't you think?"

The Leader nodded.

Goran strode towards his two companions, then turned back. "What's the problem?"

The Leader relaxed somewhat. "I'm not sure how or why, but our plans for the future seem to have been unearthed and steps taken to foil them."

Goran laughed cruelly. "The Mother is tougher than you imagined perhaps?"

"Maybe. But something – or someone – is spurring her on."

*

With the Notary in stalemate for the time being and Dubroc preparing for the Leader in the East, the Eye turned his attention to the Mother. In order for his plans to succeed, it would be necessary to eliminate her, sooner or later. Sooner suited him best.

That he had convinced her of his worthiness there was little doubt and it was almost a certainty that she would place him in a position of authority in the North, once the not-too-small matters of the Leader and the Notary had been dealt with. But would she ensure his acceptance on to the Committee and would she nominate him for President? He doubted it. What to do?

The Mother, no doubt out of gratitude, had provided the Eye with private quarters in Ludwig's castle. High up in a tower, his rooms overlooked a tributary of the river Danube. Far from being blue, it was muddy and brown and probably contaminated, but it was still a watercourse, despite Nature's intervention of six decades previously.

The Eye selected an alternative disc from Nanos's supply and quickly exchanged it for the one that presently occupied his human eye. It was in this human eye that he was most vulnerable – something he had been at pains to conceal from Kazan when she had asked the question in the West.

The new personality was very different from the old.

The Eye, not expecting to see his reflection, stood in front of a full-length mirror. This time, something stared back at him. It was not someone, it was some*thing*.

"I am the Eye," said the Eye.

"I too am the Eye," hissed the thing. The sound emanating from its throat was similar to that made by a disturbed nest of vipers.

The Eye nodded. "You are the part of me that demands obedience."

The thing made a gurgling sound. "Yes. I am Death On Two Legs."

"We have learned a great deal from the human race," said the Eye.

"Yes, you have," responded Death.

The Eye smiled resignedly. "I need to dispose of the Mother."

"Of course. You've come to the right place," said Death.

"How?"

"You'll find a way."

"I need your help."

Death sighed a sigh like the sound of a rattlesnake.

"I am you and you are me. You will help yourself."

The image in the mirror faded.

The Eye removed the disc and inserted yet

another. This time he saw no reflection.

"What the hell is going on?" General Lamar may have been past his prime, but his voice was still stentorian.

Dubroc winced. "We're mobilising for the East."

"On whose authority?"

"The Mother's and the Eye's."

Lamar's eyes flickered like a snake's forked tongue. "Who or what is the Eye?" he asked.

"He seems to have assumed an advisory capacity to the Mother." There had been a great deal of the bustle of preparation going on when Dubroc had been challenged by Lamar. It had ceased for a while, but now, on a hand signal from Dubroc, it continued. Lamar ignored the apparent challenge to his authority.

"What is the reason behind mobilisation?" the General asked.

"The Leader and the Notary have challenged the North's stability."

Lamar grinned evilly. "You mean, we've got a civil war on our hands?"

Dubroc smiled back. "Seems like it."

Lamar sighed. "I spend a few days relaxing in the snows of Scandinavia and all hell breaks loose behind my back. Where is the Leader now?"

"In the East."

"And the Notary?"

"Stuck somewhere in Italy, but trying to join up with the Leader, we imagine."

"Who stuck him in Italy?"

"The Eye."

"Ah. That name again. I look forward to meeting him."

The General paused for a moment, as if making his mind up about something. "What's the state of mobilisation?"

"We have sixty helicopters – forty action craft and twenty carrying supplies. We have two hundred Theatre and four hundred Arena troops ready to go. That's the most we can transport. If we move now, we can be on the border with the East in forty-eight hours."

Lamar gritted his teeth.

Dubroc waited.

"Move now," ordered Lamar.

There were only a dozen inhabitants of the coastal village in southern Italy, but there were seven horses. Venom shot two male villagers on the outskirts, then he and the other two troopers raced between the houses, little more than adobe huts, firing indiscriminately as they ran. There was no resistance, save from the women the two troopers were eager to despoil.

To save argument and time, Venom killed the women out of hand. The troopers were disgruntled but, mightily afraid of Venom, did not object.

The Notary was sweating as he viewed the destruction.

"Burn the village," he said. "The flames will light us on our way."

Venom nodded to the troopers and, having piled horse feed and grain next to the huts, doused these with kerosene and threw firebrands onto the roofs. The blaze was spectacular.

Venom shot two of the horses and, mounted on four of the remaining five, with the fifth carrying supplies, the quartet set off into the mud flats of the Aegean.

"There's someone who wishes to meet you," said the Mother.

She stepped aside and ushered General Lamar into the Eye's quarters. She frowned. There was something a little different about the Eye, she thought. The General greeted the Eye warily.

"So, you've made up your mind?" said the Eye matter-of-factly.

"What do you mean?" the General asked cagily.

"Come, come, Lamar, don't waste my time. You received overtures from the Leader, didn't you?"

The General began to splutter a protest.

The Eye took him firmly by the arm. "Don't play games with me, Lamar," he hissed menacingly. "You're out of your league."

Lamar was shaken and twitched with fear.

The Mother stood to one side, half astonished that Lamar might have turned against her, half incredulous that the Eye seemed to know so much.

"It's true, I was approached," said the General, "but I gave the Leader short shrift."

"I'll bet you did," sneered the Eye.

Lamar tried hard to recover his composure.

The Eye spoke to him very quietly. "You're not as young as you were and age's companion is usually fear – fear of the unknown future and how long that future might last. The best of men have been known to falter at this last hurdle."

Lamar said, apparently sincerely, "You're very wise."

The Eye seemed unimpressed by the compliment. "What is crucial," he continued, "is that you have now, as it were, seen the light."

"Oh, I have," interjected Lamar.

The Eye smiled. "I'm so glad you've decided to join the winning side."

"What makes you so sure we're going to win?" Lamar enquired, attempting humour.

The Eye's words were icy. "Well, if we don't, it will be the Leader's turn to give *you* short shrift."

Lamar swallowed. "I've ordered Dubroc to move east," he said. "The sooner we tackle the

Leader and his allies the better."

"Allies?"

Lamar looked to the Mother. She seemed to be staring at a point over his head. He looked back at the Eye. "The Leader has forged an alliance with Goran."

There was a sharp intake of breath from the Mother.

The Eye chuckled humourlessly. "Goran the Barbarian and his thousand horses. You think they'll be enough to defeat us?"

"They'll be reinforced with some of the Leader's elite Works troops. The Notary's Innuendo force could join them. The Leader still has his jet."

"It's grounded in the Ukraine," said the Eye. "If the locals haven't stripped it of its spare parts, it will be destroyed shortly."

The Mother's surprise matched that of the General.

The Eye continued, "I have despatched the Mother's jet to the East." He turned to her. "I do hope you don't mind my jumping the gun." he said with sincerity.

Parrish had taken Kazan along for the ride. The Mother's jet, in Open mode, cracked in and out of the sound barrier as it hurtled towards the Ukraine, its computers seeking the co-ordinates of the Leader's downed aircraft.

"I could get used to this," said Kazan. "It sure as hell beats walking."

Parrish smiled. He was much taken with Kazan. Most men would be. "When we've destroyed the Leader's plane, maybe we could spend some time together?" He said shyly.

Kazan feigned surprise. "Why, sir, what do you mean?"

Parrish blushed. The jet jinked slightly off course. Parrish adjusted the controls.

Kazan laughed. "Best keep your eyes on the way ahead and your hands to yourself," she said lightly. "Putting your hands on me will have to wait. We've a war to fight."

Parrish turned slightly towards her and she kissed him. Again the aircraft altered course.

Kazan said, "Right now, I reckon you've got your hands full, Mr Parrish."

"I can wait," Parrish said.

"I'll bet you're worth waiting for," said Kazan, licking her full lips.

The plane would have drifted off course again had not the computer signalled the downed jet's location. "Two minutes," shouted Parrish as he slid the aircraft into a hard left, controlled dive.

"This is better than a funfair," laughed Kazan.

The jet levelled out and overflew the Ukrainian wheatfield. The Leader's plane was clearly visible, as were the five guards attending it. "Works troops from the Urals," said Parrish.

"What are you going to do?"

"What would the Eye do?"

Kazan frowned. "I guess he'd shoot them."

"That's what I'm going to do."

Parrish switched armaments to manual, rotated two machine guns and, slowing the aircraft, flew low over the ground towards the guards.

The guards had assumed the Mother's jet was bringing reinforcement. Their mistake. Before they knew what was happening and could scatter, Parrish's machine guns had cut them to pieces.

Parrish banked the plane, armed its rockets and made another run, this time directly over the Leader's aircraft. He released all the rockets he had, certain that one at least would score a direct hit. As it happened, they all did and the Leader's jet exploded apart. The wheatfield was aflame from edge to edge.

"Wow! Guy Fawkes, eat your heart out," said Kazan.

Parrish was silent as he readjusted the controls and set a course to return them to the North.

"You OK?" enquired Kazan.

Parrish nodded. "I don't like killing my own troops," he said sadly.

"They were our enemies," said Kazan encouragingly. "They weren't your troops any more.

It's tough, but that's what a civil war's all about."

"How did it come to this, that's what I want to know."

Kazan didn't know, but she said, "It was always going to come to this. When you have something somebody else wants, sooner or later they'll come and get it. Unless you can stop them. Stopping them means doing what you've just done and it's not over yet. It just takes a little flame to start a huge conflagration. The little flame in this case is the Eye."

"Who, what and why is he and where's he from?"

"He's from the Amazon's source. Who he is, I'm not certain. He changes all the time. The changes are subtle, but they happen. What he is is the man who'll help us to victory over those who want to destroy us. Why he's doing it remains to be seen, but I have a funny feeling that he might be the dragon, rather than Saint George."

"What makes you feel that?"

Kazan smiled grimly. "Woman's intuition. The Eye's a great believer in it."

The woman was a ravishing beauty. She had a perfect figure, matched by perfect skin tone. Her eyes were large and beguilingly blue, her nose enticingly petite, her lips full and sensuous. Her breasts, though not large, were round and firm. She wore a tight leather outfit that showed off every curve. Kazan was beautiful but, compared to this woman, she looked drab.

General Lamar greeted her at his headquarters close to the North's airport. He didn't know who she was, or where she'd come from, but she'd promised important information and was the sort of woman no one, not even hardened Theatre and Arena soldiers, would turn away from the door.

"I am Lamar," said the General, almost salivating as his eyes took in the loveliness of the woman before him.

"I am Avila," the woman said, her voice soft and inviting. "May we speak alone?"

Lamar, who should have known better, threw caution to the winds and dismissed his guards. "What can I do for you?" he asked.

Avila smiled, showing perfect teeth. She perched lightly on the edge of Lamar's desk and leaned towards him, her sweet breath like a soft breeze across his cheeks. "Rather, what can I do for you?" she said.

Lamar made a movement towards her, but she was too quick for him. She slid off the edge of the desk and positioned herself close to the door.

Lamar composed himself. "Your message – marked very urgent, I might add – promised important information. What do you have to say?"

"Are we likely to be overheard?"

"This is my private office. It is quite secure. We will not be overheard."

Avila smiled seductively. The General went weak at the knees.

"I have a message from the Leader," Avila said, her voice barely above a whisper.

Lamar looked stunned.

"He's ready to make his move," went on the woman, "but you have to do something first."

Lamar's mouth gaped open, but he could not speak.

Avila moved closer. "You must see to it that the Mother dies. That a Theatre soldier is blamed for her death. That he is swiftly tried and executed. Then there must be an incident at Ludwig's castle that apparently persuades you that there are traitors in your midst. You will call upon the Leader to save the North. All Arena and Theatre troops will be withdrawn from the East and the Leader will return in triumph. A triumph you will share."

Lamar's eyes glittered. "I'm sworn to support the Mother and the Eye," he said almost proudly. "I will not shirk my duty."

Avila sighed. "The Leader thought you were his ally. That you wanted him to obtain the Presidency for you. Don't you want it?"

The General licked his lips. "I'm not certain he

can deliver."

Avila smiled wickedly. "Be assured that, if you do as he says, he can. Of course, if you decline his offer, I'll have to suggest to him that you're a turncoat." The General moved out from behind his desk and stood very close to Avila. She did not flinch. "Suppose I do as he says," whispered Lamar, "what guarantees are there that I'll get what I want?"

Avila placed an arm on his shoulder, drew him to her and brushed his cheek with her lips. "I'm part of the guarantee," she said. "Take me on account." She began to unbutton her leather blouse.

Parrish was overflying southern Italy and the Aegean. His hawk eyes searched the ground below. Kazan, strapped into the second pilot's seat beside him, was humming to herself.

"I can't contact the North," Parrish said concernedly.

"They'll get in touch when they want to. You have your instructions."

"Yes. But we seem to be living in a rapidly changing world."

"Ain't it the truth," interjected Kazan.

"Those instructions might have altered," concluded Parrish.

"OK. You keep flying and I'll keep trying to make contact." She took over the communication console and began to dial radio coordinates.

The Notary and Venom, with the two troopers keeping their horses under control, were concealed in a cave carved out of a mud mountain built by the wind. They watched as Parrish turned the Mother's jet away from them.

"He'll be back," said Venom. "He's following a search pattern."

"He's looking for us?"

Venom shook his head. "Your grasp of the obvious is staggering," he said.

The Notary scowled his displeasure.

Venom looked east. "We have company," he muttered. "Tribesmen by the look of them."

"We'd better stay hidden," said the Notary. "Maybe they'll pass us by."

"Maybe they won't."

Venom stepped out of the mud cave and waved to a group of horsemen in the distance. They spotted him immediately and spurred their mounts towards him.

"You'll get us all killed," said the Notary.

"They could be part of Goran's forces. A long distance patrol. If they are, they'll have a radio – primitive, but in working order. They can call up help from the Leader."

"And if they're not Goran's forces?"

Venom smiled. He turned to the troopers.

"Lock and load," he ordered. "If they're hostile, kill them all."

There were eight tribesmen. As they approached, they slowed their horses to a walk. Eight rifles were trained on the Notary's group. Venom spoke Arabic. The tribesmen smiled and lowered their rifles. They dismounted and embraced the Innuendo soldier.

Goran told the Leader that the Notary was in the Aegean mud basin and had made contact with one of the Tartar's outlying patrols.

"I didn't know your power spread that far," said the Leader.

Goran smiled brightly. "I'm like an octopus – I have many tentacles."

"You've despatched the helicopters to pick up the Notary?"

Goran nodded, bit into a peach and sprayed juice pretty well everywhere. He spoke with his mouth full, spitting out peach skin as he did so. "What use is he to us?"

The Leader was disgusted by Goran's eating habits, but was not in a position to voice any criticism. "No use at all," he said. "He has outlived any usefulness he might have had."

Goran's eyes widened. "Then why rescue him from the Aegean?" he spluttered.

"I like to take care of my problems personally," said the Leader. "That way I'm certain they're properly dealt with. Hearsay is no good to me. I like to *see* my opponents dead."

Goran swallowed the remains of his peach. "What about his men?"

"Oh, they'll be useful. Venom is among them."

"I don't know him."

The Leader smiled. "You'll like him. He's twice as vicious as Scarab."

Goran laughed, then almost choked. The Leader slapped him hard on the back. "Eating is like dancing, Goran. The slower the better. There's more time to enjoy the sensation."

Avila stood naked in front of a mirror. She could not see her reflection, but Lamar, lying on a couch, could – and admired what he saw. "I have someone on my staff who will kill the Mother," he said. "He's a Westerner. Coming from the West herself, she wasted no time in taking him for her lover."

Avila turned towards him. She ran her fingers over her breasts. "It must be done quickly," she said.

Lamar looked at her hungrily. "Your wish is my command."

Avila reached out and touched him. "I wouldn't have it any other way."

"Take me to the Leader," the Notary commanded one of Goran's Tartars as he stepped down from the helicopter. Venom laughed, before ordering the two Innuendo troopers to unload their equipment.

Goran and the Leader were housed in a magnificent tent pitched on the beach of the Black Sea. Goran's greeting was subdued and Venom sensed danger. Not so the Notary. He challenged the Leader. "Whose side are you on?" he yelled.

"I thought we were in this together?"

"Yes, well I changed my mind," said the Leader and shot the Notary right between the eyes with a five seveN.

Venom froze. Goran stepped outside the tent.

The Leader pointed the five seveN at Venom. "Are you with me, or against me?"

"Do I have a choice?" asked Venom drily.

"Oh, yes. Not much of one, I admit."

"What's in it for me?"

"Everything and anything he couldn't give you." The Leader indicated the Notary's corpse.

There was a long pause.

"After due consideration," said Venom pompously, "I've decided to throw in my lot with you."

The Leader thought that was very funny.

The Mother was resting. The last few days had been bewildering and exhausting. Dubroc was headed East and Lamar was controlling the situation from his headquarters. Parrish had destroyed the Leader's plane on the ground – much to the chagrin of the Ukrainian locals who coveted its spare parts – and was now in pursuit of the Notary. There was little she could do but wait for further developments. She drifted in and out of sleep.

A shadowy figure sidled into her room. For a moment, she thought it was her sometime lover, a handsome Westerner from her Theatre army. It couldn't be. He would be with Dubroc, marching eastwards. She opened her eyes wider and saw that her visitor was a beautiful woman. The Mother rose to her feet, summoning as much dignity as she could.

The intruder, Avila, smiled beguilingly. "I'm so sorry to disturb you," she said disarmingly.

"How did you get past the guards?" demanded the Mother, her curiosity overcoming her immediate anger.

"General Lamar gave me a pass." Avila waved a piece of paper in the air. "I think he's persuaded everybody that I've been promoted from who knows where to be your personal assistant."

"Why would Lamar do that?"

"Older men are so easily seduced, don't you think?" Avila was still smiling. She stepped closer to the Mother who had nowhere to retreat, save to return to the sleeping couch behind her. The Mother felt Avila's hot, sweet breath on her face. Before she could cry out, strong fingers grasped her round the throat, sharp fingernails gouged her flesh. She struggled – squirming this way and that – fighting oblivion. But she was held in an iron grip. Her life faded into death's shadow.

Avila lowered the corpse onto the couch. "Farewell my lovely," she whispered. She whirled round as someone else entered the room. It was Lamar. He quickly took in the situation. Avila seemed languid, almost uninterested, as if she had been expecting him.

There was a commotion in the corridor outside. "Get it over with," said Avila, as she turned away from him.

Lamar shot her in the back.

Parrish decided he'd had enough. "We'll never find them in this wilderness," he said.

Kazan was inclined to agree. "I still can't raise the North," she said. "What do you suppose is going on up there?"

Parrish flipped the plane on its back, executed reverse thrust, changed course, levelled off and headed north.

"Very funny," said Kazan. "I think I'm going to be sick."

Lamar had the Mother's death chamber locked

up and sent a trooper in search of the Eye. He found him in his quarters.

The trooper was puzzled. When last seen, the Eye had been at the airport. How had he returned to Ludwig's castle unobserved?

The Eye looked at him questioningly and the trooper reported the Mother's death at the hands of a beautiful stranger. The trooper couldn't be certain, but he thought the Eye wept a solitary tear.

The Eye confronted Lamar outside the Mother's room. "I'm not impressed by Theatre security," he said. "None of us are safe. Who was the assassin?"

Lamar thought himself very much in control of the situation. "She claimed to be a messenger from the Leader. She tried to seduce me with false promises of power and wealth if I arranged the Mother's murder. I concocted a plan and she – her name was Avila – went along with it. But I'm afraid she was a little cleverer than I thought. She claimed the Mother's life before I could stop her. I arrived here just too late."

"But not too late to eliminate the evidence?"

The General scowled angrily. "If I was going to betray the North, I'd have gone along with everything Avila told me and the Leader would be knocking at our gates right now."

The Eye said, "A slight exaggeration, but I take your point. May I?" He indicated the locked door. Lamar opened the door with a security card and he and the Eye stepped inside. There was a definite odour of death. Lamar wrinkled his nose. The Eye seemed unperturbed. "Did you sleep with her?" he asked.

Lamar was thrown off guard by the question, but recovered quickly. "I had to get as much information out of her as I could," he said innocently.

The Eye chuckled.

"As a matter of fact," continued the General, "there was something about her that was unreal. Our coupling was hardly pleasurable. She looked like an angel and I admit I was seduced by her beauty. But, somehow, that beauty seemed manufactured. The picture on the box was ravishing, its contents disappointing."

The Eye gave him a look of sheer loathing.

Lamar, failing to notice it, said, "I'll get some men to tidy up in here." He exited the room.

Left alone, the Eye stooped over the corpse of Avila. He placed a finger in her right eye and extracted a miniature disc.

Dubroc received the news with something approaching despair. The Mother had helped guide him along the path of his life and he had loved her daughter. When the fates conspired against him, they didn't waste time on trivia. For a moment, Dubroc wished he had never been born. But that was defeatism and Dubroc was not the kind to admit defeat, whatever the odds against him. He pulled himself out of his misery.

Lamar had communicated that an infiltrator sent by the Leader had murdered the Mother. Well, the Leader would pay a heavy price.

Arena and Theatre troops were now stationed at the very edge of the East. They had already made contact with marauding bands of Goran's Tartars and, as perturbed by the death of the Mother as Dubroc, had wasted no time in giving them a thrashing.

Eighteen of Goran's men lay dead. There were no casualties for Arena and Theatre.

Lamar communicated that the Eye, with the blessing of the Mother, was now heir to command in the North and would be joining Dubroc's forces post haste. Lamar himself would run the campaign from headquarters. Parrish and the Mother's jet would ride shotgun in the South, in case of assault from there. With the Atlantic Ocean as a barrier, any attack from the West would be signalled well in advance.

Dubroc waited impatiently for the Eye to arrive. He was anxious to wreak destruction on Goran, the Leader and the East.

Goran's primitive transmitters were powerful

enough to intercept Theatre radio traffic and he quickly learned of the Mother's death and the sudden elevation of the Eye.

The Leader strode along the Black Sea beach, Goran finding it hard to keep up with him. The first rain of the season began to fall. "We've lost control," said the Leader harshly. "The Eye, whoever or whatever he may be, has wrested it from us. We must get it back, or I'll have nowhere to go in this world. I'll have to stay here until I die."

Goran looked offended. "It's not so bad."

The Leader threw him a glance of distaste. "It's bad enough."

Goran opened his mouth to capture the falling rain.

"How ready are we?" snapped the Leader.

Goran choked on rainwater. He managed to clear his throat. "I have a thousand armed horsemen," he said, "and we have recruited close to a hundred of your Works soldiers, together with their arms. With the death of the Notary, Innuendo troops are in short supply. We have Venom and two others. Of course, we have the admirable Scarab who is well fitted for command. My troops are skirmishing on the borders as we speak."

The Leader embraced the Tartar and voiced his approval.

"Then the game's begun," he said, "and we're

risking everything on the wheel of chance. What a victory awaits us."

Goran shook his head. "You Russians are so emotional," he said sagely.

The Works

"An eye for an eye"
 Old Testament

The Eye knew that General Lamar was a liar. The more he came into contact with the human species, the more determined he became to punish them for their centuries of misdeeds. But the General was no fool. Though beguiled into treason by Avila, he had quickly cottoned on to the fact that he was being used and reacted with self-serving alacrity. The Eye had thought he might, and now he had the measure of the man he could deal with his threat at leisure. The Mother had illustrated that the meek are unlikely to inherit the Earth and the Eye would see to it that the devious and greedy wouldn't either. The Eye alone was the heir apparent.

For the time being, and time was always the Eye's closest ally, the General could be left to perform his task of organising the war in the East. Once that was concluded, the Eye had a secret weapon that could be used to bring about Lamar's fall from grace. Avila had revealed the old man's weakness. Kazan would exploit it to the full.

The Eye went east. He reached Dubroc's headquarters to find the young Theatre officer straining at the leash, eager to be upon the enemy.

"Are you ready to go?" enquired the Eye.

"I've been ready for two days or more," responded Dubroc.

"Then what are we waiting for? Let's deal the Leader a blow he'll never recover from."

Dubroc grinned enthusiastically. "I'll order the advance right now."

"They're moving," said Goran indifferently.

The Leader sighed. "It's a long way from there to here."

Goran, his eating habits as disgusting as usual, was devouring a chicken. "Why don't we meet them half way?" he mumbled as he chewed. The Leader had difficulty hearing him.

He and Goran gazed out over the Black Sea which, because the rains had come, was just beginning to resemble its former self. "They'll try to outflank us," said the Leader finally. "They'll move against the Urals, then attack us from the east and the west. It's a classic manoeuvre. It's been used since time immemorial."

"Then, while some of their troops are engaged in the Urals, we'll advance to the west, catch the remainder off their guard and wipe them out."

Goran spat a piece of gristle onto the sand.

The Leader looked at him admiringly. "You know, Goran, I think I've always underestimated you?"

Goran grunted and looked smug. "The only problem I've got is motivating my men. They're bound to suffer heavy casualties. Such sacrifice will have to be worth their while."

The Leader sighed again. "You can promise them the Earth. For that is what we shall gain once we've conquered the North. There'll be wine, women and wealth. The wine is superior to yours. The women colder, but there's great pleasure in thawing them out. And there'll be riches beyond anyone's wildest dreams."

"I suppose that will have to do." said Goran, his attempt at irony falling flat.

"Send out skirmishers," instructed the Leader.

"I already have," snorted Goran derisively.

Dubroc's helicopter was the first to go down. The pilot was killed outright and two of the four troopers on board were badly injured. "What the hell hit us?" demanded Dubroc.

One of the troopers replied, "A shoulder-held missile carrier. It will have been out of circulation for some time, but there are a few for sale if you know where to go. As far as we're concerned, they're obsolete, but they do the job."

Dubroc frowned. "Sometimes I think we're so

anxious to catch up with the new, we forget that the old wasn't exactly inferior."

Another helicopter burst into flames about a mile ahead of them.

"We'd better find this missile shooter before he wipes us out."

Venom smiled with satisfaction. Two rockets fired, two direct hits. There were two rockets left and his detachment of eight Works guards was armed with pump-action shotguns and five seveNs. They were good, hard men who had chosen to throw in their lot with the Leader rather than return to the North, a place they now considered governed by milksops. Venom knew differently but, having made their choice, he and his men would fight to the last. They had no other choice but victory or death.

Venom's deputy, a scarred veteran campaigner named Edge, called out, "There are three men on our left. They're tracking the heat from our missile shooter."

Venom swung his gaze in the enemy's direction. "Survivors from the first helicopter crash," he said. "Take two men and wipe them out. Do it quickly. Their comrades may come looking for them. We'll head south and east. Meet us at the rim of the peninsula."

Edge indicated that two of the group should follow him. Venom set off with the others.

"The missile shooter is about a mile to our right," reported one of Dubroc's men. The three of them were concealed in a thick copse of trees.

Dubroc smiled grimly. "If we've spotted them, you can be sure they've seen us. If I were their commander, I'd split my force and send troops to take us out."

"They're on their way," said the trooper. "Just three of them." He passed a pair of binoculars to Dubroc.

Dubroc focused on Edge and his men. "They're right out in the open," he said, almost incredulously. "They're either trying to draw our fire so that they can locate us, or they're damn fools."

"Maybe they're confident they can overrun us," said the trooper.

"Well, pride comes before a fall." Dubroc locked and loaded his five seveN. "Cover me," he said. "We'll turn their own tactics against them. I'll draw their fire while you take them out."

The two troopers nodded.

Dubroc burst out of the trees, firing as he came. Sometimes the direct approach is most effective. This was one of those times.

Edge reacted quickly and dived for cover. His two companions were less fortunate. Full-metal-jacketed projectiles from Dubroc's five seveN ripped one of them apart. The other fell under a hail of fire from the troopers hidden in the trees.

Dubroc found cover and waited for Edge to make his move.

Edge was cursing himself. He'd walked right into trouble and it was his own fault. Still, he remained alive. For how much longer remained to be seen. He loosed off a burst of fire into the trees and raced back towards the gully from where Venom had fired the missile shooter. He ran like the wind.

Dubroc went down on one knee, grasped his weapon two handed and fired at the retreating Edge. Bullets crept up on the fugitive, but he reached the gully and hurled himself into cover before they could cut him down.

Dubroc reloaded. "Faster than a ferret," he muttered to himself. Dodging from cover to cover, he set off towards the gully.

Edge watched him coming and smiled his satisfaction. "Come home to me," he whispered. "Have I got a surprise for you." He chambered two rounds of spreadshot in his pump-action gun. When he looked up, Dubroc was nowhere to be seen.

Edge scanned the ground in front of him. The Theatre soldier must have gone to ground, he thought. Well, Edge was a patient man and he reckoned he had the edge. He chuckled to himself. Time passed. Edge became a little agitated. "Come on," he muttered, "come on. What are you waiting for?"

A voice from behind him said, "Looking for me?"

Edge whirled round and stared into Dubroc's dark eyes as sixteen five seveN projectiles slammed into his body.

Venom scanned the land behind him with binoculars. No sign of Edge and his men. "Keep moving," Venom ordered the others. "I'll catch you up."

The five troopers, laden with the missile shooter and other equipment, walked on.

Venom spoke softly into a radio communicator. "The main force is curving round us towards the Urals," he said. "We've been overflown by eight helicopters and have brought down two. I'm going to have to leave the other six to you. Right now, I've something else on my mind." He switched off the radio and, again with the aid of binoculars, searched for any pursuers. He had a feeling Edge wouldn't be coming. Whoever had taken him down must be very good. Venom, tight lipped, looked forward to encountering him.

Dubroc had ordered his two troopers to take care of the wounded men left by the downed helicopter and to wait for support. He assumed their absence from the advance to the Crimean peninsula would soon be noted and someone would come to their rescue. Meanwhile, he set off after the remainder of the group that carried the missile shooter.

The Leader received Venom's message just in time. There was one other missile shooter and only three rockets. Goran's men, unused to the equipment, were inaccurate in the extreme and likely to cancel out any advantage the missiles might have given them.

The Leader suggested – you didn't give the Tartar orders – that Goran take his thousand horsemen to meet any advance from the west by Theatre and Arena troops. The eight, now six, helicopters would be an advance party. The main force would be marching on behind.

Goran saw the logic of the suggestion, but decided to divide his troops in case they should be tactically outwitted and the enemy fell upon their rear. Three hundred horsemen, under the Leader's temporary command, would remain by the Black Sea. The rest would surge towards the invaders. Scarab would remain as the Leader's second-in-command.

The Leader, though reluctant, had no alternative but to acquiesce.

It had been the Eye's idea to feint towards the Urals. He too was a student of military strategy and, like the Leader, was well acquainted with the great campaigns. Indeed, he had seen them flash before him and gazed in wonder as humans slaughtered humans for some petty, imagined advantage. Now it was his turn.

As the Leader had anticipated, Theatre and Arena armies had outflanked Goran and his Tartars. But not in an easterly direction, towards the Urals. Instead, the Eye had issued instructions for the North's troops to spread south and attack across the Black Sea. Now filling with water from heavy rainfall, the sea would be crossed by means of oar-driven boats like the galleys of Ancient Rome. These had been acquired from loyal Northern soldiers stationed close by what had once been Turkey, ready for the now-postponed advance into the true South.

As it was reported that Goran and his horsemen were moving west, the Eye smiled in satisfaction. The North's army was well prepared, dug in along the rim of the Crimean peninsula. Only small groups of marauders had passed through these defences and all had failed to take note of them. Twenty-two long-range helicopters, armed with rockets and machine guns, were prepared for instant take-off against the foe. They were heavily camouflaged and well protected by ground troops. Goran the Barbarian was in for a good hiding.

The Leader gazed across the sea. The heavy rains

had passed on for the moment, the sky was clear and visibility was good. Good enough for him to spot the troop-laden boats heading towards him. He cursed. Whoever it was who called himself the Eye had outmanoeuvred him. It was too late to call back Goran's seven hundred men. He'd try but, unless he could hold out with his three hundred, they were unlikely to be able to return in time. He ordered Scarab to fire missile rockets at the boats. "Do it yourself," he said. "You're more likely to hit something."

Scarab obeyed, but the boats took evasive action and the missile rockets fell harmlessly into the sea. It was Scarab's turn to curse.

The Leader lined up Goran's three hundred men to repel any attack from the boats. He didn't put too much faith in them. Used to fighting from horseback, they were likely to turn and run from a determined assault. The Leader made alternative arrangements.

He took Scarab to one side. "Have a long-range helicopter ready to take off as soon as I give the order. If things go against us, you and I are getting out of here."

"Where will we run to?"

"We'll have no alternative but to take our chances further east. He who fights and runs away, lives to fight another day."

Scarab scowled. "It'll be suicide to run east."

The Leader smiled. "It'll be suicide to stay

here. I have a feeling this Eye is not overflowing with mercy."

The Eye was informed that Dubroc's helicopter had been shot down. Delegating command of the Crimean theatre to an Arena officer, he set off in his own helicopter to find him.

The North's elite troops charged ashore onto the beaches outside Odessa. As the Leader had predicted, Goran's horsemen put up little resistance before fleeing into the interior. They suffered heavy casualties as the Northerners unleashed withering fire at their backs.

The Leader looked at Scarab. "Time to go," he said. "We'll have to travel light," he added ironically.

The pilot chosen by Scarab heaved the helicopter into the sky, narrowly evading the volley fire from the enemy troops on the ground. "Head for the Gulf," said the Leader.

The pilot shook his head. "We'll never make it."

Scarab placed the barrel of a five seveN against his neck. "At least, you can try," he said amicably.

Venom recognised Dubroc and smiled to himself.
At present, the Theatre officer was out of range, but Venom was not about to turn tail

when such an opportunity had presented itself. He could wait, watch and kill.

The helicopter flew over seemingly endless desert. The pilot was tense and deeply afraid of what Scarab might do with the five seveN. The Leader was studying something very closely.

"What's that?" asked Scarab, not entirely taking his attention off the pilot.

"I'm not sure," said the Leader. "I found it among the Notary's effects. It's a miniature disc that seems to have been programmed. It's damaged, but might be usable. For what, I can't guess."

Scarab nodded. "Venom said the Notary was anxious to show it to you."

"Well, you might have mentioned it before," the Leader scoffed. "I could have overlooked it – buried it with the Notary."

"We cremated him." said Scarab. "Anyway, I've had a lot to distract me lately."

The Leader smiled. "Well, all's well that ends well. By a happy twist of fate, I have this thing in my hand. If great oaks from little acorns grow, I wonder what we'll get from a miniature computer disc?"

The Eye grew anxious. Dubroc was proving hard to find. His smashed helicopter had been easily spotted and the four troopers, two injured, picked up. But the Theatre officer was proving elusive.

A trooper indicated to the Eye where Dubroc had eliminated Edge.

"Follow a course towards the peninsula," the Eye instructed his own helicopter pilot. The huge rotored craft, like a giant insect, headed towards the sun.

Goran spat on the ground. He had just been informed that a heavily defended redoubt lay ahead of him and that the troops he had left at Odessa had been routed by Northerners attacking from the Black Sea. His messenger looked doubtful, well aware that bringers of bad news were often blamed for it and put to death.

"What happened to the Leader?" asked the Tartar.

"He and Scarab escaped into the sky."

Goran grunted, took a scimitar from an aide and beheaded the messenger.

The aide said, "Do we retreat?"

Goran snarled his reply, "Never. Victory or death. Prepare to attack."

The aide would have liked to run for it but, as a witness to what had happened to the messenger, decided it was in his interests to remain at Goran's side. He obeyed his order and seven hundred horsemen lined up in preparation for a charge.

"What happened to the Works and Innuendo troops loyal to the Leader?" asked the aide.

Goran spat once again. "Off on a wild goose chase in the Urals. The Leader was wrong about an attack being launched from there. The North's movement was merely a distraction."

"If we lose here," the aide said, "Arena and Theatre can destroy them at their leisure."

"We haven't lost yet," snapped Goran.

Venom caught Dubroc off guard. He rose from the camouflage of scrubland and opened fire. Some sixth sense, the legacy of his upbringing in the West, warned Dubroc and he hit the ground and rolled into cover just in time.

Venom, reloading, stalked his prey.

Just then, the Eye's helicopter came roaring out of the sky. Machine-gun bullets danced over the earth, lacerating Venom's body standing in their path. Venom fell to the ground, his head blown apart like an exploded melon.

The Eye shouted in triumph. The helicopter pilot set the craft down so that Dubroc could climb aboard.

When they were airborne again, the Eye said, "There's no time to lose. We wouldn't want to miss the slaughter of the Barbarians, would we?"

Dubroc was subdued. "I'd like to steer clear of death for a while," he said quietly.

The Eye comforted him with oily sincerity. "We have no choice but to see this through to the end. It will end, have no doubt. It will end soon."

Dubroc smiled wearily. "The sooner the better."

The Leader's helicopter ran short of fuel as it entered Arabian airspace. The pilot was close to panic. Scarab was as cool as a block of ice. The Leader was speaking into a communicator. "Kubar, Kubar – come in, Kubar," he shouted above the roar of the helicopter's rotors. "Kubar, Kubar – come in Kubar."

There was a crackling sound. The Leader's eyes lit up. He had made contact. Very rapidly, he dictated the helicopter's likely landing co-ordinates into the communicator. He received a garbled response.

"Directly ahead," the Leader instructed the pilot, "about two miles. Set us down there."

The helicopter, very low on fuel, chugged through the sky. The pilot, with great skill, overcame the hazards of landing and put the craft down on the ground within yards of where he had been ordered. The Leader didn't thank him for it.

The craft and its passengers sat and waited, surrounded by the ominous silence of the desert.

Scarab instructed the pilot to step out of the

helicopter and kneel on the sand beneath. The pilot began to protest, but Scarab took him by the throat, threw him out of the craft's entry hatch and, as the pilot scrambled to his feet, shot him in the head.

"Who is Kubar?" he asked the Leader nonchalantly.

"He's a great warrior with ambitions to conquer the South. Whilst preparing my rule in the North, it was necessary to form alliances with all and sundry. Goran was to have the East, generously supplied with whatever he wanted by me. Similarly, Kubar would rule in the South. Later, we would turn our attention to the West."

"Hasn't quite worked out, has it?"

The Leader shrugged his shoulders. "One has to be philosophical about these things. We've lost a part of the game, it's true. But there's still a lot to play for. If only I knew more about the Eye." He absent-mindedly fingered the miniature disc saved from the Notary's effects.

The Eye and Dubroc arrived at the rim of the Crimean peninsula in time to witness Goran's charge. As seven hundred screaming horsemen raced towards the North's defences, more than twenty helicopter gunships rose into the sky like a flock of deadly birds. They flew over the horsemen, firing rockets and machine guns. The Eye relished the slaughter.

"This is awful," Dubroc said.

"It is awesome," said the Eye. "I haven't seen anything like this since the Middle Ages."

Dubroc wasn't sure he'd heard the Eye correctly.

The barbarian horsemen were annihilated. Not one survived.

An Arena officer brought the Eye Goran's head on a wooden platter. Dubroc looked sick. The Eye waved away the officer and his gruesome trophy.

"We must move on," said the Eye quietly. "There are more barbarians. There is still the Leader."

A solitary figure approached the helicopter. Scarab armed his five seveN. The Leader placed a restraining hand on his arm. The figure, a tall and imposing Easterner, shouted at them. "Come out Leader, wherever you are." The stranger laughed.

"Kubar's got an odd sense of humour," the Leader remarked, before jumping from the helicopter to the ground. Scarab followed him.

The newcomer eyed Scarab warily, his black eyes glittering with apprehension. Once again, the Leader placed a restraining hand on Scarab's arm.

"You come alone, Kubar?" The Leader said. "Very brave, or very foolish."

Kubar raised his arm. A few hundred feet behind him, a hundred armed men rose from the concealing sand. There was the sound of many carbines locking and loading.

"I don't believe in taking too many chances," said Kubar, his voice soft and gentle, his tone mellifluous. "It's hard to tell who one's friends are nowadays."

The Leader smiled, acknowledging the Easterner's attempt at wit. "You should hold fast to the friends you know you have," he said.

Kubar said, "Introduce me to yours." He looked at Scarab as a mongoose might look at a cobra.

"I am Scarab."

"I am Kubar."

"I'm glad to make your acquaintance."

Kubar chuckled. "That remains to be seen."

Northern troops who had wiped out Goran's charge linked up with their comrades at Odessa. The Eye sent a detachment in pursuit of the remaining barbarians and ordered the Theatre and Arena troops sent on the feint into the Urals to seek, locate and destroy any Innuendo and Works troops fielded against them by the Leader. He was furious to hear the Leader had made good his escape.

"It doesn't look as if it's going to end soon, after all," commented Dubroc.

"I've started the game," snapped the Eye, "and I intend to finish it." He smiled paternally at Dubroc. "I've ordered Parrish to use the jet to find the Leader. He can't have gone far."

Kazan said, "It's about time. I'm getting bored flying around in circles."

Parrish laughed. "I thought the novelty would soon wear off. You're an action woman."

"You better believe it. Where to?"

Parrish studied electronic maps on the computer console in front of him. "Somewhere in Arabia."

"Give me a break. There's nothing but sand there. And here. I'm sick of looking at sand."

The jet banked sharp left.

"We'll draw a line of defence cutting through Moscow," said the Eye. "North to the Baltic and south to Afghanistan. We don't know how many hungry millions will rise against us once they learn we've trespassed into their territory."

"We've kept them in check up to now," said Dubroc.

"It's as well to be prepared for any eventuality," replied the Eye. "Once you've mopped up what remains of the Leader's troops and allies, you can return to the North where, I promise you, you will be feted and become one of the elite."

"I'm not sure I'll want that."

"Oh, you'll want it once you've got it. Then you'll want more."

"You are returning to the North?"

The Eye looked determined. "Immediately. Lamar knows of our victory. I want to catch up with him before he scoffs all the fruits of that victory."

"Lamar was my teacher in the North," said Dubroc. "He treated me well and taught me a great deal."

"You learned well," said the Eye cautiously. "But you should know that Lamar is afraid – afraid of ageing and dying. What power he has accumulated he intends to utilise to stave off the inevitable. That power is considerable and has corrupted him. I didn't mention it before, but I suspect his complicity in the murder of the Mother."

Dubroc gasped.

The Eye continued before Dubroc could interrupt. "I have no proof but, if it's there, I'll find it. I hope I'm wrong, but I could be right."

Dubroc looked defeated.

Scarab could hardly believe his eyes. In the middle of the desert there was built a large, rambling palace, surrounded by outbuildings. He shook his head and looked again.

Kubar smiled at his bewilderment. "The

palace is built round an oasis," he said, "that is the only water available for many miles. The outbuildings house provisions. Some are utilised as barracks for my children. I call my armies my children. Of course, most of them prefer to pitch tented villages on the far side of the palace. You'll see."

The party moved on and Scarab became aware that the palace was built of a substance closely resembling marble. Kubar spoke again. "It looks like marble and, to all intents, it is marble, but it is reinforced with titanium."

"What about an air attack?" asked Scarab.

"Only the four Northern jets could hope to reach us and cause us damage. The Leader promised they would keep their distance. Now I understand only one jet survives. To whom must I apply to keep that at a distance?"

"Somebody called the Eye," said Scarab.

The Leader had eavesdropped on the conversation. "The Eye has no reason to attack. In any case, the North's fuel resources are low. He wouldn't want to risk his only jet this far east," he said emphatically.

Parrish flew low over the helicopter that had brought the Leader and Scarab to Arabia. "No sign of life," he said, banking for another overflight. "Nothing on our scanners either."

"You're telling me they've vanished into thin

air?" said Kazan, unconvinced.

Parrish laughed. "Something like that. Once we're at the extent of our range – and we're just about there – our detection equipment weakens. This is a vast desert area. They could be anywhere."

"They'd have needed help."

"That's for sure."

"I thought this plane could fly round the world nonstop?"

Parrish frowned. "Once upon a time, it could. But our technological expertise has declined somewhat and, more importantly, we don't have quality fuel, or enough of it. The plane's efficiency has been suitably impaired."

"You sound like a textbook."

"Sorry about that, but it's from a textbook that I learned my skills. That textbook tells me it's time to turn back. The Leader's given us the slip for the time being."

The aircraft screamed in protest as Parrish put it in reverse thrust, executed a backwards flip and set off for the North. He looked at Kazan. "Don't tell me," he said, "you're feeling sick again?"

Kazan left the flight deck and ran for the washroom in the centre of the jet.

The interior of the palace was breathtaking. Marble floors, sunken pools of water serviced by fountains, large airy rooms, carpets, divans, priceless *objets d'art*, paintings, antique weapons – a vast oasis serving Kubar and his followers as if it were a private inland sea. This hidden city was protected by two hundred desert warriors, armed to the teeth. Food looked plentiful and there were many beautiful women.

"Welcome to Paradise," said Kubar.

"Tell me something," asked Scarab. "As you've got all this, why would you want to conquer the South, or anywhere?"

Kubar looked at the Leader, then returned a benevolent gaze upon Scarab. "Greed?" he said. He and the Leader burst out laughing. After a moment, Scarab joined in.

The Eye landed in the North. He received no ecstatic welcome. Indeed, he hadn't expected one. After all, he was virtually unknown to the populace and most credit for victory in the East would belong to General Lamar. But the Eye was in no danger of underestimating the General and was aware that Lamar feared him. He would play on that fear and the General's peccadilloes and turn them to his advantage. First, though, he needed to secure an ally in the North who would extol his virtues to the people, reinforce his influence and ensure his election to the Committee. From there he would complete his takeover of Northern power and expend it in the annexation of the rest of the world. Except, perhaps, what remained of the East. The Eye had seen enough to know that out of the East could come more trouble than he was interested in handling. The area did not offer that much for him to enjoy. His anticipation was more eagerly addressed to the South and the rehabilitation of the beautiful West had become his human dream.

There still remained the problem of the Leader. He was proving to be elusive, but the threat he posed in his absence could be turned to the Eye's advantage. Anyone who can promise security, wellbeing and law and order appeals to the basic instincts of most herd-orientated humans. The Eye would promise anything and everything, could likely deliver and, in so doing, dispose of his rivals and enemies at a stroke.

The time was at hand for the second stage of the beginning of the end.

The object of the Eye's attention was a solid, shrewd little businessman named Gregor Hamlet. Hamlet had been selected by the massive computer in the basement of Ludwig's castle that stored all there was to know about the North and its inhabitants, as well as some who dwelt in the West, South and East.

Hamlet had been raised in what had once been Germany. He was well educated, clever, able to spot an opportunity ahead of his rivals, rich, ruthless, avaricious, corruptible. A perfect specimen, as far as the Eye was concerned.

Like most of those involved in the military, General Lamar scorned civilians. He would eat at their tables, accept their goods, particularly if they were armaments, pander to their egos by pretending they had influence in Committee government and take the occasional bribe. But, in his heart, he despised them and, in their hearts, they knew it.

The Eye, with the wisdom of the centuries, was more diplomatic, possessed greater skill in hiding his true feelings and was cleverer in that he was able to convince everyone that it was he who was being used by them, rather than the opposite. Hamlet took to him immediately. Sensing a fellow traveller on the road to power, he accepted the Eye as a friend and comrade without apparent question.

While Lamar bathed in the glory of victory and indulged his tastes in wine, women and anything else that took his fancy, the Eye worked silently in the background. Word spread of the Eye's contribution to the North's success and his modest acceptance of the few plaudits he received impressed the gullible, of which there were many. It was not difficult for the Eye to assume the mantle of the Mother in dealing with the domestic interests of the North. The Leader was a traitor in exile, the Notary was presumed dead, Lamar was not interested and there was no one else to fill the gap. Gregor Hamlet would like to fill it, but a true, if unwitting, disciple of the Eye, was prepared to bide his time. His own agenda could wait.

Power may very well corrupt, but it is often those who seek power who, corrupted from the start, transfer the disease to its corridors. Gregor Hamlet, like all humans, needed to be led by the nose to his destiny. That nose would quiver with excitement the closer towards the ultimate in corruption it sniffed. The Eye would be his guide.

Gregor Hamlet had the statistics of the North's economy at his fingertips. He very quickly appraised the Eye of the current situation and brought him up to date on the possibilities that lay ahead. Possibilities of which the Eye was already all too well aware.

"We have very little fuel," said Hamlet pompously. "You are aware that Nature virtually destroyed the Earth some sixty years ago?"

"I'd heard something about it," said the Eye modestly.

"Oil supplies from the East became non-existent, the North Sea dried up and the southern Americas became ungovernable," Hamlet continued. "What we have must be carefully conserved. Of course, there are other sources. Water being the most important. We can melt the snows of the Arctic and rainfall is heavier here than anywhere else. Also, we control the ice mountain at the source of the Amazon. A remarkable discovery. A dwarf called Nanos stumbled across it a decade ago. Most of the world's great discoveries are made by accident."

The Eye stifled a yawn.

"We can harness power from the Sun, we can fell trees and our progress in the field of irrigation is astonishing." The businessman was in full flow. "We can also produce natural gas from the northern Russias. Our population, after Nature's devastation, is a mere four million. Unfortunately, not many of our best minds survived and we have moved backwards in some areas. At the very best, we have stood still. Our armament production is much reduced and our capacity to wage wars of advancement, or defence, severely limited. Particularly now we have lost three of our most modern aircraft. We must depend on helicopter gunships and manpower. A few boats, perhaps. Some of these are jet fuelled, but they will swiftly become useless unless we can harness more nuclear power. We can feed, clothe, even indulge ourselves. Poverty is a thing of the past. Even so, great wealth and the power that goes with it remain in the gift of the few."

"It was ever thus," sighed the Eye, hoping

Hamlet had finished his lecture.

But the businessman was not to be put off his stride. "Any invasion of the South must be put on the back burner," he said. "We must build a wall of defence against the East. We must look to the West for any expansion."

The Eye became interested. He and Hamlet, it appeared, were very much on the same wavelength. "The few with the wealth and power to whom you refer," he said, "include us, of course?"

Hamlet smiled and nodded.

The Eye sipped from a crystal glass containing fine cognac.

"Nature herself," Hamlet said, "cannot take full responsibility for our near destruction. Over the centuries, the human race has provided its own methods of extinction. Countless diseases, endless wars."

"You're very well informed," said the Eye.

Hamlet smiled and bowed.

"I have a little power," the Eye continued modestly, "and am more than willing to share it with a worthy ally."

"Who might that be?" asked Hamlet, smirking.

The Eye returned him a conspiratorial smile and held out his glass for more cognac.

Hamlet spoke over his shoulder as he searched for another bottle of the fine liqueur. "I am at your disposal," he said, with an air of finality.

"Indeed you are," muttered the Eye.

Parrish and Kazan were kicking their heels at the North's airport. Lamar had put the jet on standby while he decided if there was any mileage in continuing the search for the Leader, a command which the Eye had concurred.

Kazan wanted action, but not the kind Parrish was presently able to offer. She wanted something to do that would make an impact. The Eye, sensing her discontent, master manipulator that he was, persuaded her to infiltrate the General's circle, search for clues of his involvement in the Mother's death and report anything of interest.

"You mean, you want me to be a spy?" Kazan was clearly unhappy.

"In a word – yes. I would remind you that espionage is one of the world's oldest professions. Without it, I suspect we'd have perished long ago. Forewarned is forearmed."

Kazan saw the sense behind the Eye's request and reluctantly agreed.

Gregor Hamlet lusted after Kazan, but was prepared to wait his turn after General Lamar, if that turn should ever come. Kazan sensed his interest and was uncomfortable in the businessman's presence. Another reason to accept the Eye's commission.

The Eye, who saw everything, made a note of

the chemistry, or lack of it, between Hamlet and Kazan and filed it in his brain for future reference. It never ceased to amaze him that men with enormous potential were so vulnerable to feminine wiles. He had glimpsed the phenomenon many times. On the grand scale, it had destroyed empires. On a somewhat lesser scale, it had damaged mankind's soul. Beware the female of the species.

It was a woman who shot Dubroc.

She was a Works trooper from the Urals. Captured by Theatre and Arena scouts, she was being interrogated when she felled one of her tormentors, grabbed his gun and shot him dead. During the course of the resultant hue and cry, she killed four other men and shot Dubroc in the back. In her turn, she was killed by a trooper wielding a scimitar captured from one of Goran's Tartars.

Dubroc was treated on the spot, but it became clear that he needed urgent hospitalisation and skilled treatment if he were to survive. A relay of helicopters carried him to Moscow where a Latvian surgeon was offered citizenship of the North if he saved Dubroc's life. He said he would try.

His task was not easy. There was a strong possibility that, even though he might live, Dubroc could be paralysed. It would require very delicate surgery to prevent that unhappy conclusion.

Instructions came from the Eye, in the North's capital, to spare no effort.

Dubroc drifted in and out of consciousness while being prepared for the hospital's theatre and the Latvian's healing hands. A pretty, young nurse, dressed in the starched white uniform of her profession mopped his brow, held his hand and administered the necessary drugs. Dubroc sometimes peered at her intently, as if she were familiar to him. He would grip her hand tightly, as if very afraid she would let him go.

The nurse brushed her soft lips over his forehead. Dubroc calmed down, drifted into sleep and dreamed the dreams of the near dead.

Among the treasures accumulated by Kubar while pillaging the East and accessible areas of North and South, were a number of computers, their operators and a specialist in miniaturisation. This latter was called Ferez.

"I studied at the feet of Nanos," he announced proudly.

"You must have had to stoop very low," commented the Leader. Scarab laughed, Kubar looked puzzled and Ferez was mortified, but held his tongue. A tongue he might very well lose if he offended his hosts.

"I remember you," said the Leader.

Ferez smiled obsequiously.

"Vaguely," added the Leader. "While Nanos

explored the Americas, didn't you lead a similar expedition into the northern tundra?"

Ferez assumed suitable modesty. "Yes, I did."

"It failed, didn't it?"

Ferez frowned.

"It was rudely interrupted," interjected Kubar, "by some of my more energetic warriors. Luckily, they kept Ferez alive."

"Lucky for him – and now for us," commented the Leader. "How good are you?"

Ferez chose his words carefully. "I am talented, but I possess nowhere near the amount of skill exhibited by Nanos."

"Yes, well the dwarf's dead, so I'm afraid you'll have to do." The Leader handed Ferez the tiny damaged disc saved from the Notary's effects. "Study this. Let me know what you come up with."

Ferez took the disc and eyed it curiously.

"You may go now. Take your time. Not too long, mind you." Ferez hesitated until Kubar repeated his instruction more emphatically than before.

Ferez backed out of the room.

The Leader watched him go beneath hooded eyes.

"What do you make of him?" asked Kubar of no one in particular.

The Leader shrugged his shoulders exaggeratedly.

"I can't understand why you haven't killed him before now," said Scarab.

Kubar sighed. "We are not all barbarians in the east. My ancestors were building golden temples when yours were studying their navels wondering if they were edible."

The Leader laughed politely. Scarab knew when to remain silent.

Kubar paced the room restlessly. "I'm tired of waiting," he said, "for something to happen, or for the chance to make something happen."

"Patience is a virtue," said the Leader.

"Not one I possess," came the reply.

The Leader seized the moment. "Your plan to invade the South is a good one," he opined, "but, once you have obtained your objective, its security would be in doubt while the North is so powerful and, alas, hostile."

"Whose fault is that?" snapped Kubar.

The Leader refused to rise to the bait. "Why not redirect your plans northwards," he continued quietly, "By reinstating me, with Scarab by my side, you will have nothing to fear and do whatever you want without impediment."

"I fear nothing as it is," said Kubar.

"Of course," the Leader was diplomacy personified, "but you must admit I have a point."

Kubar scratched his thin beard. "You're a wily devil," he said.

"You and I have a great deal in common."

The Leader smiled.

Scarab stayed out of this exchange. He would follow the Leader.

Kubar clapped his hands and several lovely young women carrying trays of food and wine entered the room.

Scarab licked his lips in anticipation. The Leader looked bored.

"Entertain yourselves while I think things over," said Kubar. "Your proposition interests me. I must consider the practicalities." He swept out of the room.

The Leader turned to his companion, but Scarab was already involved with two heavy-breasted females. Two others smiled enticingly and advanced upon him. The Leader surrendered to his fate.

The Latvian surgeon worked on Dubroc's broken body for many hours, assisted only by the pretty nurse. At length, he stood back from his task. "I have done my best," he said. "The officer outside should be informed." The nurse left the room.

The surgeon leaned over Dubroc and wiped the soldier's brow with a perfumed cloth. There was no response.

Outside the hospital theatre, Dubroc's junior officer enquired as to what should be done now. The nurse indicated that Dubroc required complete rest and constant attention. This was later confirmed by the Latvian. The officer stared hard at both of them. "If he dies, you die," he said. "If he is crippled, we will cripple you."

The nurse seemed unimpressed. The Latvian smiled wearily. He had been in the neighbourhood of death too many times to react with any kind of fear. "You've made yourself perfectly clear," he said. "And if Dubroc lives, we too will live. Not here, but in the North."

The officer nodded. "That is the promise of the Eye."

Ferez the computer miniaturist reacted like a scalded cat. He had glimpsed a part of that which had so alarmed the Notary. For a moment, he was nonplussed. Then all the training he had received so long ago from Nanos the dwarf came to his aid. He realised that, should he view the disc's programme at speed, he would expose himself to the possibility of blindness, so vivid were the colours and depictions contained in that programme. The only answer was to re-record onto fast moving videotape – videotape could be slowed to still images – and then attempt an analysis. The disc was damaged, but would surely yield some information. It would, at the very least, explain the Notary's reported alarm and, possibly, provide a clue to the reason for Nanos's horrible death. He set to work, aware that time was his enemy and Kubar its vicious instrument.

Dubroc's unconscious self looked down upon his ravaged body. Dubroc was engaged upon a flight of drugged fancy, dreaming dreams bred of his past – the what, why and wherefore of his being. The pretty nurse, breathing softly, slept on a couch beside the wounded man. She did not stir as the ghosts of Dubroc's past disturbed the room's ambience.

Dubroc's eyesight was blurred. It was as if he stared into a mist. Out of that mist there emerged a shape. The shape became a human figure. Tall and commanding, with large expressive eyes set in a weather-beaten visage dominated by a hawk nose and a firm, sensual mouth, the figure exuded the magnetic power of Dubroc's past. It beckoned. Long fingers, like those of a concert pianist, pointed a way through the mist. Dubroc could not resist, even had he wanted to.

Ferez reacted to the slow tape version of Nanos's, later the Notary's, disc with a mixture of dread excitement and eager fearfulness. This disc, its electronic impulses distorted by fire, nonetheless provided information sufficient to persuade Ferez that he might, just might, hold the key to unlimited power and undreamed-of wealth. The disc told the history of the Eye.

It led Ferez through the centuries. He saw the building of the Pyramids, the Macedonian conquest of Persia, the fall of Rome, Genghis Khan, the Wars of the Roses, and the rise of the West. From the Aztecs and the Tribes of the Great Plains to the expansion of the great white race from the Atlantic to the Pacific – until America became the greatest power on Earth.

He paused before viewing the aftermath of Nature's devastation.

The disc gave Ferez insight into the great discoveries of man, the great inventions. Discoveries yet to be made, inventiveness yet to surface in man's brain. Most importantly, Ferez could read the Eye's thoughts. He would have difficulty in interpreting them, but they allowed him to imagine that, should he handle his discovery with utmost care, he could accompany the Eye to greatness.

Ferez's entire body shivered with dread delight, as if he had been embraced by a terrible beauty.

How to keep what he had found to himself? How to escape from the palace and reach the Eye without being cut down by Kubar's legions? How to confuse and misdirect the Leader? How to persuade the Eye to permit him to serve? How, with the Eye's guidance, to rule and rebuild the world to his own design? How to become a god?

Ferez continued his viewing of the slow tape.

Nature erupted. Hundreds of millions died by drowning, burning, being buried beneath mountains of the rubble of civilisation. Disease, race and religious wars, the savage fight for survival of the fittest, reduced the population even further. The world changed in a single turn of its axis.

Ferez could see that the East was sliding into oblivion. That the South would revive, but never again have any real influence over the rest of the world. It would, perhaps, become a source of foodstuffs. Power lay with the North. But it was the West that held the greatest potential. Its great natural beauty and diversity – its great wealth of resources available to the strongest – here was a place fit for a king.

Ferez dreamed exotic dreams and those dreams were centred in the West.

Dubroc entered his past. A past centred in the West. In the barren lands of New Mexico and the red, unyielding rock of Arizona and north-east Texas – the jealously guarded stronghold of the Navajo and the Mescalero Apache.

He had no remembrance of the terrible privations suffered by his people at the hands of the white man, or of the fight for survival against the awesome forces of nature. He learned of them at the feet of the tribe's story-teller, it's historian, his father, Bosque Redondo. Bosque Redondo was a place where the Navajo had once been confined.

Dubroc's father was so named in order that, through each generation, no Navajo would ever forget the humiliation of their removal from their traditional lands to that awful place. Navajos still shivered with apprehension when the name Bosque Redondo was uttered, but they had learned to live with it and would fight to the death if anyone or anything attempted to return them there, or to anywhere like it.

For decades the largest Native American nation had lived in peace. This was not to say that the proud descendants of the great Manuelito and the eloquent Barboncito would not return to their warrior ways if sufficiently provoked. The Navajo were famed for their apparel, woven blankets of stunningly original design. This was why Dubroc was so called, his name meaning "of the brocade". A man of the people of woven cloth.

Bosque Redondo and the few Navajos who survived Nature's terrible challenge rebuilt the nation. Their once-traditional enemies, the Mescalero Apaches, were now their closest allies, Nature and the excesses of the white man both bringing them together. To have to face a Navajo was bad enough. To face a Navajo and a Mescalero Apache was inviting suicide. The white predators studiously avoided any such confrontation.

Dubroc's mother died giving him birth. She

had been twenty, his father sixty, and Bosque Redondo blamed the disparity in age for the tragedy. He fled to the mountains to mourn and Dubroc was raised by a surrogate mother, the wife of a fierce Mescalero. It was from the Apache that Dubroc learned his martial skills, his ability to use the terrain of the barren lands to his advantage and to smell out those not of his tribe. When he was sixteen, the Dog Soldiers came.

Dog Soldiers were vicious bandits who roamed the West in search of sensation. They pillaged and raped and burned and maimed without conscience. Their crossing the path of Dubroc would prove to be a mistake. As, in later years, a similar group's encounter with the Eye would prove.

Dubroc was on a hunting trip with Mangas Colorado, the Apache, when the Soldiers struck. Upon their return to the village, they discovered that many hogans had been burned to the ground, many men were dead and several women had been taken captive. The Apache, Dubroc and five others set off in pursuit.

Bosque Redondo watched the Dog Soldiers as they approached his mountain hideout. Though nearing seventy years, he was a crack shot with a .40/.60 Winchester rifle, and blew their leader out of his saddle at a thousand yards. The others – eight in all and five women hostages – took cover, their eyes scanning the hills for their attacker. But Bosque Redondo was on the move. He outflanked them and shot down two more before a fusillade of fire caused him to retreat into a red rock cave. Too late, he realised that he had trapped himself. There was no way out of the cave, save the way by which he had entered it. He blamed this mistake on the frailty of old age and loosed off several shots in the direction of the Dogs, hitting one in the face and killing him instantly.

The odds were now five to one and Bosque Redondo literally had his back to the wall. The Dog Soldiers stalked his cover. The old man checked his ammunition pouch and came up empty. His smile of resignation slowly merged into a mask of controlled fury. He threw the Winchester to one side, grasped a Bowie knife and hurled himself towards his foes. They were taken by surprise and Bosque Redondo slit the throat of one of them before the others gunned him down.

Shaken and afraid that one man, an elderly one at that, had caused such havoc amongst them, the four Dog Soldiers slaughtered their captives and rode away from the red rock formation as fast as their mounts could carry them. It would not be fast enough.

Dubroc and Mangas Colorado were close behind. They and their party circled the mound of dead women in profound silence. The Apache watched as Dubroc, bending over the body of his dead father, was racked with emotion. After what he considered a suitable time for mourning had elapsed, he said, in colloquial Navajo, "The time for tears is over." He looked at the wide land over which the Dog Soldiers had so recently ridden. "The time of death is at hand." He spurred his horse onwards.

When Dubroc was helped to his feet, he clutched Bosque Redondo's Bowie knife.

The Dog Soldiers didn't stand a chance. Their greatest weapon, surprise, was long gone. They didn't know the lie of the land and the Apache and the Navajo did. They were ridden down and took shelter in a narrow, shaded canyon. Death danced attendance.

Dubroc and Mangas Colorado flew out of the rocks like savage birds of prey. Slashing and stabbing, their knives hacked the Dogs to pieces. Not a single gunshot was fired.

It was Mangas Colorado who sent Dubroc to the North. He spoke another of the nine languages they shared: Spanish. "Our people will survive," he said, "because we have always survived. No one and nothing can kill us all. But we must fight to preserve our history. Fight to conquer the present. Fight to secure our future. You are one of our weapons and you need tempering in the North."

Dubroc, now twenty-one years old, set out on

the long journey armed with all he had been taught by Mangas Colorado, his health, his strength, his native intelligence and Bosque Redondo's Bowie knife.

The North was depressing. After the wide open spaces of Arizona and the Mexicos, its cramped cities, though few, were grimy and uninviting. Their peoples were self-centred and grasping. Ever searching for the trappings of wealth, with no time to pause to consider that there is little profit in gaining the world at the expense of a human soul.

Dubroc's talents led him to seek a position in the army of the North. Soldiering was a privileged profession and there were severe tests of suitability.

Mangas Colorado had told Dubroc that one of the members of the North's Committee of rule was of Pueblo blood and a native of the Athabascan language group. She held the title of "The Mother". The North, thanks largely to the efforts of the Mother and her immediate predecessors, had re-established itself as the commercial, spiritual and physically dominant leader of the then world. The Mother, to someone like Dubroc, seemed unapproachable but, without money or position, Dubroc was in a hurry. He gatecrashed one of her meetings with businessmen, real power-brokers of the future. He was not too successful.

Theatre troopers grabbed him, bundled him out of the conference chamber and threw him into a holding cell at the North's airport. There he was visited by an interrogator. Dubroc expected a gnarled, conscienceless veteran of torture to investigate him. Instead, his visitor was the Mother herself.

She spoke to him in an Athabascan dialect. "All I know about you," she said, "is that you are from the Navajo West. That you are young and strong and fit and that you seem to have a powerful urge to make my acquaintance. Why don't you tell me more?"

Dubroc explained his history, leaving out the gory parts. He mentioned Mangas Colorado, told her that his father was Bosque Redondo and asked to be considered for cadetship in her own Theatre army.

The Mother thought for a moment. "Our laws are strict," she said, "and I am the last person to think of overriding them. They state that any prospective Northern citizen must be sponsored. I have someone in mind. If he accepts you, you will be put through the ordeal of entrance to the Theatre army. If you succeed, we shall meet again. If not . . ." She allowed her sentence to trail away. She smiled. "I hope you succeed," she said finally.

Dubroc's sponsor turned out to be Colonel –

soon to be General – Lamar. The old warrior viewed him with distaste.

"I don't like people who use undue influence to jump the queue ahead of others who have already earned the right to try for selection for my army elite," he said disparagingly, "and I've got a feeling I'm definitely not going to like you. There's an air of confidence about you that I find distasteful."

Dubroc smiled his brightest smile. "Why don't we find out if that confidence is misplaced?" he asked insolently.

Lamar managed to conceal his smile. "Very well. The Mother has left me little choice anyway. You will undergo the test for admission to the ranks of her personal force. I presume you don't want to enlist with the subsidiary echelons?"

Dubroc, still smiling, shook his head. "No, thank you."

"Well," Lamar grunted, "at least you're polite."

Dubroc met the Theatre test-controller. Named Czar, he was a veteran of many Northern campaigns, mainly in the East. The cruelties he had witnessed, and probably indulged in, in that savage corner of the Earth had made him cynical and unbending. He would, thought Dubroc, make a staunch friend, but an implacable enemy.

"You will not complete the test," said Czar. "No one ever has, including me. How close you get is all-important."

"How close did you get?" asked Dubroc innocently.

Czar eyed him shrewdly. "Seventy-two per cent was my score."

"Has anyone ever done better?"

"One man reached seventy-eight per cent. But he lost his nerve and fell from the high grid. Otherwise, two men reached seventy-six per cent. They were younger and fitter than I was at the time."

Dubroc raised an enquiring eyebrow.

Czar sighed. "One was called Venom, the other named Scarab. You may meet them one day. For the moment, they have transferred to other troops."

"Tell me what I have to do," said Dubroc.

"You will play our Theatre game. As its name suggests, it is set in a theatre, a theatre where actors perform. Actors are professional liars. You should remember that. The game can kill you. Witness the man who fell from a great height. I am honour bound to tell you that we suffer twenty per cent casualties. Do you still want to go on?"

Dubroc smiled and nodded assent.

"What is your chosen weapon?" asked Czar. "You are allowed only one and, believe me, you will be required to use it."

Dubroc produced Bosque Redondo's Bowie knife.

Czar stepped back a pace. He looked into the young man's eyes. "You can use that knife?"

Dubroc said, "A little bit."

Czar smiled. "I believe you can. Let's find out, shall we?" He led Dubroc to the tunnel entrance of the Theatre game.

"The object is Ley, pronounced Lee," Czar said. "He is the real controller of the game. You pass through various spaces within the theatre in order to reach him. Which way you go depends on your judgement. Make a mistake and the game stops and, if you haven't reached the required percentage, you are eliminated."

"What is the percentage?"

"Sixty. From time to time, you will encounter enemies. They must be removed from your path. How you do it is up to you or, possibly, to them. You may have to kill to make progress. If you fail to kill, you yourself may die. The further you progress, the better it will be for you. Your rank in the Theatre elite depends on it. All you have to remember is that a theatre is a place of illusion. Brute strength will not carry you too far; you need to be intelligent, well-read and cleverer than your opponents. Slide down the tunnel and you are in the theatre. It's up to you whether you come out or not. Ready?"

Dubroc took a deep breath. "I'm as ready as I'll ever be," he said.

Czar helped him climb into the tunnel. "It's a time to win, or it's a time to die," he said as he propelled Dubroc forwards.

Dubroc's body gathered speed as the smooth sides of the tunnel caused him to slide uncontrollably onwards. He tried to slow himself by clutching at the surface beneath him, or by twisting his body from side to side, but to no avail. The tunnel held him in its grip and was not about to let go.

Suddenly he was disgorged into a large space, his fall from the tunnel cushioned by a soft mattress. The space was the large, elegant foyer of a theatre. Its walls were plastered with posters advertising plays and players of quality. There were portraits of great actors no longer living. There was a small box office. There was a bar. Red-velvet-covered couches were in evidence, firmly anchored to a rich, deep carpet. The whole area was a symphony of exuberant colour.

Three young women awaited him – one blonde, one brunette, one redhead. Each of them held a large key – one gold, one black, one a bright red. The women smiled, each seemingly anxious that he choose her key in preference to the others.

Dubroc hesitated. He noticed that there were

three doors leading out of the foyer. One was marked "Mantua", another marked "Verona", the last marked "Paris".

Dubroc could read the works of William Shakespeare in nine languages. He remembered that all the cities referred to were featured in, *Romeo and Juliet*. Mantua was where Romeo acquired poison. Paris was the name of the man Romeo killed before committing suicide. Verona? "In fair Verona were we lay our scene." Dubroc asked for the key that would open the door marked "Verona". The blonde and the redhead faded away like ghosts disappearing into shadow. The brunette handed him the black key. She leaned forward and kissed him on the lips. Then, she too began to fade. Dubroc reached out for her, but his hands clutched at empty air.

A skeletal hand extended from the interior of the box office. It held a theatre ticket. Dubroc took it. It was a ticket for the front stalls. The skeletal hand withdrew and hollow laughter echoed round the foyer.

There suddenly appeared a red-faced, jovial character who beckoned him towards the bar and proffered a variety of drinks. Dubroc declined the invitation and the red-faced man expressed thunderous disapproval. The jovial character became brutish. Dubroc hit him, hard and fast. The figure crumpled into dust.

"Well done," said a disembodied voice. "You

have successfully avoided death in Mantua and the death of Paris. For this, you have been awarded a score of six per cent. You have also spurned brain-deforming drink. Your score is eight per cent."

Dubroc went through the door marked "Verona". He found himself on a stage set replica of a part of what that city had once been.

"That's far enough, if you don't mind," a sneering, challenging voice remarked.

Dubroc was facing a tall, lithe young man dressed from head to toe in black. He swished a rapier blade to and fro like an expert. The swordsman lunged. Dubroc executed a hasty side-step and parried the blade with his Bowie knife. Again the lunge, again the side-step and parry. At the third attempt, the swordsman stumbled and Dubroc caught his blade on the cross hilt of the Bowie knife. He gave a sharp twist and the rapier flew into the wings of the set. The Bowie knife was at the man in black's throat. "Pax, Dubroc," he said. Dubroc released his grip. "You have done well." the young man said as he took a step backwards. "A little fortunate, perhaps?"

"Fortune favours the brave," responded Dubroc.

The swordsman smiled. "You have advanced to sixteen per cent. Go carefully, Dubroc."

"Thank you. I will."

The swordsman faded from sight.

Dubroc took in his surroundings. The set was magnificently constructed. Stage-hands had gone so far as to dig a long ditch in the earth that was the floor of the stage. An empty gondola bobbed up and down on the water that filled the ditch. At its stern lolled an aged gondolier. "Get in," said the gondolier. "Or not. It's up to you."

"Where will you take me?" asked Dubroc cautiously.

"I can offer three destinations. Venice – but that won't surprise you. It's my home town. Then there's Belmont or Cyprus."

Dubroc frowned in concentration. Venice seemed the obvious choice of destination. Too obvious, perhaps. Belmont was where Portia in *The Merchant of Venice*, chose her husband. The Merchant of Venice himself awaited a ship that didn't come.

Dubroc eyed the gondolier who was smiling evilly. "Venice is out," said Dubroc. The smile disappeared from the gondolier's face. It was replaced with a frown of concern. Dubroc remembered that Cyprus was where Othello, the Moor of Venice, fought his wars. "And I'll pass on Cyprus. Let's take a trip to Belmont."

The gondolier scowled, then sighed in resignation. "You've reached twenty-two per cent," he said, "so I suppose you might as well get in the boat."

Dubroc smiled and stepped into the gondola. Suddenly, it began to rise from the water, like a slow-moving bird taking flight. It altered direction and headed out into the theatre's auditorium. Dubroc turned to the gondolier to object but, like his predecessors, he had faded from sight. Dubroc remembered his theatre ticket – it was for the stalls. The gondola was rising towards the dress circle. Without hesitation, Dubroc jumped from the boat. Velvet-covered front stall seats broke his fall. The gondola accelerated towards the circle. It struck a pillar and shattered into pieces.

"Thirty-one per cent," said the disembodied voice.

Dubroc checked himself for injury. He was a little bruised by his fall, but the bruising affected his ego more than his body. He looked around him. There were three exits from the stalls. They were marked – "Ladies", "Gentlemen" and "Players".

Dubroc was certainly a player and considered himself a gentleman. Which exit to choose? Again, the choice, Dubroc considered, was too obvious. He went through the door marked, "Ladies". "Thirty-six per cent," a voice called after him.

On the other side of the door was a beautiful garden. There was an abundance of sweet-smelling flora and fauna, birds sang and rare butterflies danced in a clear blue sky. The three young women he had met in the theatre foyer had rematerialised and advanced towards him. Each carried a casket – one gold, one silver and one lead. Dubroc knew he would have to choose and recalled that, though silver and gold were tempting, the right choice was lead. He touched that casket. Again, two of the women faded away. The other, this time the redhead, kissed him before she too disappeared. Dubroc opened the lead casket.

Inside was a pawn ticket.

Dubroc whirled round as a voice behind him said, "I'm your man." Dubroc was confronting a dwarf. In one hand the little man held an iron bar with three balls hanging from it, in the other he struggled to hold a half broadsword. "The pawn ticket redeems the sword," said the dwarf. "Take it. You're going to need it." Dubroc handed over the ticket and hefted the half broadsword. It was a fine piece of work and a good weight. The dwarf said, "You're up to forty-two per cent. Easy, isn't it?"

Dubroc shook his head. "I have a feeling it's going to get a lot harder."

The dwarf sat on the floor and looked up at him. "Shall I tell you about Ley – pronounced Lee?"

Dubroc sat beside him. "Thank you. As he's my objective, I need all the information I can get."

"He's a monster," said the dwarf grimly. "He'll kill you, that's for sure."

"Nothing's that sure," replied Dubroc, equally grim.

The dwarf laughed. "He guards a scroll – a parchment with writings on it. Important writings."

"What are the writings?"

The dwarf snorted. "That's for you to find out. Nobody has up to now. You're good, but I don't think you're that good."

"How dangerous is Ley – pronounced Lee?" asked Dubroc.

"He's a clever man. He's too slight to fight you himself, but he can conjure up frightening weapons to turn against you."

"You mean, he's some kind of wizard?"

"That's for me to know and for you to find out," the dwarf said as he faded away, his cynical smile being the last vestige of him to disappear.

Dubroc stood up and strolled through the garden, enjoying its ambience. "You're wasting time," said the disembodied voice.

Unless he turned back, there was only one way out of the garden, a wooden gate that led to a dirt path that climbed a green hill towards a fairy-tale castle. Dubroc set off along the path.

As he approached the castle, his progress was blocked by the sudden appearance of a large, fierce-looking warrior. Dressed in light armour and wielding a sword identical to Dubroc's, the stranger said, "To reach the castle, you must dispose of me. I cannot be killed by man of woman born. Why don't you turn back?"

Dubroc realised he was facing Macbeth. He recalled that the boast was correct: he could not be killed by man of woman born. But he could be killed, as in the play, by a man untimely plucked from his mother's womb. Dubroc's mother had died giving him birth. "I'll fight," he said.

Macbeth wasted no time in launching an attack. For several minutes, there was the clash of steel. Sparks flew upwards from the blades of the half broadswords. "He's very good," Dubroc thought. "Perhaps, too good for me."

Macbeth pressed home his seeming advantage and Dubroc fell back beneath the onslaught. Dubroc lost his grip on his sword and slipped and fell. He lay prone on the ground, Macbeth towering above him. There was a pause filled with deadly silence.

Then Macbeth raised his sword in preparation for the killing blow. Dubroc reacted quickly. He plucked his Bowie knife from his belt, lunged forwards and upwards and plunged its blade into Macbeth's breast. His opponent howled in pain, dropped his sword and fell to the ground, where he writhed in agony for many seconds before dying.

Dubroc was out of breath and considerably shaken. He rested awhile. "Fifty-six per cent," said the disembodied voice. "Sixty is your minimum target. So near and yet so far."

Recovered from his exertions, Dubroc entered the castle.

No sooner had he entered than a terrible storm exploded outside. There was loud thunder, dazzling bolts of lightning and torrential rain.

The interior of the castle was luxuriously, if strangely appointed. There were artefacts from the East. There were huge pots containing many exotic plants, including massive white ferns. The air was filled with the scent of spices. At the far end of the castle's keep there was a huge sunken bath fed by golden taps that gushed cool, clear water. A naked woman was bathing.

Dubroc cleared his throat. The taps halted their flow and the woman turned and swam to the edge of the bath. Her beautiful purple eyes gazed up at him. Adjacent to the bath, there was a table laden with foodstuffs: breads, cheeses, fruits of every description, flagons of wine. The woman drifted away from the edge of the bath and floated on the surface of the water, her generous breasts pointing upwards. She was smiling. One of her hands rose slowly from the water, its fingers beckoning.

Dubroc plunged into the bath and reached for

her. She laughed a tinkling laugh as her body merged into the water and itself became liquid. "You lose two per cent," said the disembodied voice wryly.

Dubroc, laughing, scrambled out of the bath and shook himself like a dog. "It was almost worth it." he said to the air. He approached the table groaning with food and wine. He was hungry and thirsty and sorely tempted, but instinct held him back. He remembered Shakespeare's play. The woman in the bath had to be Cleopatra and she had ended her life with the poison of an asp hidden in a basket of figs. Dubroc's eyes searched the table and the food upon it, particularly the fruit.

There it was – and another – and another. Small, but deadly snakes slithered over the surface of the table. Dubroc backed away and searched the keep for an exit. There was none.

Dubroc climbed granite steps to the highest battlements of the castle. He stepped out onto a thick stone wall and braved the elements. Looking down, he saw that a moat now surrounded the castle. He wondered how deep it might be. Cleopatra's bath had been deep enough. Perhaps that was an omen? Believing he had no other choice, Dubroc launched into a dive and plummeted into the rain-lashed water below.

The moat was deep and Dubroc, gasping for

breath, was obliged to struggle mightily to resurface. In the process, his prized Bowie knife fell from his belt and sank into the sand beneath the water. Dubroc cursed as he clambered onto dry land. For the land, strangely enough, was dry. The storm had ended as suddenly as it had begun. The disembodied voice spoke. "You have retrieved the two per cent you lost for dallying with Cleopatra and gained a further nine per cent. This means you have passed the minimum mark and stand at sixty-five per cent. You may stop now."

Dubroc caught his breath. "I'll go on," he said.

The disembodied voice chuckled.

Dubroc walked back to the garden. There didn't seem anywhere else to go. He settled himself on a wooden seat and watched the birds and butterflies as he breathed the clean air.

He shifted uneasily as the dwarf suddenly materialised on the seat beside him. "You really should stop now," said the little man.

Dubroc relaxed. "Thanks for the advice, but I'm not finished yet."

The dwarf smiled and nodded. "I knew you'd say that."

"What must I face now?" asked Dubroc.

"Oh, you're into the home straight."

"That doesn't answer my question."

The dwarf stood and began to pick some

flowers. "Walk back towards the castle," he instructed, "and you'll see soon enough what you're up against."

Dubroc looked towards the peak of the green hill. As he stared, the castle slowly vanished.

"Oh, I know it's gone," continued the dwarf, "but walk in that direction. When you reach the top of the hill, you'll see what awaits you on the other side."

"Must I?"

The dwarf laughed and handed Dubroc a bunch of flowers. "If you want to increase your percentage you must," he said, as he too vanished.

Dubroc, still clutching the flowers, trudged wearily up the hill. When he reached the top, he found himself looking down on a green valley, to the right of which rose another, higher hill. To the left was a dense grouping of trees. There was nothing but silence. Dubroc began his descent into the valley, discarding his flowers one by one as he walked. When he reached the valley floor, he paused and listened. The silence was being broken by what sounded like a slow roll of thunder.

Dubroc stood very still. He recognised that sound. It was the thundering of horses' hooves.

Over the brow of the hill to his right, there appeared a mass of cavalry. Knights in armour, with long lances, swords and battle axes, were charging towards him. Dubroc ran for the shelter of the trees to his left.

The heavy cavalry charge swerved as it approached the trees and by-passed them. Dubroc, sweating and breathless, crouched in a thicket. He sweated even more when he saw that one of the knights of the charge had held back and was turning his armoured horse towards him. Dubroc stayed still. There was not a great deal else he was in any condition to do.

The knight raised his visor and spoke to Dubroc in French, a language he understood. The knight was asking whose side he was on. Dubroc hesitated. Which play was this, he wondered? It had to be *Henry V*, in which case the French were defeated.

Dubroc replied in English: "I'm on your side."

The knight smiled broadly. "Good for you," he said, also in English. "Speaking French was a trick, you see?"

"Oh, yes, I see," said Dubroc, much relieved.

"Had you responded in that language, I'd have killed you." said the knight. "As it is, you've reached seventy per cent." He lowered his lance in salute. "Au revoir," he said.

"Goodbye," said Dubroc, as the horseman rode away.

Dubroc moved deeper into the trees. He stumbled across a clearing. The clearing was another stage set and, looking up, Dubroc could see a high grid from which scenery would descend and to which lights were affixed that shone on the action below. He remembered Czar telling him that a previous player had fallen to his death from a grid. Clearly, Dubroc needed to get up there.

The setting this time was a stone-walled, spacious room in another castle. Quite different from the one Dubroc had previously experienced, this was cold and forbidding. The dwarf stood in the middle of the setting.

Dubroc, though perhaps he shouldn't have been, was surprised. "What are you doing here?" he asked.

The dwarf looked offended. "I'm only trying to be helpful," he said mournfully.

Dubroc relented. "I'm sorry," he said, "but I'm beginning to run out of steam."

"Want to stop?"

"Well, I've got this far. I might as well try and go all the way."

"You get another two per cent for your courage," said the dwarf. "That's as good as Czar."

"But not as good as Venom or Scarab."

The dwarf chuckled. "Onwards and upwards then?"

"Upwards being the operative word. How do I reach the grid?"

"You climb up there, of course," said the dwarf irritably.

"Is there a staircase, or what?" Dubroc could be just as irritable.

"There's a rope ladder."

"Where?"

"Right here." The dwarf snapped his fingers and a ladder of rope dropped down from the grid. "All you have to do is enter the set and climb the rope."

"I've got a feeling it's not quite as easy as that," Dubroc said warily.

Again, the dwarf chuckled. "Too true," he said. "There are hazards."

"Such as?"

"I'm not allowed to say." The dwarf looked coyly at Dubroc. "Am I your friend?" he asked.

Dubroc sighed, then smiled. "I would guess that, right now, you're the only friend I've got."

"Your close friend?"

"I'm a great believer in being close to my friends," said Dubroc. "I'm even closer with my enemies."

The dwarf matched Dubroc's smile. "Very wise," he said.

He stared hard at Dubroc then, certain he had his attention, his eyes drifted to a wooden chest standing against a rock wall of the castle setting. His gaze returned to Dubroc's face. The dwarf smiled mysteriously and, once again, disappeared.

Dubroc took the hint. He entered the set,

walked to the wooden chest and opened it. He frowned in confusion. The chest contained various articles of clothing. There were rubber boots, leather gloves, a heavy Kevlar vest, a tight-fitting outfit resembling a frogman's suit and wrap-around dark glasses.

The three women he had met in the theatre foyer and the garden reappeared. They each held a single weapon. The blonde carried a Bowie knife similar to that which he had lost in the castle moat. The redhead held a five seveN and the brunette brandished a water pistol. Dubroc smiled at this latter. He presumed that it was now the blonde's turn to be chosen and he could make good use of the knife she proffered to him. On the other hand, the five seveN was the most powerful handgun available and Ley, pronounced Lee, should he come across him, was certain to be such a formidable opponent that Dubroc had better be well armed.

The redhead locked and loaded the five seveN. The blonde twirled the knife in her hand like an expert thrower. The brunette just gazed at him, a fixed smile on her face.

Dubroc glanced at the contents of the chest, then looked up at the grid. The lights almost blinded him. Suddenly, he understood. Lights worked by electricity and the clothing, made of rubber and the like, would be electricity resistant. Water and electricity did not mix. On the other hand, if your opponent was likely to be a machine of some sort, powered by electricity, water could be a potent weapon. Dubroc took the water pistol out of the brunette's hand. As before, the others faded away. As before, the brunette kissed him. This time, long and lingeringly. A voice said, "Eighty per cent. The best yet."

Once the brunette had departed in the usual fashion, Dubroc dressed in the clothes available – the tight-fitting rubber suit, the rubber boots and the leather gloves. He shielded his eyes with the dark glasses. He decided the bullet-proof Kevlar vest was superfluous.

Dubroc began to climb the rope ladder. He ascended slowly, then stopped and looked down at the open, almost empty chest. The dwarf had wanted to be his friend and had provided him with the means to reach the grid and the clothing that might protect him once he got there. The Kevlar vest had to be a part of that protection. Dubroc slid down the rope ladder. He ran to the chest and wrapped the Kevlar vest round his upper body. He retraced his steps and climbed the rope ladder again.

He had almost reached the grid when he heard a noise from below. The redhead was taking aim with the five seveN. She fired sixteen shots in rapid succession. All either slammed into the Kevlar vest, or ricocheted off it. Dubroc gained a few more bruises, but was otherwise unharmed. The blonde threw the gun away in disgust. "Eighty-eight per cent," she shouted up at him, before running off into darkness.

Dubroc stood on the grid and discarded the vest. "Thanks," he muttered to no one in particular. He advanced slowly towards a door that stood ajar some hundred feet ahead of him. The grid felt warm. As well it might. A sudden charge of electricity raced through its metal supports. All the bulbs in the lamps exploded. The rubber in which Dubroc was encased smouldered somewhat, but he was otherwise unaffected. The only light now available came from the door directly ahead. A voice said, "You're cheating. Or rather, the dwarf overstepped the mark by helping you. He'll suffer for that. Why do you think he helped you?"

Dubroc said. "Perhaps he likes me better than you. Wouldn't be a tough choice, from what I've heard."

There was a silence. A blinding light flashed in Dubroc's eyes. Had he not been wearing the dark glasses, his retinas would have been burned out of his head. As it was, Dubroc continued his advance towards the open door. From behind it, the voice was screaming a variety of expletives.

Dubroc reached the door and kicked it off its hinges. He entered a small room. A young girl, painfully thin and clearly very weak, cowered in a corner. "Please don't hurt me," she said.

Dubroc's eyes searched every corner of the room. There was nothing except the girl to hold his attention.

"I am your last Shakespeare character," she said. "I am Ophelia."

Dubroc wasn't sure what to make of her. Where was Ley, pronounced Lee? Where was the scroll that, according to the dwarf, was so important?

"Ophelia" had risen to her feet. She was smiling and holding her hands out towards him. Dubroc started back. Her teeth were tiny metal daggers, the nails on her fingers were razor blades. She advanced. Dubroc retreated.

In the play *Hamlet* Ophelia drowned. Dubroc levelled his water pistol and fired. A stream of water hit the girl on the forehead. There was a crackling sound and her face burst into flames. Soon, her entire body was consumed. Dubroc didn't bother to try to put out the fire.

The room filled with light and Czar stepped through the open door-frame. He stooped and laid hold of an iron ring embedded in the floor. He tugged on the ring and a section of the floor rose, revealing a small hiding place, no more than a foot square. The hiding place was empty.

"That's ninety per cent you've got. Congratulations," he said, as he replaced the section of floor.

Dubroc wasn't pleased. "Who was that?" he asked, pointing at the smouldering corpse.

"That was Ley, pronounced Lee."

"I thought she was a 'he'."

"He or she, it doesn't really matter. All that matters is that he or she is dead."

"So why don't I get the full hundred per cent?"

"The scroll is missing. You lose ten per cent for not finding it."

"I'll keep looking."

"There's nowhere else to look. The game's over. I'll credit you with seventy-two per cent. Same as me."

"What?"

Czar smiled. "You and I know better, but it must remain our secret. If it gets out that you earned ninety per cent, you'll become famous. A famous target. I don't want to hear you've been shot in the back in the East, or carved to pieces by a mob in the West. We don't want Venom and Scarab and their masters paying you too much attention. Not yet, anyway."

Dubroc nodded understandingly. "I'll go along with that," he said, then added, "I wonder where the scroll is and who has it."

Czar shook his head. "I've no idea, but it'll turn up someday. Somebody, somewhere will probably need the Ripley scroll to save their lives."

"Is that what it's called, the Ripley scroll?"

"Well, it is now. You killed its owner – Ley, pronounced Lee – so, he rests in peace. RIP Ley."

Dubroc said, "You'll never make it in the theatre."

Czar smiled. "You have. That's all that counts."

The two men walked out of the game for testing potential Theatre recruits. Dubroc was pleased to be back in the real world.

"I'll make you a Captain," Czar said. "It's a good rank to start. Not too high up, and by no means low down. By the way, this is yours." He handed Dubroc Bosque Redondo's Bowie knife.

The Mother was pleased with Dubroc's success. Lamar, now a general, promoted in order to keep the Leader on his toes, was impressed. He appointed the new captain to his and, therefore, the Mother's personal staff. It would not be long before the Mother would call on his services. For the time being, the new general and the equally pristine captain headed East, where danger lurked in the shape of a warlord named Kubar.

At that time, Kubar had few ambitions anywhere but in his own land. It was the Leader who, quietly and insidiously, planted thoughts of grandeur that would blossom and bear a bitter fruit in the time of the Eye. As it happened, Kubar never met Dubroc, that privilege would come later. But he and the Leader met with General Lamar and, in exchange for certain favours, current and promised for the future, the three reached an accommodation. When the time was right, the Leader would become the *éminence grise* of the North, while Lamar would be President. Kubar would, in time, rule the South and, together with the Leader, possibly the West.

Kubar provided Lamar with the means of gaining kudos at home, thus strengthening his position when the time came for his bid for the Presidency. A rebel band of Easterners, small but effective, was marauding in the Urals. Kubar knew that they were low on supplies and ammunition and he could direct Lamar to their hideout. Their destruction would be a simple matter. Lamar did not hesitate to accept what amounted to a bribe to secure his future loyalty and he and Dubroc flew a dozen helicopter gunships into the foothills and wiped out a hundred men.

Upon their return to the North, it was Lamar who scooped up any plaudits. Dubroc stood quietly by, no record being entered into the main computer of his contribution and, more importantly, this time through the machinations of Czar, very little about his past and his Theatre test score was recorded. To the Leader, the Notary and many others, Dubroc would remain a shadowy figure, which suited him just fine.

The Mother called upon him. Dubroc

attended her in her private rooms in Ludwig's castle.

"I have a special mission for you," the Mother said, watching him intently.

"I'm listening," said Dubroc.

"It will mean your returning to the West. I don't suppose you would mind that?"

Dubroc favoured her with a broad smile.

"You must, having completed your mission, come back to the North," the Mother said hastily. "I – we – need you here."

"What's the mission?"

"It's dangerous."

Dubroc shrugged. "Just being alive is fairly dangerous right now."

"When I came here to the North," the Mother said quietly, "I was half the age I am now. But I left something – somebody – behind in the West. I left a child – my daughter."

Dubroc said nothing.

"I want her here with me," the Mother continued, "and I want you to go and get her."

"Sounds a simple task."

"Well, it won't be. She's a hostage of bandits. They're holding her in the hope that I'll do anything to save her and that I'll use my power here to give them everything they want in exchange for her life. Of course, I can't do that."

"Then they'll kill her, if they haven't done so already."

The Mother was on the verge of tears, but quickly pulled herself together. "I believe she's still alive. I want you to find her and bring her to me."

There was a long silence. Eventually, Dubroc said, "Where do I look?"

The Mother made a move to embrace him, but restrained herself just in time. "Czar has all the information we have. He will brief you. Czar is one of the few people I trust. He will go with you."

Dubroc nodded approvingly. "Czar will be a useful accomplice. You realise, she may be 'damaged goods' when we find her? The bandits in the West are unmatched in cruelty."

The Mother remained silent, but Dubroc could see she was disturbed. "On the other hand," he said, "they may be taking great care of her, so they have a better chance of getting what they want. Czar and I will find out."

Czar and Dubroc flew the Atlantic in the Mother's jet. It lowered them and a fully fuelled helicopter onto the west bank of the Mississippi, still a great river, if a little less than its former self. The two men flew further West.

"According to information received," said Czar, "the group we're looking for numbers less than thirty, some of them women."

"Civilians or hostiles?" asked Dubroc.

Czar smiled thinly. "Oh, hostiles, I think, don't you?"

Dubroc returned the smile. "Probably."

"We should find them somewhere in the Mexicos or Arizona," Czar went on. "It's a big country."

"It's my country," said Dubroc.

"Our information seems sound. After all, they've had to reveal something about themselves in order to blackmail the Mother. For instance, the first thing they asked for was a helicopter. In fact, two helicopters. One an armed gunship, the other for freight – ammunition and the like. It's possible they'll think we're part of the delivery."

Dubroc weaved the helicopter in and out of the mountains and red rock hills. They were flying dangerously low, but Czar said nothing. Dubroc was impressed.

At length, Dubroc said, "Two against thirty, you say? Seems the odds are about right."

Theatre

"The game is never lost till won"
George Crabbe

Dubroc put the helicopter down in a secluded arroyo. He and Czar refuelled from the extra tanks they had carried with them in lieu of extra men. Then, they both checked their weapons. Each man carried a fully loaded five seveN with eight reserve clips, a sawn-off pump-action shotgun, a dozen grenades and two knives, one for throwing. Dubroc had his Bowie knife.

"Ready to rock and roll?" said Dubroc.

"I don't really appreciate that kind of music," said Czar. "There's very little opportunity to hear any kind of music in the North. Unless, of course, you're among the privileged few. Playing equipment is hard to come by and costs a king's ransom. It wasn't always so."

"Well," said Dubroc, "right now, you'd better get ready for a little country and western."

He and Czar immobilised the helicopter and secured it against vandalism. Most importantly, they booby-trapped its armaments. Anybody who tried to take the helicopter without their permission was in for a nasty shock.

Czar led the way, studying a map as they walked. "The first rendezvous suggested by the bandits is about two miles south of here. Mescalero Apache territory."

Dubroc smiled. "I know them well," he said.

Czar looked over at him. "I'd like to meet your people sometime."

Dubroc stopped walking and indicated that Czar do likewise. "There's no time like the present," he said.

Czar looked around anxiously. "I don't see anything," he said, his breathing somewhat irregular.

"No. But they can see you." Dubroc cocked his head on one side and listened intently. "Two of them. Women, I think."

Czar looked at him in amazement. "How the hell do you know that?"

Dubroc smiled and pointed in the direction he had inclined his head. "There they are."

Czar's heart pumped feverishly. Two Apache women were approaching them. They were armed with rifles and wicked-looking knives. Czar was well aware that, had they wanted to, the women could have killed them out of hand.

The women stopped a few metres away and Dubroc spoke to them in the Apache variation of the Athasbacan tongues. Whatever it was he said made them smile. Czar, sweating profusely, sighed with relief. Dubroc introduced the women to him. "This is Kara and this is Evening," he said. Kara was attractive enough, but Evening was stunning. Czar was smitten.

The women, chatting away merrily to Dubroc, led them through defiles in the red rock until they reached a small plateau served by a river. A cascade had created a pool of swirling water. Czar had an urge to jump in, but restrained the impulse. Dubroc took him to one side.

"There are eight men here and as many women," he said. "There were children, but they were stolen or killed by bandits. The same bandits we're looking for, I suspect. Kara and Evening are the two wives of their chief. I saw you were quite taken with Evening, but I suggest you leave her alone. Unless you'd like to watch your entrails being pulled out of your belly."

Czar nodded, licked dry lips and appeared chastened.

The two men were greeted by the other fourteen Apaches, one of whom was Mangas Colorado. He and Dubroc embraced. Czar stood to one side, smiling weakly and trying to look like one of the boys.

"This is Mangas Colorado," Dubroc said. "He has been a father to me. Evening is his new wife." He winked at Czar.

Czar practically genuflected to the Apache

and Mangas Colorado laughed his appreciation. "You are welcome here," he said in English. "I will help you in your quest. I too have some business with the bandits you seek."

Kara, Evening and the other women provided food, while the men admired the weaponry their two guests carried. Dubroc gave one man his throwing knife. Taking the hint, Czar gave his to another.

All fell respectfully silent when Mangas Colorado spoke. "The bandits are hidden on the far side of Canyon de Chelly. They're well armed. Certainly, they outgun the Apache. But, of course, we the Apache sometimes do not have need of guns."

The others murmured approval. Czar smiled and joined in.

"We are safe here," Mangas Colorado continued, "where we have not been safe before. I will not abandon the safety of my people. I alone will accompany Dubroc to the Canyon. If I return, well and good. If not – my wives must be guarded by you who remain."

There were a number of protests from warriors anxious to accompany Mangas Colorado, but he remained adamant and no one dared go against the chief's wishes.

The next day, the three men – a Navajo, an Apache and a Prussian – set off for the Canyon de Chelly, ancient home of the Athabascans. Mangas Colorado led the way.

"Three against thirty," Czar muttered. "I can't help feeling the odds are against us."

Dubroc laughed. "Well, who wants to live forever?"

Czar frowned. "I for one."

They trudged on. As the light began to fade, they reached a rock formation riddled with narrow dead-end canyons and defiles. They settled on one of the dead ends and Mangas Colorado indicated they should take defensive positions. Mangas Colorado chewed tobacco.

Czar said, "I thought we were looking for the bandits?"

"We've found them," said Dubroc. "Or rather, they've found us. They've been watching us for some time."

Czar reacted nervously. "Stay still," commanded Mangas Colorado. "You have nothing to fear."

"This is not my preferred theatre of operations," said Czar. "I like to see my enemy."

Just then, a figure appeared at the head of the canyon. The setting sun behind him, he was little more than a shadow. The shadow swaggered towards them. Dubroc, covered by Mangas Colorado's rifle, rose to meet him.

The shadowy figure, a bulky, middle-aged white man who looked as tough as they come and had the scars to prove it, stopped a few feet away. He indicated that he had come unarmed.

Dubroc stepped from cover and approached him. "I am Dubroc," he said.

"I am Silvera," came the reply. "I am in command."

"Then we can do business," Dubroc said. Both men squatted on the ground. "I'm looking for a young woman."

"Isn't everybody?" Silvera laughed, showing stained, jagged teeth.

Dubroc, stony faced, said, "If you have what I'm looking for, I'm willing to trade."

Silvera scowled. "You are from the North. The North knows our terms."

"Those terms are unacceptable."

"Then the girl dies."

"If she dies, you die."

Silvera laughed a humourless laugh. "You are three men. You have no back-up. We have seen. You have the nerve to threaten me? We will bury you alive and let the ants eat their fill."

Dubroc smiled icily. "You'll have to catch us first and, while you're trying, we'll take you out. One at a time if need be." Dubroc's smile broadened. "You first, of course."

Silvera looked concerned. "If I don't return to my people within the hour, they'll slit the girl's throat."

Dubroc rose to his feet and the bandit followed suit.

"I take it she's still in one piece," Dubroc said coldly, "and that she hasn't been, shall we say, defiled in any way?"

Silvera smiled coyly. "We've had a little bit of fun with her, but nothing to worry about. She's well enough for our trade."

Dubroc tensed, then relaxed. "I'll have to see her first."

Silvera hesitated. "All right. Come with me," he said. "Leave your guns behind."

Dubroc stepped back into cover and handed his weapons to Czar. "I'll be back," he said. His Bowie knife was concealed beneath his jacket.

"I hope you're right," said Czar.

"It's the only way," muttered Mangas Colorado.

Dubroc walked out of the canyon with Silvera.

Czar made a move to follow, but Mangas Colorado held him back. "Dubroc can take care of himself," he said quietly. "He's a hard man to kill."

"I know that," said Czar. "People used to say the same about me. I'm getting softer as I get older."

Mangas Colorado smiled. "It is quite the opposite with the Apache."

When Dubroc and Silvera rounded the bluff, out

of sight of the dead end of the canyon, there were two other men waiting. Silvera acknowledged them and looked towards the top of the bluff. "There are two others up there," he said. "They'll keep an eye on your friends while we're away. There's no way out of the canyon. They're not going anywhere." He smiled triumphantly.

Dubroc followed as Silvera and the others led him through a number of narrow defiles and across a flat plateau with deep cracks, caused by the heat of the sun, that could trap a man's foot, until, after a while, they reached a series of caves set into the red rock. There, Dubroc was greeted suspiciously by more than twenty men and women, the latter as hard and rangy as their male companions. All were heavily armed with carbines, pistols and knives.

"He's here to see the girl," said Silvera. "Let him pass."

Two women stepped aside, allowing Silvera to usher Dubroc into a low-ceilinged cave. "She's cowering at the back," said Silvera. "Probably thinks you're one of my boys coming to take his pleasure."

Dubroc scowled before ducking into the cave. It was poorly lit and his eyes took their time adjusting to the gloom. At last, he could see her, as Silvera had prophesied, crouched towards the rear of the cave.

"Don't be afraid," Dubroc said gently, "I'm

here to help you – to take you home."

The young woman shifted position.

"The Mother sent me," Dubroc continued. "Your mother."

Again, the woman shifted uneasily.

"I know they've harmed you," Dubroc said anxiously, "and they'll pay for that. But at least you are alive."

Dubroc crept nearer to her. She started to shake and he feared she was having some kind of fit, but soon realised she was sobbing. He took her in his arms and rocked her to and fro, like a doting father with a new baby. The girl calmed somewhat. Dubroc said, "I am Dubroc. You are called Miranda." The woman nodded. "You must remain here for a time. Try and hold on a while longer." Dubroc tried to be encouraging but, as a man of action, wasn't doing too well. The girl shivered with apprehension, unwilling to be released from Dubroc's firm hold. Very gently, he placed her aside. "One more day," he said, "and you'll be free. You have my word." He kissed her on the forehead before scrambling out of the cave to face Silvera.

Night had fallen, but there was a full moon and visibility was good. There was a deep chill in the air.

"She's damaged goods," Dubroc said. "How many of your men have used her?"

The bandit shrugged. "Two, maybe three. It's

hard to keep real men under control. I myself did not indulge. Be realistic. It's too late to do anything about that now. How about our deal?"

"We can offer you a helicopter, fully armed and topped up with fuel."

"That's it?"

"That's it. Except, of course, I also grant you your life."

Silvera shook his head wonderingly. "You're quite a character. I could kill you now and take my time disposing of your two friends."

"They won't be easy to dispose of and you'd lose out on the helicopter. You'd be back where you started."

"Doesn't this Mother care about her daughter?"

Dubroc smiled somewhat sadly. "She cares. But the people of the North depend on her. There's only so far she can go to meet your terms."

Silvera's eyes glittered in the moonlight. Dubroc could tell he was figuring the odds. Thinking he could dispose of Dubroc and his companions, get the helicopter and still keep the girl. Dubroc stood silently by.

"OK," Silvera said, "If that's the best you can do, it's fine by me. But you must leave us all your weapons as well as the helicopter. Agreed?"

"Agreed."

"Good. There, that wasn't too hard, was it?"

Silvera chuckled evilly. "You'll stay the night, of course. Do you want to spend it with her," he indicated the cave, "or have a little fun with us?" He swept his arm in the direction of his band of thugs.

"I need to get back to my companions," Dubroc said hopefully.

"No chance." Silvera spat the words.

"Then, I'll accept your hospitality," said Dubroc. "I don't see any reason why I shouldn't take advantage of the girl. Do you?"

"Help yourself," Silvera said generously.

Mangas Colorado instructed Czar to cover his back.

"Why, where are you going?" Czar enquired nervously.

"The bandit will have left men to watch us in case we try to get out of this canyon. They'll be hidden somewhere in the red rocks. I know this place like the back of my hand. I'll be back by sun-up with their scalps." He slithered away into the gloom. Despite the full moon, strain his vision as he might, Czar could see no sign of him.

Dubroc huddled in the rear of the cave with the Mother's daughter, Miranda. They spoke to each other, very quietly and in the Navajo language. To anyone other than a native speaker, the language is impenetrable. Recognised as such, it was used throughout twentieth-century wars as an unbreakable code.

"There are twenty-eight in the camp," whispered Dubroc. "Two others are at the canyon. How many will watch outside this cave?"

Miranda snuggled close to Dubroc. "Usually just one," she said, "but you are here. That will make a difference."

Dubroc found her warmth and the soft contours of her body enticing. And, at the same time, discomfiting. He was here to get her out, not to make love to her. He listened for a moment. "I think there are two, but they're very quiet."

"There was a raid earlier today," Miranda said. "Silvera's gang returned with food and liquor."

Dubroc smiled in the darkness. "That's good. On the eve of getting part of what they want from us, they may feel inclined to celebrate. With a bit of luck they might get drunk. We'll wait and see. I'll make my move in the hour before dawn."

Miranda buried herself in Dubroc's arms. Within seconds, she was asleep.

Mangas Colorado was disgusted. The two bandits left by Silvera to watch the canyon had turned out to be easy prey. The first had been caught with his trousers down – literally – and

Mangas Colorado had disposed of him silently and efficiently with a garrotte of thin wire. The second was dozing. Mangas Colorado put him permanently to sleep with the aid of a razor-sharp flick-knife. The Apache threaded his way back to Czar. The Prussian didn't hear or see him coming and reacted with alarm when Mangas Colorado whispered in his ear. Only partially recovered when he realised who it was who had crept up on him, Czar said, "I was old before I started this. Now I've aged beyond belief."

Mangas Colorado's white teeth gleamed in the dark. "We no longer have company," he said. "It's time to visit Silvera's hideout."

"How will we find it?"

Mangas Colorado looked offended. "I'm one of the best trackers in the West," he said. "If I can't find it with the aid of a full moon, nobody can."

Czar shook his head resignedly. "Give me a pitched battle any day. Creeping about in the dark is not my scene."

"Let's go," said Mangas Colorado, scooping up his weapons and setting off for the bluff at the head of the canyon.

Dubroc did not sleep. When the hour before dawn approached, he very carefully laid Miranda aside and crept silently, as only a Navajo or Apache can, to the mouth of the cave.

There were two watchers – a man and a woman. Dubroc smiled like a tiger: the man was ravishing the woman and she was enjoying every minute of it. He was out of the cave in a split second and Bosque Redondo's Bowie knife claimed two more victims. Dubroc looked around the camp. Everyone seemed to be sleeping. He looked up towards the peaks of the rocks that surrounded the hideout. Three guards were silhouetted against the now dying Moon. Red streaks were gaining ground on the black of night in the eastern sky. Suddenly, there were only two guards. Then there was only one. Dubroc smiled to himself. Silvera would regret underestimating the Navajo and the Apache. He retreated into the cave and awakened Miranda. "Time to go," he said, "but quietly." He and the girl emerged from the cave. Now there were no guards visible, but those in the camp were stirring. Dubroc, who remembered the lie of the land as well as Mangas Colorado, led Miranda through a narrow defile, across the rocky plateau and settled her in the shade of a giant cactus. His eyes searched their surroundings, his vision aided by the brightening sky.

Mangas Colorado and Czar rose from the camouflage of the earth about fifty feet to the right. Miranda gasped.

"They're with me," said Dubroc. He held her close.

Mangas Colorado cleaned blood off his knife as he approached. "These bandits are amateurs," he said. "I'm ashamed they've been able to give us the run-around. "This is the girl?"

"This is the girl."

Czar smiled and kissed Miranda's hand. She smiled at him shyly. "I am Czar," the Prussian said gallantly.

Dubroc introduced Mangas Colorado as his father, which pleased the Apache.

In the light of day, Miranda was a pretty young woman. Though a little thin, she was well formed and her clear-skinned face was lit up by wide, startlingly blue eyes. Not an obvious beauty, she was, nonetheless, a woman of a kind a man might be prepared to die for.

Mangas Colorado read Dubroc's thoughts. "We'll die if we stay here," he said firmly. "Dubroc will take you to the helicopter, cover for your backs provided by Czar. I'll slow down any pursuit."

Dubroc made to protest, but the Apache cut him short. "You must obey your father," he said unsmilingly. "Besides, I can't fly helicopters."

Dubroc took the point. He clasped his father's hand. "They're not really amateurs. Take care."

The older man nodded.

Czar, Dubroc and Miranda made their way into the foothills.

*

Silvera was not amused. "Five dead," he said, spitting the words at a female subordinate. "We might just as well have surrendered the girl to Dubroc and waved them on their way."

The woman by his side, a tall half-breed, smiled ruefully. "You underestimated a Navajo and an Apache. Not a smart move."

Silvera smiled. "You're right, of course. Still, my plan seems to be working. They're out in the open. Let's track them down. Remember, keep the girl alive."

The woman scowled. "Leave the girl to me."

Dubroc led Czar and Miranda at a fast pace across the rugged terrain. The Prussian did his best to help the woman. Unwilling to give away the location of the Apache sanctuary, they bypassed it and headed into open, desert country.

"We're sticking out like sore thumbs," said Czar, panting from his exertions.

Dubroc said, "Keep moving. Mangas Colorado will cover us."

"One man against more than twenty?"

"One Apache," Dubroc said.

Mangas Colorado couldn't believe it. A dozen men were racing over open ground towards his hiding place among red rocks. His Winchester .40/.60 cut two of them down. The rest dived for any available cover.

The Apache checked his ammunition and thought things over. Silvera had divided his force. It was clear that he intended to keep Mangas Colorado pinned down, while he and others chased Dubroc and company. The bandit wasn't as stupid as he looked. Heavy rifle fire was aimed at the Apache. No bullet came near him, but he would be unwise to move. He swore in Athabascan.

Silvera's band had five horses. He and four others, two men and two women, rode after Dubroc, skirting the red rock hills where Mangas Colorado had gone to ground. The remainder stayed to guard the bandit encampment.

The Apache watched helplessly as the horsemen passed him by, well out of rifle range.

Miranda was out of breath, her feet were cut and bloody. She could not go on. Dubroc and Czar made her as comfortable as they could, hiding her in a clump of sagebrush. "Go on to the helicopter," instructed Dubroc. "Release the booby traps and prepare for take-off."

"You're out of your mind," said Czar forcefully.

"Maybe, but have you got a better idea? I'll follow on with Miranda."

"I'll stay and you go to the helicopter."

Dubroc smiled appreciatively. "This is my

country. I'm better equipped to deal with the situation than you are."

Czar had no choice but to concede the point. He started his run towards the arroyo where the helicopter was concealed.

The Apache flitted from rock to rock, always one step ahead of the riflemen for whom he was a target. One of Silvera's men foolishly raised his head a little too high from his ground cover. A bullet from Mangas Colorado's Winchester removed that head from its neck.

The Sun rose in the sky. Soon, the Apache thought, the men out there would become thirsty. For blood and water.

Dubroc heard the riders coming before he saw them. He made sure Miranda was concealed as well as possible, then took cover among some low outcrops of red rock about a hundred feet in advance of her hiding place.

The leading rider, a woman, caused her companions to halt their advance. She jumped from her horse and studied the ground. Her eyes followed a trail towards Dubroc's place of concealment. Dubroc leapt to his feet and fired a burst from his pump-action shotgun. One rider and his horse went down. The others scattered. The dismounted woman lost control of her mount, which bolted. She hugged the earth. Dubroc raced towards her. She rose to her feet to meet him. Dubroc threw himself at her and they both hit the ground. The woman's fingernails went for Dubroc's eyes, his Bowie knife slashed her throat. Once again, he got to his feet and raced towards cover. A horseman tried to ride him down. Dubroc turned and hauled the horse and rider to the ground. He mounted the horse and raised it to its feet. The fallen rider tried to prevent him, but was blown away by a burst from Dubroc's five seveN.

Dubroc rode hard and fast to where Miranda awaited him. He scooped her into the saddle and rode hell for leather for the arroyo, Czar and the helicopter. Silvera and his two remaining riders were in pursuit.

Mangas Colorado had killed another of Silvera's men. He was a Kiowa and had tried to creep up on the Apache. Mangas Colorado had never had any respect for Kiowas. What he did respect was that there were still eight men against him. If they were brave enough, they would rush him. He'd get one or two, but they'd finish him off for sure. The Apache shifted position and a bullet ricocheted off a rock by his head. A sliver of that rock cut his face. Mangas Colorado swore again, this time in Spanish.

Dubroc and Miranda were losing ground. One

of Silvera's riders was gaining on them. A shot rang out and Dubroc and Miranda pitched to the ground as the horse beneath them fell dead. There was a shout of triumph from behind them.

Suddenly, above the rim of the arroyo that was so near and yet so far, the helicopter gunship soared into the sky, levelled off and, machine guns blazing, overflew the fallen fugitives. Their immediate pursuer was killed instantly. Silvera and the other rider, his woman, turned tail and ran into the protection of the low red rock hills.

The helicopter reversed and floated to the ground. Czar, behind the controls, smiled with pleasure.

"Thank you," said Dubroc, as he and Miranda scrambled into the aircraft.

"Glad to be of help," said Czar. "At long last. But it's standard gunship tactics."

He set the helicopter on course for the bandit hideout.

Mangas Colorado didn't think they had the nerve to do it, but they did. Three men rushed him from either side, while two charged him from the front. These front men he took out easily with the .40/.60, but he was obliged to fight the others hand to hand. It was an uneven contest, but the Apache would not die easily. One of his assailants fired a pistol and a bullet shattered a bone in Mangas Colorado's leg. As he fell to the ground, he loosed off a fusillade of shots from his own gun. "And another one bites the dust," he thought, as the pistoleer went down. Four others, armed with knives, fell on the Apache. He slashed out at them and one of them fell away, blood gurgling from his mouth. The others killed Mangas Colorado.

Czar flew the helicopter gunship right above the scene of the Apache's death. The four bandit survivors began to run. Dubroc, leaning out of the helicopter's cockpit bubble, shot them down with his five seveN. The helicopter hovered for a few seconds and Dubroc dropped to the ground. Czar flew the gunship away, heading for Silvera's base with orders to blow it apart.

Dubroc approached the fallen Apache. He knelt, held his surrogate father in his arms and wept.

The bandits left behind by Silvera to guard the camp heard the helicopter coming and assumed their leader had accomplished his intent and was returning to base. They turned out to cheer him. Czar machine-gunned them. He dropped two phosphorus bombs on the camp, turned the aircraft around and headed back to Dubroc.

Dubroc heard the explosions and watched as a smoke of noxious fumes rose into the clear sky beyond the red rock hills. He laid Mangas Colorado's body on the ground and began to take the scalps of the men the Apache had killed.

When Czar returned with the helicopter, he and the Prussian buried the Apache, the scalps interred with him.

Silvera wanted to run as far as he could. His woman bolstered his courage. The two of them, riding back the way they had come, circled the rocks where Mangas Colorado had lain hidden. It was the woman who saw the landed helicopter first. She spurred her mount towards it, Silvera following at speed.

They were almost upon the burial party when Miranda shouted a warning. Dubroc dropped to one knee, levelled his five seveN and shot Silvera out of his saddle. Silvera's woman, firing as she rode, screamed a war cry. Czar gasped and went down.

The woman's horse reared up. Dubroc, taking careful aim and quite unruffled, waited for it to regain its balance before emptying his magazine into the woman's body.

Czar had been hit in the leg. Nothing serious, but he couldn't walk. Dubroc lifted him into the helicopter and, with Miranda beside him, flew to the home of Mangas Colorado's followers.

Dubroc shared the mourning ceremony with

Kara, Evening and the rest. Miranda cared for Czar's wound. The Apaches thanked Dubroc for burying their chief where he had fallen, with his enemies scalps at his side.

Czar asked to speak to Dubroc in private.

"If I were to take Mangas Colorado's widows as my wives, would that be acceptable?" the Prussian asked.

Dubroc looked thoughtful. "After a suitable period of mourning, it would be acceptable," he said at length.

Czar smiled. "Then, I want to stay here in the West," he said. "I'm getting too old for the trials and tribulations that await me in the North. I'd like to spend the evening of my life with . . ." the Prussian stifled a laugh, ". . . with Evening. If that's all right with you?"

"It has to be all right with Evening," said Dubroc kindly.

The Apaches accepted Czar as one of their own.

Dubroc said goodbye to each and every one of them. The Mescaleros applauded as Dubroc, with Miranda once again by his side, lifted the helicopter into the sky. Czar, leaning on a stick, waved his hand. Dubroc saluted him and the gunship turned east and north.

Miranda said in Navajo, "Does it matter to you what happened to me while I was in the hands of Silvera and his men?"

"No."

Miranda smiled. "Then I would like you to be my lover," she said with utmost sincerity.

Dubroc said nothing, but the helicopter was three days late for its rendezvous with the Mother's jet.

Back to the present. Back to the time of the Eye.

Gregor Hamlet was turning out to be an incomparable source of information. As well as knowing where he could lay his hands on virtually every luxury available, he seemed to be an encyclopaedia when it came to understanding the motivations, weaknesses and secret practices of those in a position of power in the North.

The Eye, pretending naivety, watched and listened and learned.

"Lamar is no real problem," Hamlet said. "Best leave him to his own devices. He can be President, but in name only. Otherwise, I believe there should be a Committee of two. I'll take care of the business and social problems, while you take over the army and spread your wings Westwards. I think we're a perfect combination, don't you?"

The Eye simulated delight. "Absolutely," he said.

"Then, we must celebrate our collusion," said Hamlet. "Wine, women and song."

"I'm not a lover of song," said the Eye.

"Indeed, music of any kind offends me."

Hamlet was astonished. "I find that hard to believe."

"I wish you would believe it," said the Eye. "Think about it. . ." His face was a mask of no emotion. "Music damages the ear-drums."

Gregor Hamlet laughed.

The Eye went on, "Throughout the ages, music has been used to stir the feelings of the people into broths of pseudo-patriotism and consequent violence. Marching songs, martial music of any kind – they are associated with death. Even in religion, the music of the different faiths competes. Then, and this is the most recent trend, there is the music of rebellion, of lack of conformity, of frenzy, of disrespect. The thudding of drums, the clanging of guitars, the arrogant, peacock strutting of the singers who have become icons for the young and impressionable. Such performers, worshipped like gods, could stir up more trouble than ever any recruiting poster could. They are the new danger to us all."

Gregor Hamlet needed a drink after that diatribe.

After he had downed one brandy and was sipping another, he said, "Of course, there is very little music available in the North, save of the home-made variety. Since Nature intervened, the arts, if I may include music of the kind you describe in the general understanding of what the arts may be, have suffered greatly. No cinema, of course, and theatres dark and deserted. The people prefer more physical pleasures. There are, I admit, a number of – er – musicians providing some needed entertainment. Classical music can be soothing and relaxing."

"That's acceptable, if it is really needed," said the Eye coldly, "but what about the new music? The music of strife?"

Gregor Hamlet had had enough of this one. "Well, when you are on the Committee," he said jocularly, "you can ban it."

"Oh, I will," said the Eye, smiling for the first time in a long while.

It was not difficult for Hamlet and the Eye, with the connivance of Lamar, to have themselves elected to the thoroughly vacated Committee. The Eye was very much a shadowy figure, which he preferred – for the moment. The population of the North knew little of him. What they did know suggested he was an admirable candidate for leadership. Appearances are often deceptive. Lamar, mightily indulged as President, was kept under close watch by the Eye, through his agent, Kazan. Gregor Hamlet was permitted a long leash, but the Eye could reel him back into check whenever he felt like it.

All in all, the people thought they had a good

deal. But the general public can be beguiled and history has proved that they, not infrequently, elect masters of their race who later become intolerable. Recognising totalitarianism can be a lengthy business. Opposing it, often fatal. Many wars, including at least two that have covered the world, have proved that.

The Eye was reasonably content. There remained the Leader in exile. Conjuring up – what? The new, real power in the North needed to find out.

Kubar entertained his guests with all they could desire. But luxurious indulgence can become tiresome after a while and the Leader was ready for action. Scarab, with a little less enthusiasm, was also ready to stretch his muscles. Kubar accepted that the time had come to move against the North. Plans must be laid, troops prepared and intelligence gathered.

"What progress has Ferez made with the disc?" the Leader asked.

Kubar spread his hands and adopted a sorrowful expression. "Alas, very little. The disc was much damaged."

"Are you saying it will be of no use to us?"

"For the moment. More time is needed."

The Leader, suspicion skirting the outer reaches of his mind, let the matter rest. He changed the subject. "So, what do we know about the state of the North?"

Kubar seemed to be on firmer ground. "Lamar is President."

Scarab choked on a piece of fruit he was eating. The Leader shook his head wonderingly.

"Gregor Hamlet is one Committee member . . ." the Leader's interest was aroused, ". . . the Eye is the other." Kubar said.

"The Eye," hissed the Leader. "Who or what or why is he?"

Scarab said, "It's a question we keep on asking. We need answers."

Kubar seized the moment. "An intelligence foray into the North is our immediate requirement, wouldn't you say?"

The other men nodded.

"I propose to send a small expedition," Kubar continued, rubbing his hands together gleefully, "led by Ferez."

The Leader looked confused. Scarab said nothing, merely selecting another piece of fruit.

Kubar became intense, almost manic. "Don't you see? Since the death of Nanos the dwarf, the North has had no one capable of taking his place. It is we who own Ferez. We will give him to them. He will take with him the Notary's disc."

The Leader moved to protest, but Kubar preempted him. "It's proved to be of no use to us. Ferez can pursue his research far more easily in the North and the disc is a good credential. In reality, he will be spying for us."

There was a silence.

Scarab spat out a plum stone. "Sounds good to me," he said.

The Leader's eyes narrowed. "What are you up to, Kubar?"

Their host was the picture of innocence. "If you don't like the idea, we'll abandon it. It's all the same to me. But, as far as you are concerned, how else are we to begin your assault upon the North and press your claims for its leadership?"

The Leader sighed. "You are, of course, right."

Kubar strutted towards him. "I am always right."

The nurse watched as Dubroc came out of unconsciousness. She held him close as, like a child, he held his hands out to her. She noticed there were tears in his eyes.

"You are safe, you are well, you are whole again," she said in Russian, not one of Dubroc's nine languages.

The Latvian surgeon appeared in the doorway and translated what she had said into English. "Where have you been?" he asked intently.

"I've been for a stroll through my past," Dubroc said, struggling to sit upright. The nurse helped him.

The Latvian nodded sagely. "I'm glad you're able to talk about it."

Dubroc looked solemn. "I have survived that past into the present, but not without some pain."

"Tell me about it," pressed the surgeon.

"My past is a secret place," said Dubroc.

Again, the Latvian nodded. "Then I'll leave you to the tender mercies of Natasha." He indicated the nurse. "She is good at prising secrets out of almost anybody. She also speaks French. Is that language acceptable to you?"

Dubroc nodded. "I think I can handle it."

The surgeon smiled, bowed and left the hospital room.

The nurse, Natasha, enquired in French if Dubroc required food or drink. He declined both. "Or anything else?" she asked.

Dubroc laughed and Natasha blushed.

The Eye was highly delighted to hear the news of Dubroc's recovery. He hoped that the young Theatre officer could be persuaded to become one of his closest followers. Until, that is, the Eye had achieved everything he was now setting out to achieve. He needed information. Insufficient was recorded in the main computer in Ludwig's castle. He needed to know all there was to know about his proposed protégé.

The secretary who had once served the

Notary, in more ways than one, was now the Eye's amanuensis. He had swiftly acknowledged her expertise and isolated her weakness. He would keep her as loyal as a whipped dog, with a combination of threat and promise of reward.

"Bring me the surgeon who cared for Dubroc in Moscow," he ordered. "I want all his notes. Everything he has on the patient."

"He'll take a while to get here."

"We have a jet plane. Get him here quickly."

Parrish was missing Kazan. He hadn't seen her for a while and he ached for her company. The ache was not confined to his thoughts.

The order came through to fly to Moscow. True to his word, the Eye had appointed Parrish Fleet Commander. The fact that the fleet consisted of one jet didn't spoil his pleasure at the promotion. He would not disobey the Eye. The plane, in Open mode, took to the sky and headed east.

Lamar, watching from the window of his penthouse apartment in the North's capital, followed its flight until it disappeared into the clouds.

"It's going to Moscow to pick up Dubroc," Kazan said, as she rubbed the General's back. They were both in dressing gowns, naked underneath. A bottle of champagne cooled in an ice bucket. "Happy Birthday, Mr President," Kazan whispered, stripping to the buff.

"It's not my birthday until September," said the General.

"So, what's a few months between friends?"

Between the sheets, Kazan extracted more and more pertinent information from her "lover". She learned of all his tedious ambitions, his devious and deviant nature, his tendency to try to stay on the side of the eventual winner in any conflict at whatever cost to his conscience, or the fate of others. The dead in war were but stepping-stones to his destiny, he imagined. Kazan was disgusted. The guy's destiny was over and done with. He was on the way out. What she hadn't learned was anything about the Mother's untimely death.

"You were very loyal to the Mother," she whispered as she toyed with the General's thinning hair. Lamar, sated and half asleep, merely grunted. "Was she your mistress?"

Lamar smiled. "No. Her loss, wouldn't you say?"

"Absolutely." Kazan wanted to throw up.

"She was too good for her own good, if you know what I mean," muttered the President.

"So you had her killed?"

Lamar sat up in bed and gazed at her.

Kazan held his eyes, smiled and licked her lips, like a luscious cat.

Lamar relaxed. "I was tempted to and almost did, but I backed away at the last minute."

"That last minute was a minute too late," said Kazan uncritically.

Lamar sighed. "I'm coming to the end of my days," he quoted self-indulgently. "I want what I can get out of life before death comes knocking at my door." He rubbed his brow. "Sometimes I'm confused. Led astray, if you like, by devious others."

Kazan really did think she was going to throw up, excused herself and went to the bathroom.

When she returned, Lamar had made himself more comfortable in the bed and was sipping champagne. Kazan, naked, lolled on a sofa directly in his line of sight. "Tell me about it," she said, quietly and enticingly. Well aware that most men are anxious to confess their wrongdoings to a sexual partner and talk about themselves – themselves alone – she tingled with the excitement of anticipation. She would learn the truth and complete the ugly task the Eye had given her.

"I suspect the Eye," said Lamar.

Kazan was astonished, but held her tongue.

"I can't prove anything, but I'm an old soldier and I feel it in my gut. I'm a great believer in gut feelings."

Kazan observed that his gut was certainly expansive enough.

"What I tell you does not go beyond these walls," Lamar said earnestly.

Kazan stood, came towards him and nestled on the bed beside him.

"There was a beautiful woman called Avila," the General began.

Ferez was shaking with fear as Kubar eyed him like a falcon about to dive on its prey. "No further progress with the disc?" Kubar asked.

Ferez was obsequious. "None. Other than that of which I have informed you, Excellency."

Kubar pursed his lips. "All right," he said, "perhaps you'll have better luck in the North when you present it to the Eye."

Ferez badly needed the bathroom. "Excellency?"

"You are to be my spy in the North."

Ferez felt very dizzy and began to fall. Kubar grabbed him and held him up. "Give me some help here," he cried, and Ferez was doused with cool water and led to a couch, where a pretty, bare breasted woman wafted smelling-salts beneath his prominent nose.

"Feeling better?" asked Kubar irritably.

Ferez nodded weakly.

"The woman is yours, after you have listened to what I have to say. Whatever else you get depends on your willingness to do what I want. Understood?"

Again, Ferez nodded. This time he was more alert.

"I will ensure that you gain safe passage to the North. Once there, you must see the Eye. Mention of the disc you have and of its provenance should ensure he will receive you. You must gain his confidence." Ferez looked sick. "It will not be as difficult as it sounds," Kubar went on. "With Nanos long dead, you are his only likely successor in miniaturism. I have a feeling the Eye will appreciate you for that. Once you have established yourself, you will be contacted by one of my agents and you will pass to me all relevant information."

Ferez, one of life's weaklings, but paradoxically the stronger for knowing it and admitting it to himself, knew he had no alternative but to comply with Kubar's wishes. "I am yours to command," he said bravely.

"To the death?" enquired Kubar.

Ferez tried to swallow, but his mouth was dry. "To the death," he croaked.

"Excellent!" Kubar pronounced delightedly. "Now, enjoy the woman and anything else you want. You will leave in a couple of days."

Assuming the Eye would allow a future for the world, that world's history would record that, despite heavy competition from the now dead Notary, The Leader, Goran the Barbarian and others, Kubar was the most devious mind of his time. Were it not for the Eye itself, Kubar could have gone far. As it happened, according to the Eye, he was going too far. For the time being, however, the Eye was unaware of Kubar's machinations and was more concerned with Dubroc's history and discovering the secret power of the Leader, his rival in exile.

What had the Leader to offer that permitted him to stay alive? True, there were a number of Works, even Innuendo, soldiers who remained loyal to him. But the Eye was even now purging the army. To all intents and purposes, the Leader was finished. He might as well retire to a dacha in the Eastern wilderness. But he was still a threat, a threat supported by an interesting assortment of powers. Not least among them, Kubar.

The Eye turned to the secretary. "What do you know of the Leader?"

She shrugged. "Very little. I only slept with the Notary."

"Did the Leader have a mistress?"

"Oh yes. They were many and varied."

"They?"

"At least three that I know of."

The Eye's eyes glistened. *Cherchez la femme* – this was the way of the world. "Where are they?"

"Two of them are dead. One of them committed suicide, the other died of natural causes."

"And the third?"

"Passed down the line, once he had finished with her. Venom was one of her lovers."

"Venom's dead."

"She'll be around somewhere, I expect. Regretting her past, clinging desperately to her present and dreading her future."

The Eye looked surprised. "You sound quite the philosopher," he said.

The secretary smiled sadly. "I'm merely commenting on what I am and will become."

"You're probably right," said the Eye cruelly. "Find this woman and find her quickly."

Scarab was eating food as if it was going out of fashion and drinking fine wine as if he wanted to send his liver into paroxysms. All this while pawing his naked mistress – a present from Kubar.

"From whom did you learn your table manners?" the Leader asked disgustedly. "You aren't, by any chance, related to Goran the Barbarian, are you?"

Scarab stopped everything he was doing and looked suitably shamefaced.

"Well, it's about time," said the Leader. "At last, I have your attention. Get rid of the girl."

Scarab pushed the woman away and she scampered out of the room. The Leader sat close by his subordinate. "You must go to the North," he said quietly, "and find out what Ferez, at Kubar's instigation, is up to."

"I thought Kubar was on our side."

"Put not your trust in desert princes, Scarab. In fact, put not your trust in anyone."

"Even you?"

The Leader smiled like the serpent must have smiled at Eve in the Garden of Eden. "There are exceptions," he said.

Scarab belched.

The Leader moved away from his foul breath. "You may have to kill the Eye."

Scarab laughed. "I don't know what he looks like."

The Leader did not smile. "You'll find out."

Scarab eyed him predatorily. "Why should I trust you," he asked, "when you don't appear to trust anyone?"

This time the Leader did smile. "I trust those who fear me," he said. "Or those who want something that I have."

"I don't fear you."

"You should," snapped the Leader. "One word from me and Kubar will withdraw your privileges, have you tortured, cut your body into pieces and feed you to his animals."

Scarab paled. "Why would he do that?"

"Because he wants something only I can give him."

"What's that?"

"That's for me to know and for you never to find out. Just settle for the fact that you're better off with me than with anyone else. Provided you do what I tell you, you'll live the life of a Roman emperor."

"Unless I die in the attempt."

"No pain, no gain, my friend."

Scarab made up his mind. "How can I do what you want?"

Parrish put the jet down on the landing ground outside Moscow. At one time, this city had been a thriving metropolis. Now it was a series of broken buildings, interspersed with sites preserved for the benefit of its Northern occupiers – barracks, brothels and hospitals. Parrish thought it ironic. The Notary had been criticised for pandering to his troops' sexual preferences. Here, if they weren't pandered to, the troops would riot.

Sullen Works soldiers escorted Parrish to the Latvian surgeon's quarters. "I am to take you to the Eye in the North," said Parrish abruptly. "You must bring with you all information concerning Dubroc."

The Latvian nodded assent. "There will be three others," he said.

Parrish raised his eyebrows. "Three?"

"Dubroc – he is fit enough to travel – his

nurse, Natasha and one other."

"Who is the one other?"

"He is called Ferez. He was once a citizen of the North. A student of Nanos's, he is an expert in miniaturism."

"What's he doing in this hell hole?"

"The same as me – trying to get out."

Parrish was suspicious. "Tell me more."

Once Dubroc, the nurse, the surgeon and the nervous Ferez were on board, Parrish communicated with the Eye. The new Committee member and power in the North enquired after Ferez's credentials.

"He says he has a miniature disc, like a contact lens, that was once in the possession of the Notary. He thinks it might be the work of Nanos, the dwarf."

There was a hissing sound on the other end of the line, as if Parrish was communicating with an angry cobra. Then, after a long pause; "Where did he get it?" the Eye asked, his voice neutral in tone.

"He was a prisoner of Kubar, the Leader's ally in the East. He took the disc from the Leader and escaped to Moscow."

"How very commendable," said the Eye.

"I thought it wise to bring him to you," said Parrish hesitantly.

There was laughter from the Eye. "Bring him

to me, by all means. A word to the wise. Don't let him out of your sight"

Scarab had found it harder than the miniaturist to leave Kubar's palace and reach the North.

"Why must he leave?" Kubar had been decidedly suspicious.

"Because I have assigned him a tedious, but necessary mission," said the Leader languidly.

"Which is?"

"My, you are curious, aren't you?"

Kubar sniffed. "Curiosity breeds information. Information is power."

"Yes, but it did kill the cat."

Kubar seemed puzzled. Scarab sniggered.

"If you must know," said the Leader, "Scarab is to find out what strength remains to us within the ranks of my former troops. If he accompanies Ferez part of the way to the North, he'll meet up with Works and Innuendo soldiers and be able to ask some relevant questions."

Kubar frowned. He wasn't taken in for a minute but, playing his own game, he didn't care to challenge the Leader.

"Very well," he said magnanimously, "I shall include Scarab in Ferez's entourage."

"I'm so grateful," the Leader had said smoothly.

Kazan smoked a thin, black cheroot, while

Lamar finished off the bottle of champagne.

"This woman, Avila, got close enough to the Mother because you provided her with the necessary credentials?" Kazan asked.

"Yes. But I was using her, or so I thought, to find out who was really behind her. I didn't believe it could be the Leader. He was, after all, out of the picture. It had to be someone closer at hand."

"It could have been Gregor Hamlet."

"Yes, it could. But Hamlet is not a man of action like the Eye."

Kazan blew a smoke ring. "Well, this mystery woman certainly did what she set out to do."

Lamar became animated which, considering his inebriated state, was an achievement. "And who benefited? The Eye and Gregor Hamlet."

"And you," said Kazan pointedly.

"I believe the Mother would have seconded me onto the Committee. I had nothing to gain by having her killed."

Kazan looked pensive.

"You must admit," continued Lamar, "the Eye is the oddest of creatures."

"He's taken good care of me."

"So far."

"What's that supposed to mean?"

Lamar smiled. "Do you take me for a fool? I am aware that I am not exactly an Adonis, or an Einstein. Your attraction to me has been manufactured. At the instigation of the Eye."

Kazan choked on cigar smoke. "You took advantage of it," she croaked.

Lamar roared with laughter. "No man alive would blame me for that. I'm right, aren't I?"

Kazan smiled sheepishly. "You're cleverer than I thought."

"More importantly," Lamar said quite seriously, "I'm cleverer than the Eye thinks I am."

He paused and awaited her response.

"I'm not saying that I go along with your suspicions concerning the Eye," Kazan said thoughtfully, "but I'm quite prepared to keep what you've said in mind."

"More champagne, or would you prefer something else?" Lamar said cheerfully, a glint in his eye.

Kazan clambered off the bed. "I think I'll stick to champagne."

The Latvian surgeon was ushered into the Eye's quarters.

The Eye was in no mood for pleasantries or small talk. "Your name?"

"Viktors Engel."

"How is Dubroc?"

"Well enough. He needs convalescence, but he'll survive and be whole again. He's a strong and determined young man."

"What about your nurse?"

"Natasha? She is taking care of him. They have, I believe, formed an attachment."

The Eye looked interested. "Really? That might be useful."

The Latvian said nothing.

The Eye became very friendly. "You are happy with your Northern citizenship?"

"I am. Thank you."

"You should thank me. It is in my gift. I am able to give and take away." The Eye looked at Engel for a reaction. The Latvian watched him closely. "I need all the information you have on Dubroc. Private, personal, conscious and subconscious findings."

The Latvian cleared his throat. "What do I receive in return?"

The Eye smiled. "Ah. I'm so pleased that everyone is so corruptible. It's predictable, but still satisfying," he said. "You will receive some monies from me, lavish accommodation, many privileges . . . need I go on?"

"What guarantee do I have that, once I am of no further use to you, you won't have me killed?"

"None at all." The Eye laughed. "But I shouldn't worry about it, if I were you. Your qualifications are such that I'm almost certain to need you for some time to come. Who knows, I might catch a cold."

The Latvian cut right across the Eye's

humour. "Dubroc had a spiritual journey through time," he said, "into his past."

The Eye swore. "Impossible."

"On the contrary. I have recorded everything. There is no doubt."

The Eye became pensive. "It is as I thought," he said. "Dubroc is someone special."

"Which bodes well for what you have in mind," said Engel.

The Eye gave him a look that would have chilled most men. "What do you mean?"

"It will take someone special to compete with you."

"What makes you think I'm interested in competition?"

The Latvian smiled thinly. "Anything that is won on the hazard always tastes sweeter than something hard earned."

The Eye poured Engel a drink. "You and I will get on well together," he said.

"Provided I follow and you lead."

The Eye made the drink a large one. "Very well, I'd say."

Both men smiled conspiratorially.

"What happened to Avila's body?" Kazan was fully dressed and ready to enter the fray. Always supposing she could find a fray to enter.

"I had it removed to the mortuary," said Lamar.

"Get me authorisation."

"For what?"

"To go there."

Lamar grimaced. "It's not exactly a holiday resort."

"I want to look at the body."

"Why?"

"Sometimes, the dead find it easier to yield up secrets than the living."

"What if I say no?"

Kazan leaned right into his face. "Then I'll stick to champagne and champagne only. You'll be reduced to buying naughty magazines."

Lamar sighed. "We don't publish any."

"Maybe you should start up a business. You'd make a fortune. Now, do I get the authorisation?"

When Ferez and Scarab reached Moscow, the miniaturist was snatched away by Parrish and the North's jet, leaving Scarab to fend for himself. Kubar's patronage ended here. But all was not lost. Scarab had a number of acquaintances among the Works troops stationed in what was left of Russia and, through fear or hope of reward, they could be depended upon to assist him. One such was a fadingly debonair officer named Lech.

The two men drank together in an off-limits bar run by a Russian gangster. Lech was becoming steadily drunker, his vodka purchased by Scarab. "There's a purge under way," he said.

"Who authorised it?"

"This unknown – the Eye."

"Tell me about him."

"He came from nowhere, but he seemed to know everything. He knew all about what the Leader and the Notary were up to. The Mother took him under her wing and, when she was killed, he took flight. Right to the top of the Committee tree."

Scarab eyed his friend. Perhaps he wasn't as drunk as he'd like to make out. Undoubtedly, he was spying out the lie of the land. Deciding which way to jump.

"Who killed the Mother?"

"It's rumoured the Leader had it done."

"But you think differently?"

"I wouldn't be surprised if it was the Eye who did it."

Scarab poured them both another stiff drink. "Are there others who think like you?"

"Some."

"If the Leader were to return, would they back him against the Eye?"

Lech tried to smile.

"What are you doing here?" asked the Notary's former secretary, now the Eye's assistant, as she opened the door to the mortuary.

Kazan tried to appear nonchalant. "Oh, I'm just looking around. Spending a little time with the dead makes you glad to be alive, don't you think?"

"I wouldn't know."

"What are *you* doing here?" asked Kazan boldly.

"I have authorisation."

"So have I." Kazan waved a piece of paper signed by Lamar.

The secretary smiled. "My authorisation comes from the Eye."

Kazan smiled back. "Well, if you'll pardon the pun, he and I usually see eye to eye."

The secretary frowned, as if in pain. "I know you're called Kazan," she said. "I am called Bela." She smiled again. "I also know what you've been up to with General Lamar."

Kazan snorted. "Then, we're both working for the Eye, it would seem. We're in it together. Just us girls."

"In what?"

"A heap of trouble, if my intuition is anything to go by. Where's what's left of the broad who took out the Mother?"

The secretary, Bela, gasped. Her hand flew to her mouth.

"What's wrong?"

"'What's left' is a good description. The body isn't really a body."

"Huh? How can a body not really be a body?"

Bela recovered her composure. "Come with me," she said, "and I'll show you." She led Kazan into the depths of the North's morgue.

The air was icy and both women shivered. Not just from the cold. Bela slid back a long drawer that contained a female body.

"Is this Avila?" asked Kazan. "She looks normal to me. Except that she's dead."

"Take a closer look."

Kazan did so, then stepped back quickly.

"She's hollow. No organs – nothing."

"No eyes."

"Right. How do you explain it?"

"I can't. I thought you might."

Kazan helped her shut the drawer. "What was she? Some kind of robot?"

Bela shrugged her shoulders. "Who knows? She certainly wasn't human."

Kazan laughed a hollow laugh. "Don't tell me – we're being taken over by aliens."

Bela did not laugh, hollowly or otherwise.

Kazan snorted. "I'm kidding. All right?"

"Nothing is impossible," said Bela quietly.

"What were you going to do in here?" Kazan asked suspiciously.

"I want to search the files."

"What for?"

Bela hesitated. "Can I trust you?"

Kazan seemed to think that one over. "Well,

you can't really trust anyone," she said. "But, if you're prepared to take the risk, I'm about as trustworthy as you'll find."

"The Eye wants all the information he can get on the Leader," Bela confided.

"That figures."

"Also, he wants to know everything there is to know about Dubroc."

"I've heard of him. Is he cute?"

"Lately, I received a memo from the Eye telling me to find out about you."

Kazan stared at her. "He knows a lot already," she said.

"Not enough, it would seem," came the reply.

Kazan smiled uncomfortably. "You expected to find out about me in the morgue?"

Bela chuckled. "Well, as it's turned out . . ."

"I take the point," said Kazan drily.

"I'm searching for details of the Leader's former mistresses. Two are certainly dead. I have to find the third."

"Why?"

"The Eye didn't say but, obviously, the Leader remains a threat. Any information might be useful."

"Then why don't we get to it?"

"We?"

"Remember: we're in this together."

Bela frowned. "I know. In trouble."

*

Ferez had been tortured. Racked with pain, shaking with fear, anticipating death and willing to do anything to avoid it, he was brought before the Eye.

"May I get you a drink?" asked the Eye paternally.

Ferez responded to the kindness in his tone, as the Eye knew he would. "Thank you."

"My pleasure." The Eye passed him a glass of fine cognac. Ferez drinking it down in one go, the Eye was obliged to pour him another. "Tell me about yourself," said the Eye, still apparently concerned, like a parent with a bruised child.

"There's little to tell," said Ferez.

"Well, tell me what little there is."

"I've been tortured."

The Eye looked aggrieved. "So I understand. Believe me, those responsible will be punished."

Ferez looked bewildered. "I thought you had ordered it."

The Eye smiled the most dazzling of smiles. A smile full of care, concern and friendship. "What on earth gave you that idea?"

Ferez was confused. "I don't know. I just thought . . . From what I've heard . . ."

"What have you heard?"

"That you are the master here in the North."

"And from whom did you hear that?"

Ferez looked away.

The Eye took hold of him, very gently. "Your

tormentors told me what you said. They didn't take long to break you, did they? It was the Leader, wasn't it?"

Ferez's eyes watered. "Yes," he said sorrowfully.

"Please don't cry," snapped the Eye. "I find tears tyrannical."

"I'm sorry," sniffed Ferez.

"This desert chieftain, Kubar, is hoping to deceive the Leader. I look forward to meeting him – Kubar, I mean. It's more likely to be in the next world than this."

Ferez shivered.

"Are you cold?" enquired the Eye.

"No."

"You're afraid you are going to die?"

"Yes."

"You do well to be afraid," said the Eye peremptorily. "Believe me, you would not die easily. Kubar's methods would be quite kindly compared to mine."

Ferez cringed in fear.

"Enough talk of dying, my dear Ferez. You are going to live. By my side. Sharing all that I have to give."

Ferez was silent.

"You're not impressed?" said the Eye. "You should be. Doubtless, Kubar promised you much, but I'm in a position to deliver and he isn't. I believe you have something for me?"

Ferez looked like a startled rabbit. "Yes . . . Yes . . . I do."

"Where is it?"

"I swallowed it."

The Eye frowned, then laughed. "You swallowed the Notary's disc?"

"Yes. It was the only way I could be sure I wouldn't lose it, or that it would not be found by anyone else."

The Eye couldn't stop laughing. "Have another drink," he said. "It'll act as an anaesthetic."

"What?"

"Well, we'll have to open you up to get at it, won't we?"

Ferez fainted.

"Here's something," Bela said, snatching a microfiche from a drawer. She fed it into a processor. A jumble of words appeared on the screen in front of her. "It doesn't make any sense," she said.

Kazan peered over her shoulder. "No it doesn't. Not unless you read Russian."

"Is that what it is?"

"Sure. What nationality was the Leader?"

"Russian."

"There you go," said Kazan triumphantly.

"Can you translate?" asked Bela.

"Hell, no. It takes me all my time to speak

English."

Bela sighed. "We need an interpreter."

"Anybody in mind?"

"No. We need a mechanical interpreter."

"Oh. Where do we find one?"

"General Lamar has one."

Kazan smiled broadly. "Is that a fact? Well – no problem."

The President was fast asleep and could not be disturbed. This according to one of his aides.

Kazan draped an arm round the young officer's neck. "Know who I am?" she said.

"Yes." he replied hesitantly.

"Well, that's just fine. You get on with whatever it was you were doing – hope it wasn't anything naughty – and Bela and I will check into Lamar's office."

"I can't allow that."

Kazan grabbed him by the collar. "You want me to wake him and say you tried to rape me?"

The aide smiled weakly. "I'll get the key."

The mechanical interpreter went to work.

"What does it say?" begged Kazan.

Bela read slowly. "Not much, I'm afraid."

"But enough?"

Bela smiled. "Yes. The Leader's third mistress was named Sonia Toth. He passed her on to a soldier – Scarab."

"OK. We find him."

"He's in the East. Too far away."

"Then we find her."

"Right. It's very odd." Bela bit her lip.

"What is?"

"The Leader gave her to Scarab, took her back and passed her to someone else. Nanos, the dwarf."

"He sure as hell is dead," said Kazan. "Killed by the Eye, from what I've heard," she added thoughtfully.

"Why would he do that? Nanos worked for the Notary, not the Leader."

"That's why," said Kazan forcefully. "The Leader wanted to keep tabs on the Notary and Nanos discovered the source of the Amazon. That's where the Eye had come from when I first met him."

"I'm confused," said Bela, meaning it.

"Maybe this Sonia broad can give us some answers. Where do we find her?"

Bela studied the microfiche. "There's no indication here." She thought for a long moment. "If she was the dwarf's mistress, why wouldn't she be living where Nanos lived?"

"Why didn't I think of that?"

Bela became businesslike. "Let's get going. Before the Eye thinks of it."

Ferez had been treated like a king. The Eye saw

to that. The operation, very minor, had gone well, the disc had been recovered and the miniaturist put to bed with a willing nurse.

The Eye was studying the disc in the computer room of Ludwig's castle. He saw what he had seen when he had viewed the disc's automatically filed image. But, now that he had the disc itself and better facilities, he saw something more. To the untrained eye, the disc would be an enigma never to be solved. But to the Eye itself, it revealed that, not only had Nanos recorded a personality for the Eye, but he had also, because he had inserted it in his own eye, recorded some of his own thoughts. The Eye could read the dead dwarf's mind.

He swore profusely. The damaged disc could not reveal everything, but it revealed enough. Nanos had hidden the real – the original – closed Eye and told no one of its location. The Eye, in his human form, was horrified. Could it be that he would be condemned to spend the rest of his days as a variety of humans, depending upon which disc he used? That was too much to bear. After all, humans died. The Eye had lived for thousands of years and wanted to survive a few thousand more.

The Eye sipped cognac – a present from Gregor Hamlet.

Nanos died at the source of the Amazon. Therefore, the hiding place must be there, or thereabouts. The Notary had found the charred disc. Had he found whatever it was that contained the closed Eye? It couldn't be. The Eye, in human form, was still functioning. Anyway, the Notary had been excited enough with the disc. If he had had the Eye itself, he would have been ecstatic and invincible. Perhaps he too, like the Eye, had studied the disc and learned of the hiding place, but had not had time to return to the Amazon to uncover it? More likely, perhaps he had returned North before something in Nanos's effects alerted him to the possibility of a profound discovery. In which case, to whom would he confide such information? The Eye became very still. The Notary would have confided in his then friend and accomplice – the Leader. That was why the Leader was still alive and a threat. He had something that would make him lord of all. He might not know what it was, but he knew its location. According to Ferez, he had enlisted Kubar's help to find out all he could about the Eye. But Kubar was playing his own game.

The Eye opened another bottle of fine brandy. He smiled to himself. When it came to playing games, there could be only one winner.

Sonia Toth – Nanos the dwarf's mistress, courtesy of the Leader – greeted Bela and Kazan at the door of her modest, but comfortable home on the outskirts of the North's capital city. She smiled enigmatically. "What took you so long?" she asked, not really requiring an answer.

Kazan thought the house was neat. Bela thought it cramped and unwelcoming. But a dwarf's home was unlikely to be spacious.

Sonia was probably no older than thirty, but she looked fifty. Pale and undernourished, her skin was flawed and what had once been something akin to beauty had been submerged beneath the ravages of time and stress.

Bela asked the questions. She too had been a Committee member's plaything and knew the score.

"We want to know about Nanos," she said, "Everything you can tell us."

Sonia threw back her head and laughed. "I refuse to tell you 'everything'. A girl must have her privacy – her secrets."

Bela sighed. "When Nanos discovered the source of the Amazon, were you his mistress?"

"No. I was very young at the time. I belonged to the Leader."

"OK. When did he pass you to Scarab?"

Sonia looked as though a bad taste had just affected her mouth. "After another two years. Apparently, I lasted longer with the Leader than most."

"Good for you," said Kazan sarcastically.

Sonia reacted. "I don't have to tell you anything. If you don't treat me right, I won't."

"Listen, sweetheart," Kazan said fiercely, "you talk to us or you talk to the Eye. The difference being, after you've talked to us you might stay alive."

There was a long pause. Sonia looked frightened. As well she might. Bela watched her closely, afraid that Kazan's aggression might cause her to clam up. Kazan merely smiled, not discouragingly.

Sonia calmed down and smiled back. "I thought you were a friend of the Eye. Didn't you come to the North with him?"

Kazan nodded. "Sure I did. I know something about him, but not enough. As for being a friend . . . Well, if there's one thing certain in life, it's that your supposed friends are best placed to carve you up. Let's say I don't entirely trust the Eye."

"Very wise," said Sonia. "It was Nanos who found him."

Bela leapt into the conversation. "Found him where?"

"At the source of the Amazon."

"That's right," said Kazan. "That's where he admits he came from."

Sonia offered them drinks but, becoming more and more excited by the prospect of what they might learn, Bela and Kazan declined.

"During the ten years Nanos was occupied with research," Sonia said, "he was under the thumb of the Notary. He came back home, to the North, very rarely. Sometimes I would go out to the Amazon to be with him. This without the knowledge of the Notary, but at the instigation of the Leader. He and Nanos had a lot in common. They shared the same nationality and, when the Leader snatched me back from Scarab and gave me to the dwarf, Nanos was the Leader's pawn for life. A short life, as it turned out."

"Must have been hell for you," Kazan suggested.

"On the contrary. Nanos treated me with great kindness. Most people considered him bitter and malignant. He treated me like a goddess, as if he couldn't believe his luck that I felt affection for him."

"You were a real little Snow White, huh?" said Kazan.

There was a sharp intake of breath from Bela, but Sonia was not offended.

"What did Nanos tell you about his experiments?" Bela asked.

"Very little. I wouldn't have understood what he was talking about. They were very complicated. He did tell me he had met the Eye and that, together, they would create a better world. How he met him he didn't say. I know he was trying to manufacture miniature discs. Discs that computerised personality."

"What the hell does that mean?" Kazan said.

Bela hushed her. "Did you ever see one of these discs?"

"No. And, of course, I never met the Eye. Nanos was very secretive about his whereabouts. It had to be close to the Source."

Bela looked thoughtful. "Nanos was reporting to the Leader as well as to the Notary, is that right?"

"Yes."

"So it's possible that the Eye, through Nanos, was working out some kind of deal?"

Sonia shook her head. "No. Nanos was playing his own game by this time. Welshing on the Notary and being economical with the truth as far as the Leader was concerned. Nanos was quite a guy."

It was Kazan who realised the way Sonia's mind was working. "You really do know something, don't you? Nanos's legacy to you. How about you doing a deal with us?"

Sonia hesitated. "Why don't I do a deal with the Eye?"

"Because you're scared of him. If you weren't, you'd have gone to him before now. The Notary's dead and the Leader's out of the picture. Seems to me, we girls should stick together."

Sonia smiled. She walked to a sideboard, opened a drawer and extracted a small wooden box. She opened it and took out a round, flat, silver disc.

"What are you going to do?" asked Kazan. "Play us some of our best-loved tunes?"

Sonia's smile became wan. "There's very little music in anyone's life nowadays. The Eye will make sure it's lost to us forever. Nanos told me – the Eye hates music of any kind. It's a tremendous irritation to him. He becomes quite frenzied."

"So, he's a critic?" joked Kazan.

"It isn't funny," said Bela.

"No, it isn't." Sonia handed Bela the disc. "I don't know exactly what's on it," she said, "because it's coded. You'll have to break that code. I know I can't. All I know is that it contains information as to where Nanos hid the Eye."

"But the Eye's here in the North," protested Kazan.

"Is he? Think about it," said Sonia. "Nanos was trying to code personality – or personalities – onto miniature discs. Discs small enough to fit into someone's—"

Kazan didn't let her finish. "Into someone's eye."

"Quite. Why would he do that? How could he do that? With whose connivance would he do that?"

Bela interrupted, "Because the Eye isn't

human. Like the corpse of the Mother's assassin isn't human. Nanos was creating personalities for the Eye."

"I'm way off base here," said Kazan. "If the Eye isn't the Eye, what is he? Hell, I'm confusing myself."

Sonia said, quite coldly, "The Eye is an 'it'."

Kazan said, "How about that drink? I think I need one."

Sonia poured three glasses of wine. Kazan downed hers in one go and held her glass out for more.

"I think I follow," said Bela. "When the Notary returned from the Amazon, after Nanos's death, he was very secretive. He'd found something in Nanos's laboratory. What if it was one of these discs?"

Sonia ignored her wine. "Then he would have tried to decode it. But, soon after his return, he ran to the East."

"To join the Leader," said Kazan.

"Therefore, if there was a disc the Leader has it now."

"Maybe," said Bela, "but he wouldn't know how to decode it."

Kazan had finished her second glass of wine. She frowned. "Tell me something." She spoke directly to Sonia. "Nanos left you this coded disc. Now, it's nothing like the miniature discs he was manufacturing, but it's supposed to tell you something. How were you supposed to glean anything from it?"

"A man called Ferez could decode it. He was Nanos's assistant for a while."

Bela froze. The other women were momentarily alarmed.

"Ferez is a prisoner of the Eye," Bela said anxiously. "He's defected from the East and the Leader to here in the North."

The three women were silent for a long time.

"Curiouser and curiouser," said Kazan finally.

The Eye's human eyes opened. He had closed them in the hope that darkness might help him think more clearly. Now he had something in mind. He scurried to a safe that he had had set into the wall of his quarters. It protected the box that contained Nanos's discs. He selected a disc, placed it in his human eye and turned to a mirror. Death On Two Legs appeared. "What do you want?" Death hissed.

"Your help."

"You mean, you want me to help you help yourself?" Death might have been laughing. The Eye couldn't tell.

"You are part of me," said the Eye, "therefore, without you, I am not quite whole and unable to bring all of my – our – powers to bear on the conundrum."

"Which is?"

"The Notary obtained one of the dwarf's discs and passed it on to the Leader."

"I know that," hissed Death impatiently. "I am you and you are me and, therefore, I know what you know."

"Ferez has returned the disc to me."

Death On Two Legs hissed disapprovingly. "Get on with it. Please, get on with it."

"You may know as much as I do," said the Eye acidly, "but you are unable to speculate as I can. Nanos has concealed us, our original self."

Death On Two Legs, whose eyes, like a snake's, never closed, stared out of the mirror at the Eye, its *alter ego*.

"I believe he secreted that information," the Eye continued, unfazed. "It is possible, however, that the Leader knows something. Hence his longevity, against the odds."

Death may have smiled. Again, the Eye couldn't tell.

"You're saying we don't know where we're hiding, but someone else might?

The Eye did smile.

"You are probably right about the Leader," Death said. "He knows something, but not enough. He's moving against us, but slowly. Therefore he is not in possession of everything he needs to know to destroy us. Time, as ever, is on our side. On the other hand, there may be – must be – someone else who knows of the secret. Who could that be, I wonder?"

"Nanos knew and is dead. The Notary may have known and he is dead. The Leader suspects, as you suggest, but does not know for certain." The Eye's brow furrowed in concentration.

Death On Two Legs sighed. "You're beginning to disappoint me, which means I'm beginning to disappoint myself," it hissed.

The Eye looked directly into the mirror. "Someone close to Nanos must hold the key." he said.

"*Cherchez la femme*," Death said.

Bela, the Notary's former mistress, now supposedly at the beck and call of the Eye, was nowhere to be found. The Arena soldier who reported this trembled before the Eye's wrath. "If you can't find her," the Eye said grittily, "perhaps your superior might. Fetch General Lamar."

The Soldier looked aghast. "He is the President."

"Oh, well, in that case," said the Eye, "ask if he will kindly grant me an audience. Suggest to him that I would appreciate that audience right away." His voice dripped sarcasm.

The soldier was anxious to get out of the room and pass the buck concerning the disappearance of Bela. "Very good, sir."

"Also," commanded the Eye, "send Ferez to me."

"We've got to get Sonia out of sight," said Kazan. "We've found her, so the Eye won't be far behind."

"Except that I'm the one he detailed to look for her," said Bela. "He'll wait for my report."

"I wouldn't count on it," said Kazan hastily. "If what Sonia's told us about the dwarf is true, it won't take the Eye long to begin to put two and two together and come up with five."

"This is what is most important," said Bela, holding up the silver disc. "We've got to get it to Ferez, so that he can decode it."

Kazan snorted derisively. "He's the Eye's man. He sure as hell won't do us any favours."

"We'll force him to," said Bela, a new determination about her.

Kazan shrugged. "OK. I'll go along for the ride."

Sonia, who had been out of the room preparing food for her guests, returned with a tray laden with cheeses, fruit and bread.

"We have to get you out of here," said Kazan.

Sonia was unmoved. "We'll eat first."

"Yeah, well we'd better make it quick, or this could be our last supper."

"What were your instructions to Bela?" asked

Lamar, half dressed and much disgruntled that his sleep had been disturbed.

"I thought it a good idea to look into the Leader's background," said the Eye smoothly. "The secretary was checking up on his former mistresses."

"Well, perhaps she's still checking?"

"In the middle of the night?"

"Maybe she couldn't sleep." The General chuckled.

The Eye didn't see the joke. "I want her found," he said, "and I want her found before it gets light."

Lamar found the Eye's manner disturbing. He was frightening enough when normal. "She'll be in your power by dawn," said the General, exiting the room with what dignity he could muster.

Shortly after he had gone, Ferez was ushered into the Eye's presence.

The Eye placed his arm round the miniaturist's shoulder and held him tight and close. "What else did the Leader have belonging to the Notary, apart from the disc?" he asked in friendly fashion.

Ferez, who had been disturbed in the act of making love to a maid employed in the castle kitchen, smiled weakly. "Nothing, Excellency."

The Eye clasped him very tightly, almost choking the smaller man. "Think, Ferez, think. Think or die."

"There was something," gasped Ferez.

The Eye let him go.

"You know that I was Kubar's hostage?" Ferez continued.

The Eye nodded impatiently.

"Well, it was his idea I should come here and act as a spy in the North."

The Eye snapped at him. "You confessed as much under torture. Get on with it."

Ferez spoke hurriedly. "Of course, the Leader knew of this plan and approved it but, as you are aware, Excellency, the Leader is a devious opponent. He arranged for one of his minions to accompany me part of the way. I'm certain he was meant to follow me into the North and keep an eye out for the Leader's interests."

The Eye smiled. "Keep an eye out . . . I like that."

Ferez, ever the sycophant, joined in the Eye's laughter.

"What was the name of this minion?" the Eye asked.

"Scarab."

If it hadn't been for the nurse, Natasha, Dubroc would have felt neglected. Apart from initial and perfunctory interest in his well-being, no one had come near him. Still, Natasha was proving to be adequate compensation. They lay in each other's arms on a soft, goosedown mattress.

"Tell me about Miranda," the nurse said in French.

Dubroc replied in the same language. "She lived, she loved, she died. I will never talk about her."

Natasha rolled on top of him and looked into his eyes. "You loved, you lived, you didn't die."

"No. Maybe I should have."

Natasha placed her fingers on his lips. "Never say that. Your life is too precious."

Dubroc sighed. "A lot of people have to die to preserve the lives of the few. I know. I've killed more than my fair share."

"That's your job."

Dubroc smiled. "The Mother once said that to me."

"Well, then...?"

"It doesn't make killing easier."

Natasha kissed him.

A bell rang.

Dubroc laughed. "That's clever. How did you manage that?"

Natasha smiled and rolled off him. Dubroc snatched up a small mobile telephone. He listened to a voice on the other end of the line for a few moments, then broke the connection.

"I have to go somewhere," he said.

Natasha protested: "But you're meant to be recovering from a near-death injury."

"I'm well enough."

"Where do you have to go?"

"I have to go looking for someone. Someone called Scarab."

Lamar looked smug. "I've found her, the Leader's ex-mistress."

The Eye pretended gratitude and patience. "How clever of you. May I ask where?"

"At Nanos the dwarf's house. The Leader passed her on to him."

The Eye, walking to his desk, appeared to stumble.

"Are you all right? A little too much to drink perhaps?" the General enquired, a twinkle in his eye.

The Eye, had he been able to, would have blushed. "What about Bela?"

"It was by pursuing Bela's line of enquiry about the Leader's former mistresses that I came across this woman – Sonia Toth."

"Did you come across Bela herself in this 'pursuit'?"

Lamar looked uncomfortable. "They're missing."

"They?"

"Bela and the Toth woman. Looks as though they left Nanos's house in a hurry."

"What you're telling me," said the Eye, his voice as cold as winter, "is that not only have you failed to discover Bela's whereabouts, as you promised you would, but you have also lost this other woman. Very careless, Mr President, if I may say so."

Lamar remained silent.

The Eye suddenly became friendly. "I'm sorry," he said, almost gushing, "I'm sure you did your best."

Lamar wiped his brow. "It's hard to keep up with you. Your personality seems to change by the second," he said innocently.

The Eye bared his teeth in a feral smile.

Scarab had promised Lech the earth. Whether or not his friend expected to inherit it hadn't made much difference. He acquired for Scarab a long-range helicopter with extra fuel tanks. This was serviced by some Works troops who were Lech's underlings. "Nurse this thing along and it'll get you to the North," Lech had said. "You'll have to make other arrangements to reach the capital. This'll run out of gas at the border. Roughly where Prague used to be."

Indeed it had. Scarab had had to steal electric cycles in order to complete his journey. Begging or borrowing them wasn't in his nature. He'd had to kill a couple of disgruntled owners.

Scarab went looking for the contact whose name the Leader had given him.

The Eye questioned Ferez in detail. He was

beginning to suspect that the miniaturist might have outwitted his torturers and held something back. Of course, this would not be surprising. Torture in the twenty-first century was nothing like it had been a thousand or two thousand years before. It was to the Eye's advantage that he could recall the methods of long ago.

"Let me make you an offer, Ferez," said the Eye. "Abandon everyone who has influenced you in the past and throw in your lot with me."

"You said something about an offer?" Ferez replied cagily.

The Eye managed to control his instinct to hit out at the man. Instead he smiled his now famous smile – the smile to be found on the face of the tiger once his prey has been brought down. "I propose to rule in the North and, later, in the West. The East will be ignored, unless the population there troubles me. In which case, I will mobilise our army and teach another hard lesson. The South needs thinking about. Of course, you know all this, don't you? You have read the disc."

Ferez, on the very brink of what he had set out to achieve, held his breath and remained silent.

The Eye, sure of the capture of Ferez's soul, continued. "That disc, formerly in the possession of the Notary and the Leader, I have now destroyed. There are others." The Eye glanced at Ferez, watching for any reaction. There was none. The miniaturist seemed frozen to the spot.

"Nanos and I created the discs," said the Eye. "But you will have guessed that already. I need someone to maintain those discs. Someone to give me complete and unquestioning support in my mission. I have chosen you. The rewards . . . ? Well, I will leave you to imagine them for yourself." The Eye paused for effect. "The alternatives to my offer do not bear thinking about," he said. "Kubar has tried to use you and has failed. The Leader has been misled by you. If you should fall into either of their hands again . . ." the Eye acted out horror. "I fear you would be much misused," he concluded tamely.

Ferez shifted uneasily. "I am yours to command, Excellency," he said sincerely.

The Eye laughed. "I'm sure you say that to everyone who threatens you."

Ferez winced.

The Eye stood very close to him. "Whatever you think might happen to you should the Leader or Kubar find you, multiply by a thousand times and you will still come nowhere near imagining the pain I am able to inflict."

Ferez panicked. "The Leader and Kubar have many agents in the North. I am afraid of them."

"Do try to relax," said the Eye easily. "Once you are in my employ and become my close confidant, no one will dare touch you." He chuckled to himself. "I will keep an eye on you." The chuckle became a laugh.

Ferez tried to assume a mantle of dignity. "I will always obey you," he said. "I know that what you promise will be delivered. Not so with the Leader or Kubar."

The Eye stopped laughing and became deadly serious. "What does the Leader know that allows him to continue to dictate terms to such as Kubar?"

Ferez took a step backwards, such was the intensity of the question. "He knows nothing."

The Eye's manner became chilly. "You must not lie to me, Ferez."

"I do not lie," said Ferez anxiously. "He is not privy to what was on the disc. He has no inkling of Nanos's secret."

The Eye looked at him sharply. "What secret?" he asked, his voice barely above a whisper.

"The hiding place of something that, once found, releases all the power in the world."

The Eye didn't move a muscle. "And what might that 'something' be, I wonder?"

If Ferez was acting innocence he deserved some kind of an award. "I don't know. All I learned from the disc was a fragment of Nanos's thought that suggested this hiding place. Of course, I learned that you, the Eye, have watched over the world. I would guess that that which is hidden is of importance to you."

The Eye remained deathly still. "You will help me find it?" he asked.

Ferez responded enthusiastically, "You are my master, I am your slave."

There was a pause. At length, the Eye said, "What then is the power the Leader possesses?"

"He has an ally here in the North. Without the Leader, no one can approach him."

"Him?"

"Or her – I don't know."

"This ally of the Leader's must be powerful in his, or her, own right?"

"Yes indeed."

"And you have no idea who it might be?"

"No. But he, or she, shouldn't be hard to find."

"Oh?"

"He, or she, will be Scarab's contact here. Find Scarab and he will lead you to him. Or her."

The Eye smiled appreciatively. "I have already set in motion a search for Scarab."

Ferez smiled back. "You are always one step ahead of the rest of the world, Excellency."

The Eye laughed. "Yes. Sometimes I outpace myself. I quite misunderstood the Leader's source of influence. Still, with you by my side, I shall not too easily jump to errant conclusions."

"I am your humble servant, Excellency," whined Ferez.

The Eye frowned. "Don't overdo it."

According to a publication of Gregor Hamlet's, there were four million, two hundred thousand inhabitants of the North. Fourteen thousand, or thereabouts, lived in the capital city. Scarab was one of them and Dubroc was looking for him.

The nurse, Natasha, had insisted on accompanying him.

"The odds are fourteen thousand to one against my finding him," said Dubroc.

"Not at all," said Natasha. "Of those fourteen thousand, half are women. There are two thousand children and at least a thousand inhabitants are immigrants."

Dubroc smiled. "All right then. The odds are four thousand to one."

She smiled back at him. "Better, no?"

"Better, yes."

"Where do we start?"

Dubroc thought for a moment. "All likely entry points from the East."

"Why does not your superior offer you help in finding this man?" Natasha asked innocently.

Dubroc shrugged. "He has his reasons. He doesn't trust too many people. He's probably right."

"I thought it was suggested he had some hand in the Mother's death?"

"Suggested by whom?"

Natasha backed off. "Oh. I heard it somewhere."

The Eye entertained Dubroc's surgeon, Viktors Engel.

"I'm so pleased you are now a member of my small, but exclusive, team," the Eye said expansively.

Engel smiled and nodded.

"I feel like the Emperor Nero," the Eye went on. "Everyone I have invited to the ball is dancing to my tune."

"The Emperor was much misunderstood by history," ventured Engel.

"How very true. It seems to be forgotten that he was a great patron of the arts. Of course, he was an execrable musician. Not that I would know: all music is anathema to me."

Engel made a mental note of that comment.

The Eye was lost in the past. "Rome was destroyed by him. Those that play with fire must expect to get burned." He stared intently at Engel, as if searching his very soul. The surgeon was alarmed. "Tell me about Dubroc," said the Eye.

Engel said, "I have his entire history, a personality printout and am able, to a certain extent, to read the contents of his mind."

"How certain is that extent?"

Engel smiled knowingly. "A lot of it is guesswork, I admit, but there are certain clues that make any guesses educated ones."

"You will provide me with all details of his past in the West and assess his likely attitude to such as Lamar and, of course, myself. How would you quantify his depth of loyalty?"

Engel thought for a moment. "If he believes in something or someone, his loyalty would know no depth."

"You mean, he would follow blindly?"

"Until and unless his eyes were opened to the truth."

The Eye smiled. "What is truth? It is the lie told by the victor."

Only because Kazan had used almost all of her powers of persuasion had Parrish agreed to provide sanctuary for Sonia Toth and Bela. He knew nothing of the silver compact disc bequeathed by Nanos the dwarf, but had been led to believe that Bela was trying to escape the lascivious designs of Lamar and that Sonia was an illegal immigrant from the South.

Parrish took Kazan on one side. "They can't stay long."

Kazan kissed him lightly on the lips. "Take it easy, Baby. They'll be here no more than two days – you have my word on that."

"Where will you be?"

"I'm out there looking for something. When I

find it, I'll hot foot it back here to you."

"Let me help you."

"You're helping enough as it is." Kazan rubbed her body against his. "This guy Ferez, the one you brought back from Moscow, where is he?"

Parrish looked concerned. "The castle guards messed him about a bit. Then the Eye stepped in and, it seems, they've become bosom pals."

"That doesn't answer my question, Sweetie."

"Ferez has rooms in Ludwig's castle's basement. There's a well equipped laboratory next door. Ferez is an expert in nanotechnology." Parrish smiled. Kazan was arousing him and he didn't want her to leave.

Well aware of her sexual powers, Kazan knew exactly what she was doing and, very gently, pushed him away. "I'll be back," she whispered.

"What's Ferez got that I haven't?" Parrish asked flippantly.

"When I find out, I'll let you know."

Kubar was displeased. "I have heard nothing from Ferez," he stormed.

The Leader smiled sympathetically. "It's so difficult to hire decent employees nowadays," he said laconically.

"Don't try to be funny, Leader," responded Kubar. "I'm not in the vein. My agents tell me that Ferez has succeeded in gaining the Eye's confidence. If that is so, why hasn't he passed on any information?"

"Perhaps your agents haven't asked him for any? Perhaps they find it difficult to gain his ear, now that he is firmly ensconced in Ludwig's castle? Have they made physical contact?"

"No. They have merely reported what they have learned from castle gossip and the like."

"Well then?"

Kubar was pensive. "If Ferez has changed sides . . ."

"Yet again," interjected the Leader.

". . . then my agents will be at risk."

"What better way to find out?"

Kubar sighed. "You are right." His eyes glinted. "If Ferez is no longer under my control, my plan will have failed."

"Yes, well the best laid plans of mice and men . . . as the saying goes," said the Leader.

"What of your plan, my dear Leader?"

The Leader feigned innocence. "What plan? I have no plan. Other, that is, than to support you in any way I can."

"Shall we stop playing games with one another?" Kubar hissed.

The Leader scowled. "Get to the point, Kubar. What do you want?"

"I think you have enjoyed my hospitality long enough. Now is the time for you to begin to repay."

"I don't respond too well to threats," said the Leader coldly.

"It's not a threat. Think of it as a suggestion."

The Leader's smile was a chilly one. "I am aware that the only reason I am allowed to live is because I have something you want. A powerful contact in the North."

"Is it not time to reach out to him? Then our plans could proceed."

"Our plans? I thought you had your agenda and I had mine and, like East and West, never the twain would meet?"

Kubar looked penitent. "Let us put aside our different agendas, our different plans, and combine all our forces. United, we will stand and conquer – divided, we may fall."

"Very eloquently put," said the Leader. "Let us decide to trust one another."

Kubar appeared delighted. "Now, what about your ally in the North? Shall we set things in motion and make contact?"

The Leader shook his head wearily. "I'm very fond of you, Kubar," he said, "but you can sometimes be a little slow on the uptake. Where do you think Scarab is at this moment?"

Kubar frowned. "Checking up on the loyalty of your Works troops."

"At this moment, he is making the contact that will begin the last part of our adventure together. He is meeting with our friend in the North."

Perhaps the Leader hadn't taken account of the time difference between the desert and the industrial North, but Scarab was still far from making any kind of contact. For one thing, the Leader's "friend" was very hard to reach. For another, he sensed danger. He was a known Innuendo officer and could, at any time, be recognised and his whereabouts reported to the Theatre and Arena troops now loyal to the Eye.

He chose to proceed slowly, make contact as soon as, and in any way, he could and await developments, whilst at the same time, preserving his liberty. He needed someone he could trust to carry a message for him. The only person he could think of was his former mistress, Sonia Toth. He knew where she lived.

Kazan found it very easy to enter Ludwig's castle. Most guards and employees knew, or suspected, that she had the ear of the Eye and was his special agent. Which, of course, to some extent was true.

The sergeant who had greeted her so coldly on her very first day in the North was on duty. He eyed her warily as she swaggered towards him, her hips waving hello. "How's it going?" she asked.

The sergeant was immune to her charms. "As well as can be expected," he said.

Kazan suspected she might not get anywhere with this man. "I need a pass for the basement apartments," she said. "How about writing one out for me?"

The sergeant favoured her with an evil grin. "Why should I do that?"

"Because I'm asking you nicely?"

The sergeant shook his head. "Not good enough."

"Or because, if you don't, I'll scream blue murder and the Eye, or General Lamar, or both, will come running and you'll be busted to the lower ranks so fast even your privates will feel the pain," Kazan said sweetly.

The sergeant licked dry lips. "You're some kind of a bitch, aren't you?"

Kazan said, "You better believe it. Now, write out the pass."

The sergeant scribbled a few words on a piece of paper. He handed the pass to her.

"There – that wasn't so difficult, was it?" Kazan said over her shoulder as she strolled towards the castle's basement steps.

The sergeant pulled a face at her back. When she had gone, he used a mobile telephone to communicate with the Eye's quarters. A voice said, "The Eye cannot be disturbed. He is the guest of Committee Member, Gregor Hamlet." The sergeant tried another number, only to be informed by another disembodied voice that the

President, General Lamar, had left for his estates in Scandinavia. The sergeant swore all the oaths the army had taught him.

Gregor Hamlet was throwing a dinner party for those with influence, or potential influence, in the business community of the North. The Eye was guest of honour.

Before everyone, including the Eye, had arrived, Hamlet made certain that the occasion would be memorable. The food and wine was of the finest and in sufficient quantities to feed many of those on the brink of starvation in the East. Beautiful women and handsome young men would dance attendance on the guests, indulging their every whim. There would be lavish entertainment – a sword swallower, a fire-eater, a clown, a spectacular firework display and, for those so inclined, private rooms for the indulgence of sexual proclivities. There would be no music. Although Hamlet, ever curious, would try to persuade the Eye to listen to some at a later date, so that he might form a judgement of the relevance of the Eye's reaction.

With everything prepared and nothing overlooked, Hamlet preened in anticipation of an event that would shape the North's, later the world's, future. A future that Hamlet himself would have a large part in shaping.

*

Ferez thought that Kazan was another bedroom companion provided by the Eye. She had to slap him around a little to persuade him otherwise. The miniaturist cowered on the floor as she stood over him. "Sorry about that," she said. "You can look, but you mustn't touch. OK?"

Ferez nodded compliantly.

"Good. Now we understand one another," Kazan went on, "we can get down to business."

Ferez, frightened, looked up at her enquiringly.

She smiled down at him. "I have a little job for you." She flourished the silver disc obtained from Sonia Toth. "I need you to translate what's on this."

Kazan stooped and helped Ferez to his feet. "Let's get one thing straight," she said, with all the menace she could muster. "You play fair by me and I'll play fair by you. Mess me about on this and I'll come back here and wipe you out. You already know how easy it is for me to get to you. *Comprendez*?"

"We will need to go to the computer bank," Ferez said quietly.

"Gee, why didn't I think of that?"

Ferez, his arm held in Kazan's iron grip, led the way to the laboratory in an adjacent room. Kazan released him so that he could bring the computer he had selected for the job on line. He held out his hand for the silver disc.

"Remember," Kazan said as she passed it to him, "I'll know if you're trying to lead me into the boonies."

Ferez activated the computer's discovery mode.

Scarab was cooling his heels at Sonia Toth's house. A big man, he found its rooms cramped, its atmosphere claustrophobic. It was clear to him that Sonia had left in a hurry, which suggested it would be a while before she came back.

Scarab thought things over. Where had she gone? Why? and What for? were questions that could wait. How had she got to where she was going? That was a good question. Scarab set out to find the answer.

If she had walked he was likely to be out of luck but, chances were, she had used transportation. Did she possess an electrically powered cycle? Scarab checked the contents of an adjoining building. There was an electrical battery-charger set into its wall. The cycle had a range of twenty miles before it needed recharging, always assuming it was fully charged to start with. Scarab took readings from the charger on the wall. He smiled to himself. The instrument indicated that the cycle had started off on half power. That cut its range to ten miles – five miles out, five miles back. What lay within five miles of Sonia Toth's home that might attract her? Scarab sighed.

It was too obvious. The airport for the North was three miles distant. If she was running away from something in the North, it was the logical place to head for. But Sonia Toth would not be able to fly any type of aircraft. She would require the services of a pilot and, assuming that she wanted to get as far away as possible in the shortest possible time, as her hasty exit from her home suggested, she'd want someone who could pilot a jet – the only jet extant – Parrish's jet.

The Eye was enjoying himself. Hamlet's party was an organisational *tour de force*. Everything seemed perfect – even the other guests. These were businessmen, each an expert in his own field, who controlled all of the resources needed to sustain a nation at war. Gregor Hamlet was gearing up for the solid protection of the North and the rapid invasion of the West. One of the guests, a plump armaments manufacturer with eyes that had died long ago, was holding forth. "There is now under construction a wall of steel that will protect us from the East," he said. "The Easterners are a disorganised rabble and have little chance of breaching it. Even should they do so, we would receive timely warning. Warning timely enough to launch missiles to destroy them."

"We have no nuclear capacity," another guest remarked drily.

"We have warheads that carry chemicals,

viruses, any disease you care to name," the armaments manufacturer snapped at him. "And we have the means to deliver those warheads."

"One jet aircraft?" The heckler was not to be put off.

"Six massive guns with a range of a thousand miles."

There was scattered applause. The heckler buried his face in his glass of fine wine. Hamlet beamed at everybody. The Eye was becoming bored.

"They must be very big guns," a female guest commented.

The armaments manufacturer seized his cue. "The biggest ever made. Their barrels are a mile long."

"I remember them," said the Eye. Everyone looked at him, their expressions puzzled. "At the end of the last century," he said, "one was manufactured here in the North and supplied to the East. It didn't work: it ran out of spare parts."

Hamlet said, "The Eye's knowledge of history is unsurpassed."

"Those who do not know history are condemned to repeat it," quoted the Eye.

Another businessman intervened. "It is I who will supply the spare parts required," he said proudly. "Rest assured, they will never be in short supply." There was a further scattering of applause.

Other guests rose to their feet and announced their contributions to the adventure that lay ahead. Small arms, uniform supply, helicopter manufacture, fuel collection and conservation, troop training and indoctrination, ground transportation, boat building – the list was endless and the Eye was becoming jaded, until Hamlet said, "We must not forget the preparation of our élite corps. The test – the game – I have prepared will select none but the bravest, the strongest and those certain to remain blindly obedient to all of us here."

"Game?" the Eye enquired. "What sort of game?"

The others remained silent while Hamlet explained.

"It's merely a sophisticated version of the tests we used in the past to select the troops best suited to guard members of the Committee."

The Eye looked uneasily about him. He knew nothing of these tests, or games. An unfortunate admission for someone who claimed to know everything and intended to rule the world. The Eye covered his tracks well, though. He smiled knowledgeably. "Of course," he said, "of course. And you, Gregor – you have refined the selection process?"

"Indeed I have." Hamlet bathed in the admiring attention of his guests. "Come with me to the Dome tomorrow and I will give you a demonstration."

The Dome? This was something else of which the Eye was ignorant. He kept silent for the moment, but determined to bring himself up to date on these relevant matters as soon as he returned to Ludwig's castle.

It wasn't hard for Scarab to find Parrish's apartment. He had two choices: to knock on the door and hope to be admitted, or to barge in unannounced, his five seveN locked and loaded and ready for use. The choice was obvious.

Scarab shot the lock off the apartment door and kicked it open. Assuming the correct Seek and Locate stance, he raced from room to room. It was in a bedroom that he found Sonia Toth.

Sonia had been sleeping and her rude awakening was worsened as Scarab's muscular arm seized her round the throat. "Is there anyone else here?" Scarab demanded.

Sonia could hardly breath, but managed to gasp, "No."

Scarab threw her on the bed. "Where's Parrish?"

Sonia choked and coughed before replying. "He was ordered to fly the President to Scandinavia."

Scarab grunted. "You'd better be right, or you'll be dead."

"I'm telling you the truth."

"Anyone else around?""

Sonia shook her head.

Scarab slapped her across the face. "You're lying."

Sonia began to sob. Through her tears she said, "There were two other women. One's gone to the castle, the other's gone to the mortuary."

Scarab said, "That's where you'll end up if you're lying again."

"I really am telling you the truth."

Scarab sat on the bed next to the woman, his five seveN clutched in his hand. "I've come from the Leader," he said.

Sonia controlled herself. "I guessed as much. What does he want?"

"What do you think he wants?"

"Not my body – not any more."

Scarab sneered at her. "I doubt there are many who would want that."

Sonia scrambled off the bed. Scarab clutched her naked body from behind. "I'm the exception," he said.

She turned into him. "Now who's lying?"

Scarab let her go. "I don't have time to prove I'm not," he said. "I need to get a message to the Leader's contact here in the North."

"What message?" Sonia was suddenly alert.

Scarab snorted. "You don't need to know. I have to meet with the contact and report back to the Leader. That's all."

"Why should I help you?" Sonia snapped.

"For old time's sake?"

Sonia didn't smile. "The Leader treated me like a piece of trash," she said feelingly. "I had to endure his fumblings, then your bestiality." She shivered, not with cold.

"He gave you Nanos." Scarab said quietly.

Sonia weakened. "Yes. That was the best thing that's happened to me."

Scarab took her in his arms. "Better things lie ahead."

She looked into his eyes. His lips brushed hers. "Such as?" she asked.

"When the Leader is truly our leader again, he won't forget those who helped him."

"How's he going to regain his power?"

"Wait and see."

Sonia broke away from him. "The Leader will have to confront the Eye."

Scarab shrugged. "He's eliminated his enemies in the past. The Eye will be just another notch on his gun. He's only human."

Sonia threw back her head and laughed. "Are you quite sure about that?"

The silver disc was blank.

Kazan swore. Ferez did likewise. She swore in Spanish, he in Arabic. "I don't understand it," said the miniaturist.

"Well, if you don't, nobody will," said Kazan irritably.

"You say Nanos composed this disc?"

"I've said it countless times."

Ferez shook his head and pursed his lips. "Nanos was a genius," he said finally.

"And you're not?"

"Not in the same class, I regret to say."

Kazan paced up and down in the laboratory. "Let's think this through," she said. "Nanos gave the disc to his lover, Sonia Toth. It was supposed to be some kind of insurance for her. Now, he wasn't to know that you'd be available, so he had to assume that Sonia would be able to interpret the disc herself. Ergo – there's got to be a simple way of deciphering its contents."

It suddenly dawned on Ferez. Kazan noticed his expression change. "What is it?" she said sharply.

Ferez, very pleased with himself, said, "We're assuming that the computer can scan the disc. That its contents are visually encoded. What if it's an audio disc?"

Kazan said, "I think I'm going to be sick."

Dubroc and Natasha were getting nowhere. They had found Scarab's point of entry to the North – an abandoned electric cycle and a dead Arena border guard testified to that – but of Scarab himself there was no trace.

"Where might he go?" Natasha asked.

Dubroc said, "Your guess is as good as mine. A lot depends on why he's here."

"You have said he was with the Leader, so he must be here on the Leader's business."

"Whatever that might be."

"Perhaps he is here as an assassin?"

"That's possible. More likely, he's here to contact someone. Someone in the North's establishment who is of use to the Leader."

"He would have to be powerful." Natasha said helpfully.

"Yes, he would. Well, it's unlikely to be the Eye."

"That leaves Gregor Hamlet and the President."

"Just the two?" Dubroc looked at her steadily.

"They are on the Committee."

"It could be anyone just below them. Any number of influential businessmen. Anyone who has convinced the Eye of his worthiness. It could be Viktors Engel, for example."

Natasha returned his steady gaze. "Yes, it could," she said, "but who is most likely?"

Dubroc tensed. "The President, General Lamar. It was always thought that he might be in the Leader's pocket and the Eye mentioned that he might have had something to do with the Mother's death."

"Viktors Engel suspects the Eye."

Dubroc was uncertain. "You've said that before. What makes Engel think so?"

"The Eye has made Viktors his vassal. His first task was to provide all information concerning you when you were under his care. When you were asleep, or drugged, or both. When you had your out-of-body experience in the West."

Dubroc was unimpressed. "That was a dream."

"A nightmare, more like."

"All right," accepted Dubroc. "We won't place our entire trust in the Eye. But, until he does something to suggest he's up to no good, I'm prepared to give him the benefit of any doubt. I think Scarab's most likely contact is Lamar. Let's find out."

Sonia Toth had two choices. She could lead Scarab astray, or she could throw in her lot with him and betray Bela and Kazan and surrender Nanos's secret to the Leader. Either way, she figured, she would be likely to end up dead. She took what was for her the easy way out.

Having promised to lead Scarab to Kazan, she excused herself and entered Parrish's apartment's bathroom. When Scarab, alarmed by the length of time she was taking, broke down the bathroom door, he found that she had taken a razor to the veins in her wrists and her lifeblood was ebbing away into a bath of water. Scarab swore, took out his five seveN and shot the dying woman between the eyes.

Where had Sonia said the others had gone? The mortuary was one destination. Scarab smiled grimly. It was as good a place to start as any. Making contact with the Leader's ally in the North would have to wait.

Dubroc and Natasha were informed by staff at the airport that the President had left for Scandinavia in the North's jet, piloted by Parrish.

"If he's Scarab's contact, he's not making it easy for our friend, is he?" Natasha remarked drily.

"Perhaps he doesn't know Scarab wants to meet him."

Natasha said nothing.

Dubroc began to stride away across the runway. Natasha trailed behind him. "Where are we going?" She called after him.

"Parrish's apartment. He'll have a flight log there. Anyway, as pilot of the only jet available, I'd like to know what he's been up to lately."

The door of the apartment was unlocked and opened to Dubroc's touch. Much as Scarab had, Dubroc locked and loaded his five seveN and searched each room. The sound of running water, a precious commodity, alerted him that the bathroom must be his ultimate destination. Very cautiously, he pushed open the door. Just behind him, Natasha gasped in horror. Dubroc turned aside, shocked by what he had seen. The nurse rushed to the bath side, turned off the water faucet and, lifting Sonia Toth's soaking body into her arms, examined it for any sign of life. There was none.

Dubroc felt sick. Not yet fully recovered from his wounding, he found it hard to be impervious to the horror of his surroundings.

Natasha replaced the corpse in the bath and helped Dubroc into the apartment's main room. She sat him down, searched for and found a bottle of brandy and forced him to take a drink.

"She was, I think, committing suicide," the nurse said quietly, "in the Roman way. Somebody fired a bullet into her face to speed up the process."

Dubroc gulped brandy, shivering as the liquid fired his gullet and said, "It was Scarab."

"Probably. What was he doing here?"

"Looking for General Lamar."

Natasha frowned. "He couldn't know he would be here. The airport guards told us it was a last-minute decision to fly to Scandinavia."

"Then he was looking for Parrish."

"He had no reason to. Think, Dubroc, think. It was the woman."

"Who was she?"

Natasha searched the apartment until she found a purse belonging to the deceased. "Her name was Sonia Toth. This identity card has her picture. It gives her address and a reference." The nurse's brow creased in concentration. "It's difficult to read, but her reference was the Leader, then Scarab, then Nanos the dwarf."

Dubroc leaped to his feet. "She must have been Scarab's contact."

Natasha shook her head. "You're still not thinking straight. She wasn't powerful enough."

"Then she must have been a courier. Someone to introduce Scarab to the Leader's ally."

Natasha smiled. "That's more like it. Question is – how do we find out who Scarab is so anxious to meet? Let's face it, the answer's unlikely to be here."

"Do we have her home address?" Dubroc asked.

Natasha's smile grew broader. "You're getting better and better," she said admiringly.

The Notary's former mistress and secretary had decided to return to the North's mortuary to take another look at Avila's corpse and to check the computer for any other information concerning the Leader. Kazan had tried to persuade her to stay with Sonia, but she was on edge and needed to be doing something.

The husk that was Avila's body seemed to be disintegrating. "Ashes to ashes, dust to dust," muttered Bela to herself. She looked very closely at where Avila's eyes had been. Something very tiny, clasped by an eyelash, glinted in the light. Bela found a powerful magnifying glass. With a pair of tweezers, she extracted a minute particle of transparent plastic from the lash. She held it closer to the light and recognised it as a part of a contact lens or disc.

She tingled with a mixture of excitement and dread. Could this be a remnant of a disc created by Nanos? She moved rapidly to the morgue's computer bank. Because forensics required state-of-the-art equipment to analyse any findings, one of the computers would be able to tell her something about this fragment. She set a computer on line, placed the tiny piece of plastic beneath a medical magnifying glass and linked it to the computer's power source. She instructed the machine to conduct an analysis. The information she received, a list of the disc part's constituents, was of little help. She instructed the computer to source the material. The answer came back – the Amazon. Bela became more excited. She asked the computer if the piece of disc had any imprint of its user.

After what seemed an eternity, the computer threw up a number of distorted images. Bela slowed and magnified the computer's visual aid.

She gasped. Although fragmented, there in front of her were a series of pictures that told a terrible story: Lamar lying naked on a bed. Lamar signing some kind of document. The Mother in close up, her face twisted in agony. Lamar with a gun. A blank screen. Then the Eye leaning into sharp focus. Whorls of a fingerprint. A blank screen.

Bela sat back, almost exhausted. The Eye had plucked the disc from Avila's retina but, in doing so, had damaged it somewhat and left this tiny piece behind.

The mortuary was cool enough, but the temperature dropped further for a moment as an interior door opened. Bela whirled round. Scarab punched her and she fell in an unconscious heap.

Dubroc and Natasha searched Sonia Toth's home from top to bottom and found nothing of interest. Dubroc was disheartened and ready to give up, but Natasha persuaded him to search all over again. Eventually, even she was ready to admit defeat. She sat on a sofa, toying with Sonia's mobile phone, while Dubroc helped himself to a drink.

Natasha said, "Why would she leave her communicator behind?"

"If she was hoping to get out of the North she wouldn't need it." Dubroc sat down heavily.

Still not fully recovered, he felt bone weary.

Natasha's eyes widened. "Would this have a memory?" she asked.

"Probably." Dubroc and she jumped to the same conclusion at the same time. He rushed to her side as she punched numbers into the communicator. "Got it!" she pronounced triumphantly,

"Three numbers are logged in."

"Let me see." Dubroc scanned the numbers on the communicator's screen. "One is Ludwig's castle," he said. "The others I don't know."

"Is there any way to find out?"

Dubroc sighed. "All I really want to do is go to bed."

Natasha's eyes sparkled. "Me too," she said.

Dubroc didn't know whether to laugh or cry. He got to his feet. "We have work to do," he said firmly, but not too convincingly.

Kazan and Ferez had reached the conclusion that the dead dwarf, Nanos, was playing one last joke. The silver audio disc had played nothing but music for nearly an hour. From ancient hymns, through baroque, all stages of classical symphonies, sonatas and such, to heavy metal, reggae, rap and rock 'n' roll. Kazan even joined in on some of the songs familiar to her. Ferez looked at her as if she were mad.

Suddenly the music stopped and there was a

deathly silence. It was as if the world was standing still and every creature was holding its breath in fearful anticipation.

Nanos's voice came from the speaker. "I hope you enjoyed the concert," the voice, carefully modulated and precisely articulated, said. "It may be the last concert you will ever hear. Why? Because the Eye hates music. Ask him. He's quite prepared to admit it. Why does he hate it so? Your guess is as good as mine, but there is little doubt he has the potential to deal most viciously with those who compose, play or sing. He claims that music stirs savagery rather than soothing it. In a way, he's right. Fifes, kettledrums, bagpipes and sickly songs of home have all been musical appendages to war. As for the music of the last century . . . well, it creates frenzy, tribalism and rebellion." Nanos chuckled. "So, the Eye has a weakness. It is not the only one." There was a long silence and Kazan thought for a moment that the disc's message had ended. Then, Nanos spoke again, this time very gently and soothingly. "Sonia, if you are listening to this . . . I am dead. If anyone else is listening . . . I say, greetings to you who are about to die. You imagine you will live forever?" Again, Nanos chuckled. "Not while the Eye exists. Of course, he – or rather, it – may permit you to survive, but only so that he may toy with you, like a cat with a mouse, a spider with a fly, a mischievous god with us mere humans. I thought I could outwit him but, clearly, I was wrong. Can anyone outwit, defeat him? Nothing is impossible, but this is as close to the impossible as you are likely to get. Who, what and why is the Eye? He is many personalities. I know: I helped create them for him. What he is is an evil presence in the world. The day of the monster has arrived. The beast has arisen from hell. I do not exaggerate. If you think I do, take him on and find out your mistake the hard way." It seemed that, at this point, the dwarf was interrupted, for there was a scuffling sound followed by abrupt silence. Ferez and Kazan waited patiently.

Suddenly there was sound again – a powerful, strident rock 'n' roll performance. As the music faded away, Nanos could be heard to be chuckling again. "That's just in case the Eye is listening to this," he said. "A captive audience for my kind of music." The disc stopped. Ferez leapt to his feet in alarm. "It's finished," he said anxiously.

Kazan said, "Try turning it over. Let's listen to the B side."

Lamar, the President, instructed Parrish to alter course.

"Not Scandinavia?" the pilot said.

Lamar smiled knowingly. "No. Turn east. Enter Stealth mode – I don't want us detected."

Parrish looked aggrieved. "We may not have sufficient fuel."

"Don't try and pull that one on me, Parrish," Lamar said crossly. "I checked the load before we took off."

"Where to in the East?"

"Oh, you've been there before. Moscow."

"I couldn't wait to get out of that place," muttered Parrish.

"I don't blame you. We won't be staying long."

The pilot looked at the General. "Then – Scandinavia?"

Lamar was coy. "Possibly. I'll let you know."

Scarab had hit Bela a little too hard. It took him a while to bring her round. "Speak to me," he said, "or I'll cut out your tongue."

Bela was still groggy and found it hard to open her mouth and form any words. Scarab stood patiently, but menacingly by. Bela spat in his face. This time Scarab really did hit her too hard. The Notary's ex-mistress, her head striking the hard edge of the computer console, died instantly. When Scarab realised what he had done, he swore softly. "Give my regards to the Notary," he said mockingly. Then he began to search the data bank in front of him.

The easiest way of finding out who owned the

communication numbers logged in Sonia Toth's telephone's memory was to dial them. From one there was no answer. The other was a computer analysis company on the outskirts of the capital city.

"What would she want a computer analyst for?" Dubroc said, to himself really.

Natasha sighed regretfully. "You're not thinking again. She wanted something analysed – a computer programme, perhaps."

"A programme on a disc," Dubroc said, smiling slightly. "Nanos, her lover, was an expert."

"So, he left her a disc and she needs someone, an expert, to reveal its contents."

Dubroc kissed the nurse. "Natasha – I don't have to think. You're doing enough for both of us." Natasha kissed him back.

Scarab was beginning to think he was on the wrong side. It was clear from the information in front of him that the Eye was no ordinary human. In fact, he was almost inhuman.

The Innuendo soldier had served the Notary well and had been of considerable assistance to the Leader. They both owed him something. The Notary would never repay and the Leader might not be in a position to. That left the possibility of a switch of allegiance – to the Eye. Scarab needed to give the matter some thought. Immediately, however, he searched Bela's lifeless body and found a notebook. He scanned its pages and realised it was a diary. The entry for that day indicated that Bela and Sonia Toth had made contact. There was another name: Kazan.

Scarab switched computers and asked for a trace. He learned that Kazan had entered the North with the Eye, that she was considered to be his ally, that she had a connection with General Lamar and that she had access to Ludwig's castle. The castle was the obvious place to look for further information. After all, the Leader's contact was powerful enough to have accommodation there and, Scarab thought, with a bit of luck he might bump into this woman Kazan. Having taken note of her statistical details and admired her computer picture, he thought that could be an interesting encounter.

The Eye, used to being one step ahead of the game, couldn't bear the thought of being even half a step behind. Having excused himself early from the party, pleading pressures of state – which drew an odd look from Gregor Hamlet – he commandeered an electric cycle and went in search of the Dome. It was not hard to find. In fact, it was an obvious feature of the capital city's architecture. The Eye had assumed that it was some kind of training quarters for the North's army and nothing else. Training quarters it was, but it was certainly something else.

Entry to the building was gained with an ease that surprised him. There seemed to be no one about. No lights shone. There was nothing but pitch darkness. Of course, the Eye did not need light and paid little attention to the difference between day and night. He observed that the Dome was well named.

It was literally as described – a massive dome of steel sheltering a huge arena. There was a raised area that he presumed was a stage. Was this a theatre? Hamlet had said all theatres were dark. From the roof above hung massive arc lights, extinguished for the present. The Eye saw that there was a tunnel that led to the side of the, stage. He entered it. There were several doors off it that opened into dressing rooms, bathrooms, equipment stores and audio/televisual control rooms. Most of the equipment that was required for musical presentation, instruments and the like. The Eye recoiled in horror.

One of the control rooms possessed a large picture window with a view of the entire Dome's arena. The Eye gazed out into stillness and the dark. He sensed, more than heard, a movement behind. He turned round. A very pale, thin man with a professorial air stood before him. The newcomer appeared quite unthreatening. Not that the Eye would have had any difficulty dealing with him.

"You are the Eye," said the man. "I have been

waiting for you." His voice was cultured, its tone appealing.

"And you are?" asked the Eye.

"No-one."

"What does that mean?"

"It means I am not someone."

"A riddle?" enquired the Eye. "I'm not sure I have the time or the patience."

"No, really. No-one is my name."

"How unfortunate for you."

"A rose by any other name would smell as sweet."

The Eye was getting tired of this conversation. "What are you doing here?"

"I am the keeper of the Dome. The Game Keeper."

"Which means?"

"Which means, I watch over all the games played here. The innocent games, as well as the games of death."

The Eye pondered for a moment. "Games organised by whom?"

"Whomsoever wishes. Provided they have the resources, the manpower and sufficient wealth. Gregor Hamlet stages games here. The various troops of soldiery – Innuendo, Works, Arena and Theatre – used to have their own variations." No-one shook his head. "They were very hard games to win. In fact, nobody ever did win. Some progressed quite far, though."

"Such as?"

No-one seemed deep in thought. "Scarab and Venom were very good," he said, his memory dredged. "Czar was the best of the older generation. Dubroc was best of all."

"Dubroc?" The Eye's attention had been grabbed.

"Yes. The Navajo. You would do well to call upon his expertise when you attempt to conquer the West."

The Eye was genuinely surprised. "Why would you think I intend to do that?"

The Game Keeper tapped the side of his nose and smiled conspiratorially. "Take the disc out of your human eye," he said.

The Eye was astonished. "What disc?" he spluttered.

"Now who's trying our patience with riddles?" No-one said, but not impatiently.

"Who are you?" The Eye peered at him intently.

"I have said."

"Your answer was not satisfactory."

"Take out the disc and you'll find out."

The Eye hesitated, almost demurred, but finally slipped the personality disc out of his human eye. For a moment, he could see nothing at all. Then vague images took shape. One became No-one. "Well?" demanded the Eye, but without his usual authority. "Who are you?"

No-one faded from view. There was a flash of brilliant light. The voice of Death On Two Legs said, "Here we are at last."

The Eye spun round.

Death hissed, "There's no point looking for me, I am within you. We are one and the same, remember?"

"Then who was No-one?"

Death said, "You have just answered your own question."

The Eye began to compose himself, to set his mind in order. "What are we doing here?" He asked.

Death said, "Looking around, deciding if this might be the venue for our own game, our game of oblivion for the human race. Or not, as the case may be."

"Well, it's either oblivion for the human race, or it's not," the Eye said sarcastically.

"There's no need to be unpleasant," said Death. "You are merely bruising your own ego."

"All right," said the Eye, "show me the way."

"You are the Eye. It is you who should show me."

The Eye held his temper while Death chuckled to himself. The chuckle sounded like a puff adder preparing to strike.

"You are Death," the Eye said, "the conclusion of all things. I wish to reach some kind of conclusion."

"You mean, you want the gain without the pain?"

"Stop playing games with me."

"Why?" asked Death sharply. "That's what we're here for, isn't it?"

The Eye strode out of the control room, raced along the tunnel and entered the arena. He looked up at the stage.

"What happens there?" He asked.

"You wouldn't like it," said Death. "The young people of the North – some of the older ones, for that matter – seek entertainment here. Musical entertainment. The ending of the world could begin here, if we're not careful."

"The ending of the world has already begun. With me."

"You mean with 'Us', of course. I forgive you the oversight."

"What sort of game did Dubroc play?" The Eye asked quietly.

If Death could have summoned enthusiasm, he would have shouted with pleasure. Instead, he merely hissed, "Oh, you'd really like that one. We must develop a variation on its theme. Gregor Hamlet already has, but we will take it further."

"For what purpose?"

"Because we want to."

"Why would we want to?"

There was a silence from Death, so the Eye

repeated the question.

At length, Death said, "We must have our playthings, our toys. We win nothing if we merely accept the world. It must be inhabited by a select few. A few selected by us. Those few will entertain us. They will play our games, much as humans play innocent games to pass the time of day."

"Someone must win the game."

"Oh, we'll always win."

"Then what's the point of playing?"

Again there was a long silence from Death before he said, "The point you make about the point of playing is a good one. The human – the selected human – must have a chance of winning."

The Eye said, "Then we might lose."

"True. We must, therefore, be very careful about the selection process of our opponents."

"How do we do that?"

"Why – by playing a game, of course."

"There is a lot of good in the world," the Eye said very quietly.

Death said, "We will put an end to the world as it is."

"Why?"

"If we do not, the world will put an end to us."

The Eye said, "What do I – we – do now?"

"You must find out Nanos's secret before it is

too late. You must prepare for our future, a future that will stretch into eternity. You must not be seduced by the human race. Beneath the apparently benign exteriors of most men lies . . . the real face of humanity. That is where you will find us."

"This is not the way to the computer analyst's," said Natasha.

"On the contrary. It is the way to Ludwig's castle. There we'll find the best analyst alive. His name is Ferez. If you remember, he flew here with us from the East."

Natasha frowned. "Why didn't I think of that?"

"Perhaps your thinking capacity is in decline, while mine is making a rapid recovery?"

Natasha smiled shyly. "*Touché*, Dubroc, *touché*."

Kazan and Ferez listened, with increasing impatience and frustration, to the ramblings of Nanos, the deceased dwarf. All the bitterness and pain of his life surged from the audio speakers.

"I think this guy is better off dead," said Kazan. "Can't we fast forward, or something?"

Ferez shook his head. "We might miss something."

"Well, I wish he'd get to the point."

Nanos stopped speaking. Apart from a barely audible hiss, the disc was silent. Then, there was another, sudden burst of music. This time, a fanfare. Nanos said, "Now, at last, what you have been waiting for. The secret of the Eye."

Although it was unnecessary, Kazan and Ferez leaned forward.

"The real Eye is hidden. How to find it will be revealed by one of the human Eye's personality discs. Look for the blind disc, act on what it tells you and you might, just might, have a future. If I have failed and it is the Eye itself listening to this, then I say 'we will meet in hell, for that is where we both belong'." There followed the sound of weeping. Gradually, this faded away to be replaced, this time finally, by silence.

Ferez and Kazan looked at one another.

"I don't know about you," Kazan said, "but I'm beginning to see the light. The Eye's personality changes come about because he's able to insert a variety of Nanos's discs into his human eye. That explains a lot. The 'original' Eye is the real villain of the piece. Take that out of the equation and the Eye we know and love might turn out to be our benefactor – ours and the world's."

"I hate optimists," said Ferez.

Kazan laughed, then became serious. "Now we have to find the Eye's disc collection. We sure as hell aren't going to find any rock 'n' roll."

"It will be in his quarters."

"Of course. Where is he now?"

"Gregor Hamlet is entertaining him," Ferez said.

"Then we'd better get moving."

Ferez reacted with alarm. "We can't burgle the Eye's quarters now."

"You mean, we can at some other time?"

"I mean, it's too dangerous."

Kazan acted tough. "It is dangerous I'll admit. Whether or not it's too dangerous, we're about to find out. If you won't come with me, I'll go alone." She strode out of the laboratory. With extreme reluctance, Ferez followed on.

Scarab killed a Theatre guard and, dressed in the dead man's uniform, entered Ludwig's castle. It being the middle of the night, security was somewhat lax and anyway no one appeared to recognise the former Innuendo officer. No one, that is, except the sergeant with whom Kazan had so recently clashed. The sergeant went for his five seveN, but Scarab, one of those who had shown their mettle in the Theatre game, was too quick for him. His fist, knuckles extended, smashed into the bridge of the sergeant's nose. Bones cracked and blood flew into the sergeant's eyes, blinding him to the remainder of Scarab's assault. A savage blow from the hardened edge of a hand struck the sergeant on the left side of his neck, killing him instantly. Scarab regained his breath and looked around. Nothing stirred. "I could take over the North by myself, at this rate," Scarab thought. He wrote out a pass for the castle's basement and set off for the stairs. At the foot of the stairs he was challenged by two Theatre guards. The pass got him through into the basement proper. There, his luck ran out. Ferez and Kazan were on their way to the Eye's quarters. Ferez screamed in a combination of terror and fury, "It's Scarab. We must run. Kill him."

"Which is it to be?" questioned Kazan, a split second before she aimed a kung fu kick at Scarab's head.

In the narrow space allowed by the basement area, the Innuendo man just avoided it and retaliated with an open-handed double thrust at Kazan's throat. She whirled away from him and Scarab followed through with a series of kicks of his own. The woman was like a will-o'-the-wisp, he thought, as she danced away from him. Kazan turned and raced off, deeper into the basement proper. Scarab pursued. Ferez had already taken to his heels and was well ahead of them.

Kazan led Scarab into the laboratory and turned to face him in the more open space. She needn't have bothered. Ferez, summoning up courage he'd never thought he had, had seized a bottle of acid. He threw its contents into Scarab's face. Scarab screamed in agony as his flesh melted and drained away. He collapsed and writhed on the floor. Kazan watched in horror, Ferez with satisfaction. When Scarab died he was unrecognisable. His head had become skeletal.

Kazan held her breath for a moment. Ferez gazed in horror upon what he had done. "How did he get in here?" the miniaturist asked.

Kazan shrugged. "It doesn't really matter. What does is that he's not getting out."

Ferez looked as if he were about to faint.

"Pull yourself together," Kazan said. "We've still got a job to do, remember?"

Parrish was instructed to wait for his President at the Moscow airfield until Lamar returned.

The General, escorted by Works guards upon whose loyalty he felt he could rely, rode in a convoy of electric cycles to what had once been the Lubyanka prison. He was ushered into a cell that had been refurbished and was now a luxurious suite.

"Good of you to come," Kubar said.

Both men embraced. "It's been a long time," said Lamar, smiling.

"If there's anything you want, you only have to ask."

Lamar thanked his host. "I mustn't stay long. A little caviare, some vodka perhaps?"

Kubar clapped his hands and an attendant appeared. He instructed him to bring the food and drink.

"If we could commandeer your jet," Kubar said slyly, "we could conquer the North in one fell swoop."

Lamar nodded. "Yes, we could. Except that the plane is not fully armed."

Kubar scowled. "Why is that?"

"You must ask the Eye."

"He seems to think of everything."

"That is why I propose we join forces with him."

Kubar would have said something, but the attendant returned with the ordered caviare and vodka.

When he had gone, Lamar spoke hurriedly, afraid of interruption. "Hear me out, Kubar. This is the moment we have been waiting for. Years ago, I made you a promise. It is about to be fulfilled."

"That promise was made to me and, by inference, to the Leader," Kubar said, his eyes narrowing.

Lamar pressed on: "Yes, well that's a promise that can safely be broken. The Leader imagines he still has power in the North because he has an influential ally. Indeed he does, but the only ally worth having is the Eye. The Notary and the Mother are dead, the Leader's life is in your hands and, although I hold the title of President, it is held upon the whim of the Eye. He is already in charge in the North. Soon, he will rule the world. We can, and we must, stand by his side."

"You are very persuasive," said Kubar. "Why would you wish to share the world with me?"

"Two minds are better than one. We shall need both our wits to keep pace with the Eye."

"What about the Leader?"

"What about him?"

"Why not choose him to be part of this triumvirate you envisage?"

Lamar chuckled. "The Leader has lost his stake and is out of the game."

"While he is alive he remains a threat."

"Yes, well nobody wants to live forever. I'm sure the Leader can be encouraged to take early retirement, as it were."

"Everybody makes the mistake of underestimating you, Mr President," Kubar said admiringly.

Lamar stuffed caviare into his mouth and followed it with a stiff shot of vodka.

"What of the Leader's contact in the North? How powerful is he? How dangerous to our plans?" Kubar asked.

Lamar choked, then took a deep breath. "Any time now," he said, "the Eye will have him at his mercy. The Eye, I should not need to tell you, is merciless."

"What is his name?"

"You'll find out soon enough."

Kubar became angry. "Why not tell me now?"

Lamar matched him. "Because your security is about as effective as a sieve. I don't want to return North to find out that a coup has been staged in my absence."

Kubar seemed affronted. "My intelligence is very good," he said lamely.

"Your personal intelligence is not in question," Lamar said soothingly. "It is the way of your world, I'm afraid, that means you cannot trust anyone."

"Except you?"

"United, we shall conquer – divided, we shall fall," Lamar said expansively.

"I've heard that somewhere before," Kubar said ironically.

The irony was lost on the General. "Ferez belongs to the Eye," he said. "Your agents, had they attempted to contact him, would have been committing suicide. As it is, I was able to use them as a conduit to you."

"I'm very grateful."

"There's no need to be. That's what friends are for."

The two men gazed into each others eyes like lovers.

"What shall I do with the Leader?" Kubar enquired at length.

Lamar feigned surprise. "I thought he was no longer of this world?"

"I see," said Kubar. "Well, rest assured, it won't be long before he isn't."

Kazan and Ferez entered the Eye's apartments. They were occupied. Ferez recoiled in fright. Kazan punched out and Viktors Engel fell to the floor.

"Lock the door," said Kazan. Ferez obeyed.

Kazan helped the groggy surgeon to his feet. "What are you doing here?"

"I might ask the same of you," said Engel.

"Yeah, well let's not pussyfoot around and cut to the chase, shall we?"

"I don't believe we've met," said the Latvian, recovering his composure.

"I'm Kazan. Ferez you already know."

Engel frowned with concern. "You are with the Eye," he said.

"Aren't you?"

There was a silence.

"We're looking for some discs," said Kazan. "Any idea where we might find them?"

Engel paused before finally making up his mind. He raised a box from beneath the Eye's desk and held it out.

Kazan took it and looked inside. "Well, well, well. Welcome to Aladdin's cave. Here you are, Genie, read these and weep." She handed the box to Ferez.

"I can scan these in the laboratory," the miniaturist said.

"There's a dead body in there."

Ferez did not flinch.

"OK," said Kazan. "If it doesn't bother you, it doesn't bother me." She turned her gaze on the Latvian. "Do I take it we're in this together?"

"If we want to find out all we can about the Eye."

Kazan smiled. "Curiosity killed the cat."

Engel smiled back. "I'm prepared to use up one of my nine lives." He held up a miniature contact lens. Before Kazan could stop him, or Ferez open his mouth to shout a warning, he placed it in his eye.

There was a flash like lightning and the Eye's full length mirror shattered into a thousand pieces. Death On Two Legs stalked the room. He took hold of Engel in a lover's embrace and the Latvian felt the sting of a thousand vipers' tongues.

Ferez raced out of the door. Kazan leapt through a window and plunged into the Danube tributary below.

The surgeon's eyes bulged. He gasped for air. Death On Two Legs, like a python, crushed the life out of him.

Dubroc and Natasha arrived at Ludwig's castle and entered a tumult. A Theatre guard was dead in the grounds, the sergeant had been killed, there was an unidentified corpse in Ferez's laboratory and the Eye's private quarters had been vandalised. A fourth body had been discovered there. The castle guards were running around like headless chickens.

"This is like the last act of a Jacobean drama," Dubroc commented, before asserting his authority and taking command of the situation.

Soon it became clear that Ferez was missing, that one of the dead was Viktors Engel and that the other, which was not Ferez, had to be identified. Dubroc ordered a computer scan of the remains.

The Eye arrived on the scene. Once informed of what had happened, he rushed to his quarters. When he discovered that the box of disc lenses was missing, he slumped in a chair and looked for all the world as if he were about to burst into tears. Dubroc indicated that Natasha should attend him, but the Eye recoiled from her touch.

A Theatre soldier burst into the room and announced that the mystery corpse was the Innuendo officer, Scarab.

The Eye was transformed into a man of action. "I want the whole city on alert," he ordered. "Finding Ferez is a priority." He turned to Dubroc. "There are so few who are as trustworthy as you," he said modestly. "Will you help me?"

Natasha found his manner nauseating, but Dubroc merely nodded acquiescence.

Kazan hauled herself out of the filthy water of the Danube's tributary and swore softly. She would have sworn loudly, but all hell was breaking out in the castle behind her and she didn't want to draw attention to herself. She set off towards the mortuary in the hope of rejoining forces with Bela.

A sound, other than the din from the castle, attracted her attention. She crouched in readiness for an assault. Ferez, much dishevelled, emerged from a clump of bushes. He still held the box containing the Eye's discs. His nose wrinkled. "You smell," he said.

"Yeah. Well you don't exactly reek of Chanel Number Five," Kazan replied. "Let's get going."

"Where to? I need a computer. We daren't go back to my laboratory."

"To the morgue. There are computers there."

Ferez hesitated. "That's the last place I want to go."

Kazan gritted her teeth and took a firm hold of him. "Pretty well everybody would agree with you but right now we have no other choice." She pulled him along beside her, away from the commotion in the castle.

Natasha knelt by the body of Viktors Engel. She

studied his eyes. It is sometimes thought that the image of a murderer is imprinted on his victim's retina. She noticed the small contact lens, but said nothing to the Eye or Dubroc.

The Eye was watching her carefully. He knew what she had seen. Natasha, afraid, knew that he knew.

"What is missing?" asked Dubroc.

"Some discs – lenses. They are for my eyes."

Dubroc frowned. "And you think Ferez has them?"

The Eye nodded. "I would be grateful for eternity for their return," he said emotionally.

"I will help you find Ferez," Natasha said to Dubroc, anxious to leave the room and avoid the Eye's presence. "As a nanotechnologist, he will require the use of computers. We can assume he won't return to his laboratory. Where else would he find what he needs, other than at the computer analysts on the outskirts of the city?"

"The mortuary," said Dubroc.

"Go there now," instructed the Eye, "and see if she is right. If she is, take Ferez alive and handle my eye discs with care."

"Will you be all right?" Dubroc asked, genuinely concerned.

The Eye looked abashed. "Thank you, yes. I shall not forget you, Dubroc. Go now. I'll be just fine."

Natasha couldn't wait to leave. Dubroc took his time.

When they had gone the Eye called out. "Where are you?"

Death On Two Legs stepped out of the shadows at the far end of the room. "Careless," he hissed, "very careless."

"What happened?"

"The surgeon wanted to be you – us. He inserted a lens and paid the price. We must find the remainder quickly and at whatever cost."

"Does Ferez have them?"

"Yes," said Death, "and his accomplice."

"His accomplice?"

"The woman – Kazan."

Ferez tripped over Bela's body.

Kazan swore. "I feel as if I'm crawling from charnel house to charnel house," she said with feeling.

"Scarab was here before us," Ferez commented. "This is certainly his handiwork."

"And where Scarab has been, others will surely follow," said Kazan. "How do we find the blind disc among this lot?" She indicated the box the miniaturist was holding.

"I'll feed them all into the computer tracking device and instruct it to select it."

"What about the rest?"

"We don't have time to study them. Even if we

did, I'd be reluctant after what happened to Engel."

"Yeah. Right. We just want the blind one. Go find it."

Ferez extracted the tiny discs from the box with the aid of tweezers. This took time and Kazan became agitated, but she managed to hold her tongue. The computer swallowed the discs and Ferez punched in his instructions.

"Now what?" said Kazan.

"We wait."

"For how long?"

"For as long as it takes."

Eighteen minutes after the North's remaining jet took off from Moscow it exploded in mid-air. There were no survivors. Wreckage from the stricken plane even killed innocents on the ground. When informed of this, Kubar said, "There is no such thing as an innocent. We are all guilty."

Within an hour of the explosion and consequent deaths of Lamar and Parrish, a slim young man, his face and body slippery with oil, slid into the Leader's sleeping chamber. He placed a knotted rope around the Leader's neck, gave it a short, vicious tug and his victim never awakened from an unpleasant dream.

Within two hours, a message arrived at Ludwig's castle addressed to the Eye. It offered the undying allegiance of Prince Kubar and his Eastern legions.

"I've got it," said Ferez. He extracted all the discs from the computer, carefully placing them back in their box. All, save one. This he held up to the light. "This is it."

"OK," said Kazan. "I don't want to worry you, but time's running out. What next?"

"We could decipher it here."

Kazan shivered. "Take it from me, we need to get out of here."

"All right," said Ferez, surprisingly calm in the circumstances. "We'll take a laptop with us. That's a small—"

"I know what it is," interrupted Kazan. "What about the rest?"

Ferez thought for a moment. "We'll leave them behind. Then, when they're found, the Eye will call off any pursuit. We'll still have the one disc that really counts."

Kazan matched his thoughtful pause. "OK," she said eventually. "You're smarter than you look. Now, let's be on our way."

Had they known what was going on, the people of the North might have gone into mourning. Or not, as the case may be. As it was, Gregor Hamlet looked suitably solemn for any funeral. The Eye and he stood together in the castle grounds, close by the spot where Kazan had emerged from her soaking in the river. It was daytime, but heavy clouds threatening rain darkened the sky and it might as well have been dusk.

"We are all that is left," said Hamlet mournfully. "Who would have thought things would have turned out like this?"

"The fact that nobody thought of it doesn't matter," the Eye said snappily. "The important fact is that things couldn't have turned out better."

Hamlet decided it was as well to go along with him. "Oh, I agree," he said. "Lamar had to be got rid of sometime. The Leader was a nuisance. From a distance, but a nuisance just the same. This man who calls himself Prince Kubar? We owe him a favour, perhaps. How shall we repay him?"

The Eye smiled his favourite smile. "Those who live by the sword shall die by the sword," he said pithily.

Dubroc accepted the mission without question.

The Eye was at his most paternal. "The man Kubar," he said, "remains our only threat. We are fortunate to be able to identify him. Think how different history would have been had we been able to detect those who would bring horrors to the world. Kubar must be eliminated, or who knows what horrors he has in mind for us."

"Where and how?" asked Dubroc.

"Moscow. I have sent a message to Kubar promising to meet him there. He is expecting that we will divide the world between us. How is up to you. You're the best. I know you will not fail me. I mean, you will not fail the world."

"We have no jet. It will take a long while for me to get to him."

"It'll do him good to wait." The Eye chuckled.

Dubroc felt uncomfortable, but it didn't occur to him to dispute the Eye's motives. "The discs are safe?" he asked.

"Yes," said the Eye musingly. "Having gone to so much trouble to get them, one wonders why Ferez became so careless as to abandon them."

"Are there any missing?"

The Eye looked sharply at Dubroc. In his brain, there was a hissing sound. Death On Two Legs was stirring. "I'll look into it," said the Eye.

"Here, you'd better take these," said Ferez, offering Kazan the laptop computer and the tiny blind disc. "Whoever is after us will want me first, because I am a so-called expert." He smiled resignedly.

Kazan saw the wisdom of the gesture. "OK. But how can I interpret what's on the disc?"

"It should be very simple. Nanos will not have complicated matters. You saw how I used the main computer. Just follow those steps, on a smaller scale, and you should find out all you need to know."

Kazan looked concerned. "Nothing's going to happen to you, Ferez."

The miniaturist shrugged. "If it is written, it will. I have nowhere to go and, anyway, I'm tired of running."

"You think we should split up?"

Ferez nodded. "Absolutely. You must go West. I'll lead our enemies astray."

"West?"

"Of course. That is where the real Eye will be hidden. You'll be on familiar territory."

Again, Kazan took the point. "OK. I'm out of here." She snatched up the laptop, carefully concealed the tiny disc in the fold of her bosom and made to leave their hiding place. She turned back momentarily. "*Au revoir*, Ferez."

Ferez said, "Goodbye."

The nurse, Natasha, lay asleep on a rumpled bed. Dubroc had left for the East. The door to her room opened, but she did not stir. The Eye watched her gentle breathing and the rise and fall of her breasts. Because he was the Eye, he was not aroused. Death On Two Legs hissed in his brain. Death's bloodlust rose like bile in the Eye's throat. He stepped closer to the bed. Natasha awakened suddenly, as if from a bad dream. She was about to enter a nightmare. Modestly, she tried to cover her exposed body with a cotton sheet.

"Very becoming," said the Eye, with a voice filled with such cold that the room's temperature seemed to drop abruptly. "The sheet will be your shroud."

Natasha cringed away from him. The bed was situated against a wall. There was nowhere she could escape to. She tried to scream, but her throat was dry and she could utter no sound. The Eye drew closer. He seemed to be in a daze, as if he was not controlling his own actions. His mouth was agape, his tongue in constant movement. He emitted a terrible hissing sound. She closed her eyes in terror, hoping against hope that she was still dreaming. When she opened them again, she was confronted by Death On Two Legs. This time she did scream. It was the last sound she ever made and nobody heard it.

Kazan reached the North's airport where she learned of the deaths of Lamar and Parrish and that there was a search under way for her and for Ferez. The Arena trooper who imparted this information arrested her then and there. But Kazan, like a wild animal, was hard to cage. She lashed out at the trooper who, foolishly underestimating the power of a woman, paid the price with a broken neck.

Kazan did not mourn Lamar and could not take the time to spare a tear for Parrish. Avoiding the airport staff, she made her way to a helicopter parked in shadow away from the main terminal building. Security was slack. Apart from the trooper she had had to kill, everybody seemed more concerned with what had happened at Ludwig's castle than with what was going on under their noses. When they did pay attention, it was too late. Kazan took to the air like a bird escaping certain captivity. Troops on the ground organised pursuit gunships, but Kazan had a good start and the lightweight helicopter she had purloined could probably outrun them. She headed west.

Dubroc's progress east was slow. Reversing Scarab's route into the North, he used electric cycles and a series of helicopter flights to reach Moscow. Shortage of fuel and the priority given to the building of the wall of steel to deter any Eastern advance made his journey more frustrating than it should have been. At last he met with Kubar in the apartment in the Lubyanka.

"You took your time," scolded the Easterner. "Time and tide wait for no man.

"Well, you waited for me and I'm grateful," said Dubroc.

Kubar got down to business. "What is the Eye prepared to offer?" he asked.

Dubroc appeared quite relaxed. Too relaxed. "Nothing," he said.

"Nothing?" Kubar almost exploded.

"The Eye considers you superfluous to his needs. He believes you are a threat to the stability of the North and, for that matter, the rest of the world."

Kubar managed to control his anger. "Nothing shall come of nothing," he said harshly.

"Well, that's the message," said Dubroc.

Kubar was puzzled by the man's nonchalance. "Do you imagine you will get out of Moscow alive?" he asked.

"Oh, I can imagine it," responded Dubroc. "Whether or not I actually make it is up to you."

"Indeed it is. I can have you killed now."

"What good would it do?"

"It would give me a deal of personal satisfaction."

Dubroc smiled. "I sympathise with your feeling," he said, "but, in the long run, by killing me you'd be signing your own death warrant. Even now the Eye has long guns pointing from the North in this direction. If you think the East is suffering now, wait until those guns are fired. You ain't seen nothing yet."

Kubar became agitated. "How do you know all this?"

"I made it my business to find out before I left the North on this mission."

"What precisely is your mission?"

"To kill you."

Kubar laughed a genuine laugh. "You're welcome to try."

"I'm glad you say that," said Dubroc calmly, "because I have a proposition to put to you."

Kubar's laughter faded away. "What proposition?"

"You and I will fight. If I win, I will have carried out the Eye's instructions to the letter and your followers will slink away to the East. If you win, the Eye promises uninterrupted food supplies for you and your legions, provided you stay in the East and in one or two areas of the South that he is prepared to concede."

"So, you lied. He does offer something."

"I'm making you that offer, not the Eye. But he'll honour the deal. He is an honourable man. Anyway, there won't be a problem. I intend to win."

Both men smiled, but for different reasons.

"What if I refuse or renege on the deal?" Kubar asked slyly.

"Then the guns will start blazing before I'm cold in the ground."

Kubar gave the matter some thought. "Our contest will be a spectacle for my followers," he said at last. "I am a practical man. My followers are my children. I will not leave them without a father. When and where shall we fight?"

"Winter is here," said Dubroc. "Heavy rains in the South, snow in Moscow. The Moskva river is frozen over. What would you say to a knife fight on the ice?"

Kubar smiled. "I would say – yes."

The Eye was in conference with Gregor Hamlet. The businessman was trying to persuade him to visit the Dome.

"There is a game I have developed," said Hamlet, "that I'm certain you will enjoy. It serves two purposes. We select the entrants from those we consider, shall we say, not entirely committed to our cause. If they win the game, we might consider sparing and re-educating them. If they lose, they die and the North is free of their dissidence."

The Eye spoke coldly, "If they win, then they are the more dangerous because they are the more competent."

Hamlet was quick to answer. "Therefore we will have learned their true potential to cause us harm. We merely redirect that potential. In other words, we seduce them. Every man has a price, a weakness, something that makes him manipulable."

The Eye trod warily. "I'll give it some thought," he said. Of course, he had his own agenda where games were concerned and it did not include the participation of Gregor Hamlet, once the businessman had outlived his usefulness. That time was fast approaching.

Gregor Hamlet and the Eye were interrupted by a message from Theatre troops that the runaway Ferez had been apprehended while trying to steal an electric cycle. It was also reported that Kazan had fled in a westerly direction.

The Eye turned to Hamlet, a gleam in his human eye. "I believe we have found a likely guinea pig for your game," he said.

Hamlet said, somewhat hesitantly, "When would you like him to play?"

The Eye, with Death On Two Legs squirming in his brain, said, "Within the hour. The contestant's name is Ferez."

The helicopter ran out of fuel over the ditch that was once the Sleeve, or the English Channel. But Kazan was a survivor. She managed to settle the aircraft on a bank of mud without too much difficulty and without causing any damage. The machine's navigation equipment informed her that she was some two miles from solid earth. She set off to reach it. As she walked, she heard helicopter gunships, in search pattern, droning overhead. She smiled to herself. If the helicopter hadn't run out of fuel, she'd still be in the sky and about to be blasted out of it. Every cloud has a silver lining.

She reached what was still called France and

sought refuge in an out-of-the-way farmhouse. The land all about was pitiful, only capable of yielding a minimal harvest. Still, the owner was likely to possess an electric cycle and Kazan intended to take it off him. At gunpoint if she had to.

She had to. The farmer was most unwilling and she was obliged to knock him out and tie him to his bedstead, so she would have sufficient time to make good her escape before he could raise the alarm. The cycle was fully charged and she set off westward, ever westward.

The Eye interviewed Ferez. The miniaturist, to the Eye's surprise, seemed uninhibited, as if resigned to his fate. A resignation fortified with some courage. This was odd and the Eye didn't like it. "You stole some of my lens discs," he said, like a schoolmaster dealing with a recalcitrant pupil."

"Just one," said Ferez, too insolently for the Eye's liking.

The Eye searched the box in which he kept Nanos's miniature creations. He began to laugh. "You stole the blind one," he spluttered. "The only one in the box that is of no use."

"It may be of no use to you, but it has a tale to tell to someone."

The Eye stopped laughing. "What do you mean?"

"Where are you?" said Ferez.

"I am here," said the Eye, confused by the question.

"The real you is elsewhere," said Ferez, a hint of triumph in his voice. "The blind disc shows the way."

The human Eye remained calm. Inside him, Death On Two Legs writhed in agitation. "Who has the disc?"

Ferez said, "Guess."

The Eye shook his head. "I don't know where you've found your courage, Ferez, but it won't make life, or rather, death any easier for you. Kazan has the disc."

"And the means of deciphering it."

The Eye frowned. Kazan was escaping to the West. She was running towards the Americas and, sooner or later, would move to the source of the Amazon. Where the Eye had begun, there she would try to end Its existence. Unless she was stopped. He returned his attention to Ferez. "Would you like to play a game?" He asked kindly.

The ice on the Moskva river was treacherous. In some places solid, in others dangerously thin. Kubar and Dubroc trod gingerly, each armed with a knife. Kubar had a small, scimitar-shaped blade that was razor sharp. Dubroc held Bosque Redondo's Bowie knife. The two men reached the centre of the frozen river and turned to face each other. "On the count of three, we will begin," said Kubar confidently.

"You call it," replied Dubroc.

The banks of the river were lined with Kubar's followers and some Works and Innuendo troops. Arena soldiers, supervisors of the new defences, watched both sets of spectators with care.

On the count of two, Kubar lunged forward, aiming for Dubroc's neck. Suspecting Kubar might bend the rules a little, Dubroc was ready for him and side-stepped the thrust. He countered by whirling the Bowie knife in his fingers so that it resembled a deadly Catherine wheel. Kubar retreated in haste, stepped onto a patch of thin ice and slipped into cold water. Dubroc went after him. Thrashing about like great white sharks, the two men grappled with each other. Kubar plunged his dagger into Dubroc's left arm. Dubroc slashed the Bowie knife across his opponent's eyes. Momentarily blinded by his own blood, Kubar retreated further, scrambling onto solid ice.

Dubroc remained floundering in a mixture of ice and water. Kubar, having cleared his sight, sensed his opportunity. He leaned forward, offering his hand to pull Dubroc free of the slush of the river. Dubroc took it. Kubar's other hand, in which he clasped his knife, snaked forward, the blade aiming for Dubroc's face. Again suspecting foul play, Dubroc was ready. Before the blade could touch him, he heaved Kubar into the watery ice. Both men disappeared beneath the surface of the river. The spectators craned their necks to see exactly what was happening. Dubroc burst from beneath the water and, hurling himself clear of the widening patch of thinning and broken ice, skidded onto a solid patch. He scrambled to his feet and held his Bowie knife high in the air for all to see. The knife dripped blood.

A mournful cry rose from Kubar's followers. Arena troops locked and loaded their weapons. Works and Innuendo troops began to applaud.

Kazan reached the Atlantic coast. An old-fashioned steamboat was due to leave for the West. Kazan didn't ask where the captain got his coal from and he didn't tell her. The crew looked a swarthy lot, but Kazan was unafraid. Her martial arts expertise, a wicked looking knife and a fully loaded five seveN would protect her virtue. She smiled at the thought.

There was time to try to read the miniature disc.

Gregor Hamlet introduced the Eye to No-one at the Dome. Neither the Game Keeper nor the Eye acknowledged that they had met before.

Hamlet led the Eye to an electrically controlled balcony in the centre of the arena. This allowed them to spectate from ground level or, as the balcony rose, from any height up to one hundred feet. "It will be necessary to clear the floor of the arena at some point," said Hamlet. "We would not wish to become involved in any part of this game. We are merely here to observe."

The Eye gave No-one a sidelong glance. The Dome's caretaker indicated, by the slightest movement, that he should detach himself from Hamlet. No-one had something to say that was for the Eye's ears alone.

Gregor Hamlet was holding forth, as was his wont: "The games devised as tests for entry into the various arms of the North's forces were good, even very good, but we have taken them a stage further. This you will see. We will, in due course, take them to further stages, for our greater enjoyment and to discover greater excellence in performance."

"Are preparations complete?" asked the Eye with an air of boredom.

Hamlet, anxious to please, excused himself, promising the "entertainment" would begin within five minutes. The Eye took the opportunity to confer with No-one. "Well?" He spoke irritably.

No-one smiled. "You've forgotten something," he said.

"I'm sure I've forgotten a lot of things. When you've been around as long as I have, there's a lot to forget. Please, remind me."

"In a very short space of time – seconds, in your lifetime – you have almost reached your goal. As you suspected, the human race, in its foolishness and greed, has helped more than hindered you. The Mother, the Notary, the Leader, the last President, the new President, Goran the Barbarian, Kubar – all major players who stood in your way, not to mention the smaller roles, have been eliminated."

"How do you know about Kubar? The message from Dubroc was only recently transmitted and in an unbreakable code."

No-one sighed. "You forget who I am."

"You are no one."

"Which could mean I am two, or three, or four. I am a part of you. I exist parallel to you. Most humans have aspects of personality that they call instinct, or conscience. I am your instinct," he smiled slightly. "Alas, we have no conscience."

"Is that what I've forgotten?"

"How could you forget what you didn't know?" responded No-one archly. "Think awhile. Most of your enemies are destroyed. What remains?"

"There is Kazan and the blind disc. I was anxious that Dubroc would pursue her, but he has been wounded by Kubar and was otherwise not fully fit. But I have made alternative arrangements."

No-one raised an insolent eyebrow.

"All right. All right," spluttered the Eye. "Tell me what I want to know."

"The Leader's contact here in the North is still at large."

The Eye snorted. "He, or she, is impotent now."

"Hardly. It's a he, by the way."

The Eye looked deeply into No-one's eyes. He saw nothing.

"The nurse, Natasha, Dubroc's lover – she aided him in his search for Scarab. You didn't bother to study the details of that search. Some might consider that careless. Had you done so, you would have discovered that they had found a communicator. The communicator's memory log contained three numbers. One was for Ludwig's castle, the second for a computer analyst; from the third, they received no reply. The Leader's ally in the North was temporarily incommunicado. He was hosting a very important gathering."

"Ready when you are," called Gregor Hamlet from the viewing balcony in the arena.

The Eye and No-one turned to look at him, their faces expressionless.

Kazan cracked the blind disc's code. A child

could have done it, which meant it took Kazan over an hour. The disc revealed a diagram: a tall, statuesque woman next to a waterfall. An Amazon and water – the Amazon river. "Tell me something I don't know," muttered Kazan to herself. She peered closer. There was an eye watching from the centre of the waterfall. "So," Kazan thought, "the real Eye's in the Amazon, encased by a waterfall. Or does that mean encased in a block of ice, as is more logical?" Another diagram appeared. It showed a pool of water beneath the cascade. "OK, OK," she thought. "The ice has melted and the Eye will be in the pool of water." She peered even closer. Sure enough, the Eye was now in the pool of water. "Fine," Kazan thought. "Nanos hid the Eye in ice, the ice melts and, abracadabra, we can drown the thing."

It seemed too easy. There had to be more to Nanos's message. Kazan would have to wait until she reached the Amazon to find out what it was. In the mean time, she would have to deal with a swarthy, leering crew member who was making unwanted advances.

The Eye joined Gregor Hamlet on the balcony. Hamlet clapped his hands and the arena went dark. Very slowly, an artificial sun began to rise. Into the arena ran a naked man, his body glistening with oil. He held a lighted firebrand. He bowed to the two spectators, then swallowed the fire, before running off again. The artificial sun continued to rise. A huge man replaced the fire-eater. He was dressed like a Roman gladiator, armed with a weighted casting net and a stabbing sword. Another gladiator, not as big, entered the arena. He was armed with a trident. The men circled each other and began to fight. The contest was brief. The smaller man was soon trapped in the net, his trident broken. The big man cut off his head with his sword.

"What do you think?" asked Hamlet excitedly.

"I've seen it all before," said the Eye, stifling a yawn.

Four tigresses were whipped into the arena by a handler.

"Normally," said Hamlet cautiously, "we would have music, special effects and the like. It adds to the excitement."

"Really?" commented the Eye. "It wouldn't excite me."

The handler withdrew and the tigresses prowled hungrily. The balcony rose a dozen feet above the ground. "Just to be on the safe side," muttered Hamlet.

A human being was thrust into the arena. It was Ferez. The Eye's interest was kindled.

The tigresses began to stalk their human prey. Some crouching, ready to leap. Others slinking along the edges of the arena. Ferez stood stock still, his eyes closed, an enigmatic smile on his lips.

"Oh dear," said Hamlet. "He's not going to run or fight. I'm afraid that spoils the spectacle."

"I've seen that before as well," said the Eye.

One of the tigresses rushed at Ferez. The others, taking their cue, followed suit. It didn't take long for Ferez to die. Later, the dominant tigress fought off the rest and dragged his corpse to a corner of the arena for a private feast. The handler reappeared and whipped the animals out of sight.

"What happens in my variation," said Hamlet, "is that our contestant fights his way to this point. He must eat fire, overcome the gladiator and fend off the tigers."

"With his bare hands? Ferez didn't have a weapon."

"The foolish man declined one. Our entrant will be armed with a weapon of his choice."

"I'd choose a five seveN," said the Eye unsmilingly.

Hamlet sensed that this exhibition wasn't going down too well. "It would be a sword, a knife, an axe, not a gun."

"Ah. What next?"

Hamlet cleared his throat. The balcony rose to fifty feet. "We need to be well clear of the ground for this part," he said, the perspiration of anticipation on his brow.

The artificial sun was now very bright. A moving basket was lowered from above until it was level with the balcony. The brightness of the artificial sun made it difficult to see why the basket was moving. A pretty, scantily-dressed young woman ran into the arena. "This is the Mother's daughter," said Hamlet. "I've been saving her for this special occasion."

The Eye shifted position uneasily. "She was Dubroc's. She died."

Hamlet tittered. "Look a little closer. Is she the Mother's daughter?"

"I'll take your word for it."

"Why do you think the Mother failed to dispose of the Leader? It was only when you came on the scene that her hopes were raised. She'd been through a hostage situation with her daughter once before and wasn't thinking straight. She kept her secret from Dubroc. Miranda – that was the girl's name – has been a kind of insurance policy. Once the Mother had been dealt with, the Leader would have used this Miranda to bring Dubroc to heel. That may be academic now."

"When Dubroc gets to hear of it, it might not be."

Hamlet smiled. "He won't get to hear of it, will he? He will remain our faithful and loyal servant."

No-one called out, "Are you ready to continue, sir?"

Hamlet clapped his hands. The moving basket split open and more than twenty deadly snakes plunged to the ground. They squirmed and hissed and wriggled. Miranda screamed. Just then, a tall, fit young man armed with a Bowie knife entered the arena. The Eye gasped. "It's Dubroc."

"Close, but no cigar," said Hamlet. "Not a bad likeness though, is it?"

Miranda ran blindly round the arena, hysterically seeking escape. The Dubroc look-alike grabbed a cobra by its neck, held it in the air and cut it in half. Hamlet applauded. The young man raced after Miranda, took hold of her and shielded her with his body. A fer de lance rose up and threw itself towards them. Stepping aside, the young man placed his foot on the snake, trapping it, then killed it. Once again, Hamlet applauded.

The Eye looked towards the wings. No-one looked at Hamlet, looked at the snakes below, then looked back at the Eye. He winked.

The young man had killed two more snakes, a taipan and a coral. But the remainder, as if able to communicate with each other, were gathering together for a concerted attack. Hamlet leaned over the balcony, his eyes gleaming with lust – for blood and for Miranda. The Eye took hold of him by the waist and, with a mighty heave, pitched him among the snakes. Hamlet screamed horribly. There was a terrible hissing and threshing.

No-one applauded.

The Dubroc look-alike turned on Miranda, about to cut her throat. "No, don't," shouted the Eye. No-one shot the young man in the back with a single round from a five SeveN. Miranda screamed. The Eye, immune to snakebite, jumped to the ground from the balcony. Miranda's eyes widened. The jump was easily fifty feet. No-one smiled knowledgeably. The Eye took Miranda in his arms. "You are safe now, my dear," he said tenderly. His human eyes glistened. The hissing of the disappointed snakes in the arena was matched by that of Death On Two Legs in the Eye's brain.

Kazan disposed of the threat to her virtue far more easily and in less time than she took to crack Nanos's code. The crew member, drawn in close by an enticing smile and a glimpse of creamy coloured breast, received a savage blow to his genitals that would likely keep him celibate for some time to come.

Kazan used the laptop once more. The drawing of the tall woman now showed her as naked. The next drawing had her plunging into the pool below the waterfall. The Eye, still below the surface, watched her every move. What is this? thought Kazan. Are we into voyeurism or something? The woman appeared to be bathing in the pool. The Eye rose up and became huge. The woman was now swimming in its tear ducts. She disappeared from sight, assimilated into the Eye. "Ugh," said Kazan aloud. "Not a nice way to go."

Dubroc's wounds were tended by none other than Scarab's erstwhile friend, Lech. "I'm impressed," he said, as he cauterised the gaping flesh-wound created by Kubar's knife. "So impressed, I'd like to serve with you. Serve the Eye."

Dubroc said, "I'm not impressed. Not impressed by your credentials."

Lech shrugged and continued his work with surprising delicacy. "The trouble with the North's troops," he said, "in my opinion, is that we were corrupted by success. Apart from the Mother, we weren't too clever when it came to electing our leaders. We fell for the promises of quick wealth and glory. It didn't quite work out that way."

Dubroc ignored the pain of the repairing of his wound. "Why should the Eye put his trust in you?"

Lech smiled. "Everybody who has so far hasn't been let down. Not by me, anyway. You could say they let themselves down. I served the Leader because I was in his Works force. I helped Scarab because he was a friend. I did what I had to do. I'll serve and help you too, if you'll let me."

"You could betray me."

"I could. But you'll have to trust me first. I'll tell you something you should know. As an act of good faith."

Dubroc gave him his full attention.

"Miranda may be alive."

Dubroc cried out, not in pain from his wound, but in a different agony. He lashed out, caught Lech a blow to the head and sent him spinning to the floor.

Lech got slowly to his feet. He rubbed his cheek. "You hit hard," he said, not belligerently, "very hard. I'm telling you what I've heard."

Dubroc's eyes were blazing.

Lech approached him cautiously. "The Leader's ally in the North takes care of her. If it is her."

Dubroc's voice was like a rasp. "His name?"

Lech shook his head. "I honestly don't know. But the Eye could find out."

Dubroc took control of himself. "I need to get back to the North," he said.

Lech smiled. "No problem."

"Apart from everything else," asked No-one, "what did you think of the game?"

"Promising," said the Eye.

"Something to work on anyway. You and I

and Death can see to it."

"What have you done with the girl?"

"Miranda? Well, she should really sleep with the fishes, but I gather you'd like to keep her alive for Dubroc's benefit?"

"You don't think that's a good idea?"

No-one looked thoughtful. "For the moment, perhaps. After all, when our games are staged, Dubroc is likely to be our first contestant."

"What makes you think that?"

"The same thing that makes you think it."

Death On Two Legs stirred and the Eye looked uncomfortable.

"We will preserve this Miranda," No-one went on. "She'll be an opening skirmish for her lover. An introduction to the game. The pilot, Parrish, sadly no longer with us, had an apartment. We'll house her there."

The Eye sighed wistfully. "We are surrounded by death, aren't we?"

No-one looked at him severely. "The human race invented death and exploits its invention. Compared to the monsters of Earth's history, you are almost angelic. Human sentimentality does not become you."

Death On Two Legs hissed agreement.

"Now, to business," said No-one briskly. "How to reach the Amazon in time to greet Kazan."

"Must she die too?" the Eye asked plaintively.

"Of course not. She will be the second contestant in our games."

"Jet boats," said the Eye.

No-name clapped his hands. "Excellent. Why didn't I think of that?"

The Eye scowled. "Yes, why didn't you?"

Kazan set foot on Brazilian soil. She swore as the filthy mud of the Amazon river's bank oozed over the top of her boots. "What a dump!" she said very loudly, but nobody heard her.

The steamboat captain had kept his promise and, apart from the admirer she had kicked in his private parts, she had experienced no difficulties. The captain, though, suspected something – what, she knew not – and kept his distance. He seemed glad to be rid of her, as if she were tainted. A Jonah, perhaps?

"The hell with him," muttered Kazan. She set off in search of a different kind of boat. One that would take her to the Amazon's source.

She preferred to steer clear of the North's troops in the area and chose instead to approach a group of Indians, savage inhabitants of the interior who had come to the coast to trade. Big and blonde, a true Amazon, Kazan imposed herself on the natives. They seemed in awe of her and chattered among themselves. One of them, their leader, approached. He spoke some English and Portuguese which, being similar to Spanish, permitted Kazan to communicate with him. "You are a goddess," he said respectfully.

Kazan preened. "Whatever you say, Charlie."

"How may we serve you?"

Kazan indicated that she wished to be taken into the jungles, to the Source.

The chief nodded. "Your will shall be done," he said.

Kazan was beginning to enjoy this. She hefted her five seveN and fired a single shot into the trees. "Just in case you have any other ideas," she said.

The chief seemed unmoved. "We will serve and obey," he said sincerely.

Kazan smiled. "Well, that's fine by me."

The Indians, about ten of them, led her to a long dugout canoe. Laden with supplies, it looked ready to sink. The chief indicated her place in the dugout. "Oh well," she thought, "beggars can't be choosers."

The canoe was surprisingly buoyant and, propelled by the strong arms of the Indians, cut through the waters of the Amazon like a knife through butter. Kazan was exhilarated. The natives began to sing. "The Eye wouldn't like this," Kazan thought.

Lech was a born scrounger. He acquired weaponry, survival equipment and a fast, long-distance helicopter. "General Lamar left this here as a gift for Kubar. He didn't know at the time that the Prince had planted a load of Semtex on his plane."

"So many who have died," Dubroc said sorrowfully.

"And more to come," responded Lech.

"How do you live with yourself?" Dubroc was genuinely curious.

"How do you?" Lech smiled. "I drink a lot. It numbs my feelings, makes me come to terms with what is."

Dubroc said, "It wouldn't work for me."

"Well, you should try something else to take your mind off it. The tender arms of Miranda, maybe."

Dubroc tensed. "When I find her."

Lech smiled approvingly. "I like that. You have no doubt. 'When', not 'if'. We'll find her."

"Maybe now that we have the Eye the world might be a better place," said Dubroc.

Lech nodded. "Yes, but it's a big 'maybe'."

"Of course, the Eye isn't perfect." Dubroc seemed deep in thought.

"Who is? But, from what I've heard, he could be the best we've got."

Dubroc nodded his head in agreement.

Of course, both men couldn't have been more wrong.

The Eye was informed that Dubroc, whom he

thought was recuperating in Moscow, had disappeared. He pondered the significance. Dubroc was looking for something, or someone. The Eye smiled secretly. He would make the trip to the West to foil Kazan.

Accompanied by No-one, the Eye set off by helicopter gunship to the Atlantic coast, there to board a jet-propelled ship similar to that which had once belonged to the Notary. This ship towed another. When the first ran out of fuel, including its reserve tanks, it would be abandoned and the crew transferred to the fully fuelled back-up. By this means, the Eye and No-one reached the mouth of the Amazon hot on Kazan's heels. There, they refuelled and set off at speed upstream.

Kazan heard them coming. She swore in Spanish and the Indian chief, understanding, looked at her with a combination of alarm, admiration and inquiry.

"Pull over," said Kazan. "I mean, duck into the river bank and take cover. There's somebody coming up behind I want to avoid." The chief issued rapid instructions and the canoe altered course, sliding under the overhanging fronds of huge, prehistoric trees that lined the river side. Kazan put her fingers to her lips. The Indians giggled in unison, then frowned and remained utterly silent. Only the lapping of the river waters could be heard. Until, that is, the jet boat raced past, leaving a mini tidal wave in its wake. The Indians struggled to keep the canoe afloat. Two of them fell into the water and there was considerable merriment as they were dragged aboard and the dugout steadied. Kazan swore again. The Indian chief touched her gently on the shoulder. "What may we do to ease your pain?" he asked.

Kazan smiled at him. "I need to get to the Source." She gestured in the direction of the long-gone jet boat. "They'll get there ahead of me, that's for sure. But I don't want to be far behind. Anything you can do about that?"

The chief huddled in conference with the other Indians. There was much chattering, like a wilderness of monkeys, before a decision was reached. The chief said to Kazan, "We will go through the forest. We will carry the dugout. We will reach the Source more quickly."

Kazan looked into the thick jungle. "Are you quite sure about that?" she asked apprehensively.

The Indian chief smiled and nodded encouragingly. "As the crow flies, the Source is closer this way."

Kazan said. "That's all very well, but I'm no crow."

The chief thought that was the funniest thing he'd heard and conveyed the joke to the rest.

There was much hysterical laughter. Kazan really wanted to cry, but she joined in with the general good humour anyway. She didn't want to offend her hosts and possibly end up in their cooking pot.

The Indians hoisted the canoe onto their shoulders and, the chief and Kazan in the lead, set off into the rain forest. The chief seemed to have an uncanny sense of direction and was able to find relatively easy passage through the thick-boled trees, trailing vines and dense undergrowth. Once, they were confronted by an anaconda. Twenty-six feet long and as thick as a tree trunk, it impressed Kazan so much she was ready to make a run for it. The chief took her by the arm and they strolled round the giant snake as if it wasn't there. "If left alone," the chief said, "he will not harm us. Here in the jungle, we have learned to respect each other. We live and let live."

"That's great," said Kazan, still sweating.

"It is essential," said the chief sagely.

Suddenly, they were back on the river bank and the canoe was relaunched. The air was fetid and the water movement slow. The Indians needed all their muscle to keep the dugout moving.

The chief pointed straight ahead. "Ten clicks," he said, "to the Source."

The Eye and No-one were disappointed. There

was no sign of Kazan and not one Northern soldier or Source worker had any idea where Nanos the dwarf might have stored or hidden anything.

The Eye seemed depressed. No-one admonished him. "You have been too long as a human," he said sternly. "Remember what you are. We will search for ourselves until Kazan is taken."

The Eye had no choice but to agree. "Where to begin?" he asked.

No-one began an examination of the ground where Nanos's laboratory had once stood. He called out to the Eye: "Go into the cave. Study the ice mountain. We must not overlook the obvious. Nanos may have returned us to our original resting place."

The Eye was not hopeful and, therefore, was not surprised or disappointed to see that the ice mountain in the glorious cave consisted of nothing but frozen water. Huge lumps of ice were being hacked off the mountain and loaded into refrigerated storage tanks ready for transportation to all points north. The Eye muttered encouragement to the workers. They applauded his presence amongst them, clearly appreciating him as a worthy leader.

No-one had found nothing. The Eye refrained from commenting, "I could have told you so."

No-one's brow was deeply furrowed in clearly

painful thought. "Cold water," he said enigmatically. "That is what is required. A block of ice would be better, but cold water would suffice."

"The only block of ice is the mountain and the river, if anything, is warm," said the Eye tersely.

No-one said, "It's sometimes possible to find pools of cool, even cold, water, fed by snow from mountains or by underground streams, even in the warmest of climates. We must study a computer read-out of the local terrain."

They were almost at the Source, maybe three clicks away, when Kazan spotted the tributary. She indicated to the chief that he should slow the impetus of the canoe. The Indians stopped paddling and the dugout drifted towards the narrow inlet, partially hidden by trailing branches and thick bushes.

"Where does that go?" Kazan asked.

The chief smiled. "You are truly who we think you are," he said. There was much mumbling among the rest. "It leads to the Goddess pool."

Kazan remembered the laptop computer graphics. "Where better for a goddess to go?" she said.

The Indians set to with relish and the dugout raced into the tributary.

Dubroc was not amused. The Eye had left for the Amazon, everyone else with any authority was dead, dying, or under the close scrutiny of Theatre and Arena intelligence units and he couldn't find Miranda. It was confirmed by an Arena officer that the Eye had ordered a purge. The North's army, supported by the people, eagerly awaited its conclusion. It seemed that the Eye had captured the imagination of everyone and everyone's imagination now considered him to be the obvious and acclaimed new leader in the North. "From nowhere to the ultimate somewhere in no time," commented Lech.

"Where has he hidden Miranda? And why?"

Lech shrugged. "Why is obvious. To keep her safe. Where? Your guess is as good as mine."

Dubroc paced to and fro in the conference room of Ludwig's castle.

"At least the Eye saved you the trouble of killing Gregor Hamlet," said Lech.

The Arena officer nodded his agreement. "Hamlet was willing to sell us out to the Leader and other traitors. It is thanks to the Eye that the integrity of the North has been preserved."

Lech smiled to himself. Here was an officer who had swiftly adapted to the Eye's party line. How often had history thrown up such people? People who latched onto false prophets and followed them blindly through repeated follies into new hells on Earth. Lech knew: he had nearly done it himself when following the Leader.

"Miranda is not at Hamlet's estate?" Dubroc asked.

The Arena man shook his head.

"Someone must know where she is." Dubroc eyed the officer keenly. The Arena officer reddened slightly. "You know, don't you?" said Dubroc.

"I am not permitted to reveal her whereabouts," came the stiff reply.

Lech punched him in the stomach and, as the man doubled over, Dubroc grabbed his hair, raised his head and peered into his eyes. The Arena officer was terrified. Dubroc's eyes were full of danger. "Speak to me," Dubroc said, his tone ominous.

Lech said, "Leave him to me. I'll get the information we need in five minutes."

Dubroc forced the officer to his knees.

The man's spirit was broken. "She's at the pilot Parrish's apartment. There are two men guarding her with orders to kill intruders on sight."

Dubroc cast the officer aside.

Lech said, "Members of the Eye's new order should be made of sterner stuff." He kicked the man while he was down, before following Dubroc out of the room.

The pool in a clearing in the Amazon jungle was about as close to paradise in the middle of hell as anyone could hope to get. As in Nanos's graphic, there was a gentle cascade that fed its cool, clear water. A strip of golden sand led to the water's edge, this sand sloping down to form the bottom of the pool. Kazan studied the whole pool area. There was no sign of the Eye. She took out the laptop and searched Nanos's disc for further clues. There was one other computerised picture – that of the Eye being closed.

The Indians were fascinated. Kazan handed the laptop to their chief. "A gift from a goddess," she said good humouredly.

The chief was ecstatic. He reacted as if she had handed him the keys to the kingdom. Perhaps she had.

"Well, I don't know about you boys," she said in Spanish, "but I'm filthy and I'm going to wash my sins away in the pool. No peeking now." She stripped naked and plunged into the water.

The Indians gasped in admiration of her nerve, as well as her statuesque figure. Here was a goddess indeed.

No-one indicated the location of the Goddess pool on the computer map. "It's near enough for Nanos to have carried us there," he said. "It would seem it's cool enough for our preservation. That wasn't too difficult, was it?"

"Too easy, perhaps?"

No-one smiled. "Never overlook the obvious.

It is the simplest and often the most effective method of concealment."

"We must go there," said the Eye.

"Just we two, I think."

The Eye concurred.

As Dubroc and Lech approached Parrish's apartment, Miranda's two guards opened fire. Lech was hit in the leg and Dubroc struggled to bring him to cover. Lech swore in Russian. Dubroc couldn't understand what he was saying, but got the drift.

"Kill them," Lech said, through teeth gritted with pain.

"I'd rather not. After all, they're on our side."

Lech spat blood. "Kill them anyway."

Dubroc shouted to the guards. His answer was another hail of bullets.

"See what I mean?" Lech said grimly.

Dubroc made him as comfortable as he could and, using all his training and Navajo instinct, slipped out of cover.

Arena

"Ut imago est animi voltus sic indices oculi"
Cicero

Dubroc had timed his approach well. Darkness fell as suddenly as a lamp fusing and it began to rain. Miranda's guards sent up a flare, but Dubroc had already reached the main building and was mounting its fire-escape. All the flare revealed was the grimy apartment block surroundings. It also drew a hail of bullets from the wounded Lech's five seveN.

Dubroc was on the roof. One of the guards had guessed as much and the two men clashed on its slippery surface. The guard fired at Dubroc, but his shot was inaccurate and the bullet ricocheted off into the night. Dubroc fell on the man before he could fire again and Bosque Redondo's Bowie knife claimed another victim. Once more, there was a burst of covering fire from Lech's gun below. Dubroc entered the building through a skylight.

Miranda's second guard had had enough. He waited in the corridor outside Parrish's apartment and, as soon as he felt Dubroc's presence, shouted out his surrender, placing his gun on the floor. Dubroc picked it up and told the man to wait in the lobby of the building. "I wouldn't go outside if I were you," he said. "There's a wounded Works soldier out there who'd love to blow you away." The man ran off.

Dubroc, somewhat hesitantly, pushed open the door to the apartment. "Miranda?" He said her name softly. "Miranda?"

She came out of the darkness of the interior and fell into his arms. Dubroc let his two guns fall to the floor. He kissed Miranda's hair, her neck her mouth – he brushed the tears from her eyes. "Oh, my love," he whispered, "I thought I had lost you." She pulled him into the darkened room, her agile fingers tearing at his clothes. Dubroc returned the compliment and, by the time they reached the bedroom, they were both naked. All the pain and longing that had consumed Dubroc dissipated as he made love to Miranda. He held her close and tightly, never wanting to let her go again. He spoke to her in Navajo, expressing his undying love. She did not reply.

Dubroc thrust her away from him and, like lightning, rolled off the bed and raced from the room. He touched a lamp and light flooded the apartment. Miranda, her face a mask of hatred, was coming for him with Bosque Redondo's knife. Dubroc couldn't have been more vulnerable. He grabbed a chair and, like a lion-tamer, dodged round the room fending off the thrusts and jabs of the deadly sharp weapon. Miranda – except that it wasn't Miranda – was screaming with rage. She lashed out with all her strength and the chair flew from Dubroc's hands. Miranda was on top of him, the knife's edge searching for his throat. Dubroc sweated and struggled, but she was as strong as a tigress in heat and the knife drew closer. It gouged his cheek and blood ran. Miranda squealed in triumph. Her fingernails sought his eyes, the knife began to slice into his neck. A single shot rang out.

Miranda's breath rushed out of her, like a ghost of the night escaping the dawn. She choked and collapsed on top of him. Dubroc pushed her lifeless body to one side and staggered to his feet. "Thank you," he said, almost breathlessly.

"No problem," said Lech casually. He was leaning against the doorpost, a smoking five seveN in his hand. "I hadn't heard from you for a while and was beginning to miss you." Both men smiled. "You'd better get dressed," said Lech. "If the vice squad suddenly turned up, we could be in trouble."

"What the hell is that?" said Dubroc, indicating Miranda's corpse.

Lech sighed. "Well, I'd guess it isn't Miranda."

"You'd guess right."

"Then, she's a trained look-alike. Somebody's been playing games with you. They knew you'd have to get this close to her to discover she was a fraud. Too close for comfort."

"Thanks again."

"Again, no problem."

"Let's get out of here," suggested Dubroc. "We'll have the whole Northern army on us in a minute. I'm surprised they're not here already."

"They are – well, some of them."

"What?"

"I heard them arriving as I limped up the stairs. We'd better leave quietly and discreetly, if we don't want to end up dead or in jail."

"How the hell are we going to manage that?"

"There's a light helicopter on the roof. Why do you think the other guard went up there?"

"I thought he was looking for me."

"That, and trying to keep you away from the aircraft."

"All right. Let's go," said Dubroc.

"Aren't you forgetting something? If you don't get dressed, you'll catch your death of cold."

Dubroc smiled. Both men heard troops climbing the stairs. Dubroc scooped up his clothes, his guns and the Bowie knife. "I'll dress on the plane," he said. "You're wounded. Can you fly it?"

Lech said, "No problem."

Kazan ducked below the surface of the pool's cool water. Her eyes searched for anything unusual, but the golden sand that formed the bed of the pool was undisturbed. She surfaced and gasped in air. Her Indian audience applauded. She waved at them, then dived below the surface once again. Again, no disturbance. Either Nanos's computer graphic description of the location of the real Eye was faulty, or she had picked the wrong place. Anyway, the spot was idyllic. The Sun warmed her, the water cooled her down. She swam about using a lazy breast stroke. Once again, her audience applauded.

The Eye and No-one strolled through the jungle towards the Goddess pool. The Eye stopped and listened. "Can you hear that?" he asked.

No-one, who was feeling the heat, snapped back irritably, "Hear what? The chattering of monkeys?"

"It sounded like people clapping."

"Well, there you are."

They proceeded on their way.

An Indian raced out of the trees and sought out the chief. After a hurried conversation, the chief waved to Kazan, indicating she should leave the water. She failed to see him. The chief stripped naked and dived into the pool. Kazan, seeing him cutting through the water like a shark, became alarmed. In the middle of the Amazon jungle, with a group of Indians for company, she could hardly cry "rape". She went underwater. The chief followed suit. The sand at the bottom of the pool erupted and a huge eyelid slid back to reveal a bloodshot, evil Eye. The chief was immediately sucked into the Eye's tearducts. Kazan, thrashing in the water like a barracuda, shot to the surface and swam flat out for the pool's beach. The Indian spectators stood stock still. As she climbed out of the pool, water cascading from her naked body, they applauded once again, then cast around for their chief. With a mixture of fast sign language and pidgin Indian dialect, she convinced them of danger. Two Indians plunged into the water. The one who had come out of the jungle spoke rapidly to the others. From their dugout canoe they collected weapons – blow pipes, bows and arrows, ugly looking axes. Kazan locked and loaded her five seveN. The two Indians emerged from the water with the body of their chief. He looked as if he was sleeping. There was not a mark on him and his facial expression was one of sublime peace. The Indians managed to convey to Kazan that whatever had killed him and that had frightened her was no longer in evidence. Nevertheless, the bulk of the group took cover in the thick jungle. Kazan, standing over the body of the chief, awaited any new arrivals.

A fusillade of gunfire followed the light helicopter as it took off from the roof of the apartment block. The airport guard commander detected a distinct feeling of *déjà vu* as he launched gunships in pursuit.

Dubroc, with difficulty, was dressing himself. "Where are we heading?" he called out over the noise of the craft's rotors.

"Well, anywhere will do for the moment," replied Lech coolly. "Anywhere where we're unlikely to get wasted. Got any ideas?"

"I'll leave it to you."

Lech flew the helicopter dangerously low at maximum speed. In other circumstances this would have been a nightmare ride. As it was, Dubroc gritted his teeth, uttered a silent Navajo prayer and trusted to the skill of the pilot.

Lech was enjoying himself. "I'm really good at this," he said proudly. "They'll never catch us."

A rocket from a gunship exploded directly above them. Dubroc stayed silent as Lech cursed and altered course as fast as a fox evading hounds. "We'll go South," he shouted.

"Why?"

"Why not? It's the only place you haven't been lately."

"What about fuel?"

A rocket exploded to their right.

"What about it?" said Lech. "Right now, fuel's the least of our worries."

The gunship was hot on their tail.

Lech swore many oaths. "He's good," he said grudgingly, "he's very good. Let's see if he's good enough."

The helicopter raced right and left, in a zigzag pattern through the sky. The gunship dropped back a little, but still had them in its sights. Rockets exploded on either side of the smaller craft.

"He's straddling us," said Dubroc anxiously. "The next shot could be a direct hit."

"You think I don't know that?" Lech wrenched on the control stick and the helicopter executed a sickeningly slow flip over. The rotors stalled. The pursuing gunship overflew them. The helicopter righted itself and the rotors roared back into action. Lech shouted in triumph. "Got you," he cried, his elation infectious enough to make Dubroc smile in admiration. "Now I'm on your tail." He frowned. "Not that it's going to do us much good. This crate is unarmed." He turned the helicopter violently to the left and lost height so they brushed the tips of bushes and flew in and out of tall trees at alarming speed. Dubroc held his breath. There was a maniacal look in Lech's eyes. The tip of a rotor touched the branch of a tree. "Whoops!"

said Lech. The helicopter smashed sideways into a sequoia and fell to the ground in a crumpled heap of twisted metal. Dubroc and Lech crawled clear of the debris. The remains of the aircraft burst into flames.

Above them, the gunship pilot reported to his commander that the fleeing helicopter had been destroyed and that he was returning to base.

"You all right?" Asked Lech.

"Of course I'm not all right," said Dubroc. "I'm bruised, cut and frightened almost to death. How about you?"

"You know the leg I was shot in?"

"Yes."

"Well, I don't think I've got it any more."

Dubroc examined him. Lech was right. His leg had been severed from his torso as if by a surgeon's knife. Dubroc did his best to staunch the flow of blood. "I need to get you to a doctor."

Lech swore. "No, thank you. The only doctors round here are likely to be of the witch variety."

"Then I'll tend you myself." Dubroc started a small fire from pieces of undergrowth.

"You sure you know what you're doing?"

"Well, when I was in the West with the Athabascans I learned a few things. But, you're right. I'm not really sure."

"Oh, well," said Lech philosophically, "the show must go on, I suppose."

Bosque Redondo's knife, red with heat, cauterised Lech's wound. The Works soldier passed out.

The Eye and No-one walked out of the jungle onto the Goddess pool's strand of beach.

Kazan raised her five seveN and took careful aim. "That's far enough," she said. Though naked and dripping wet, she was a commanding presence.

No-one smirked. The Eye smiled. They stood quite still.

"Isn't this what is called an impasse?" enquired the Eye politely.

"Hardly. I'm armed and you're not," Kazan responded defiantly. "Who's your friend?"

"No-one," said No-one.

"I thought we were friends," said the Eye seductively.

"Yeah, well, according to Nanos, with a friend like you I won't need enemies."

No-one took a step towards her.

"I'm warning you!" Kazan called out. "I know how to use this." She made a big show of relocking, reloading the five seveN. No-one kept on coming. Kazan opened fire. Half a dozen full-metal-jacketed projectiles passed right through No-one's body. He kept advancing towards her.

"I told you I was No-one," he said.

Kazan seemed frozen to the spot.

"Wait a moment," said the Eye.

No-one stopped walking and the Eye stood alongside him. Without taking his human eyes off Kazan, the hard edge of the Eye's hand karate chopped No-one's neck. The Eye's instinct, his *alter ego*, fell to the sand unconscious.

"There, that's better," said the Eye cordially. "Now we can have an uninterrupted conversation. Although I must admit your state of undress is distracting."

Kazan was stunned. "What the hell's going on?" she asked wonderingly.

The Eye assumed a serious, sincere expression. "I am a prisoner," he said, "but, with your help, I can be released. Become free again to help the North, even the world."

The water of the Goddess pool became turbulent. Kazan turned and shrieked in horror. Rising from the waters, like the wrath of all the gods, was Death On Two Legs.

Kazan emptied the magazine of her five seveN into the monster. Death staggered and squirmed and hissed, but reached dry land. Kazan ran for the safety of the jungle trees. Death followed on. The Eye seemed in a daze, as if asleep on his feet.

Arrows and blow darts tipped with poison rained on Death On Two Legs. It brushed them aside as if they were nothing more than a swarm of harmless flies.

The Eye said, "We must stop now."

Death stopped in his tracks. "The game is not yet over," it hissed.

The Eye confronted him. "Which of us is the strongest?" he asked.

Death On Two Legs squirmed. "There is only one way to find out. But, in doing so, we would be committing suicide."

A brave Indian fired an arrow from his jungle concealment. It struck the Eye in his human eye. The human eye that held the Nanos manufactured lens. The Eye was in agony. In desperation, he tried to pluck out the missile. Death On Two Legs began to retreat towards the water.

The Eye was on his knees.

No-one's unconscious body began to disintegrate, becoming part of the sand on which it was lying.

Death On Two Legs slipped into the Goddess pool, sank below its surface and disappeared.

Kazan ran from cover and took hold of the Eye. She helped him remove the arrow. The Eye, blood coursing down his cheeks like tears, was blind.

The Indians ran to the water's edge and began a war dance of victory.

"Help me, help me," pleaded the Eye.

Kazan took him in her arms and rocked him to and fro like a mother with her child.

No-one's body had merged with the sand. Ashes to ashes, dust to dust.

One of the Indians plunged into the water in search of the monster. When he emerged, he reported that the Goddess pool was deserted. Other Indians placed mud and palm leaves on the sockets that were all that remained of the Eye's human eyes. His pain eased and he drifted into sleep, still held in Kazan's tender arms.

Dubroc carried Lech out of the glade of sequoias. He had no idea where they had crash-landed but, true to Lech's directions, headed south. He and his burden had not gone far when a group of men and women, tall, handsome and black, rose up in front of them as if they had sprung from the earth itself. Dubroc counted ten, men and women of equal number. They were armed with long spears and tapered oval shields. Their dress consisted of simple loin cloths. Their skins glistened with the sweat caused by the heat of the rapidly rising Sun.

Dubroc tried all of his nine languages. He had reached the eighth, Arabic, before he got any reaction. The ten men and women smiled and bowed in his direction. Two men stepped forward and relieved him of the burden of Lech. Two women began to fuss over the unconscious soldier.

Dubroc was offered water and food and sanctuary. He thanked his benefactors. "Why would I need sanctuary?" he asked.

The oldest of the men, presumably their leader, stepped forward. "We are about to be invaded by the North," he said concernedly. "You have escaped from there. You are welcome to fight and die with us, here in the South."

Dubroc thanked him. "I'd rather stay alive for a while longer," he said. "There will be no invasion from the North."

The Elder looked dubious.

"I speak the truth," said Dubroc earnestly. "The Eye has set his sights on the West, not the South."

At the mention of the Eye there was a strong reaction from the group. The Elder stepped back in alarm. The men began banging their spears against their shields. The women emitted a high warbling sound.

Dubroc tried to be conciliatory. "The Eye wishes you no harm," he said, hoping he was right. "The North is no threat. Under the Eye, we seek peace, not war."

The men stopped banging their shields, the women stopped wailing. The Elder said, "How do you know this?"

"Because I know the Eye. Even now, he is in the West. He has no designs on the South."

The Elder withdrew and the handsome warriors went into a huddle. There was much gesticulating from the men. The women, casting occasional appraising glances at Dubroc, seemed calmer.

The Elder approached him. "We will accept your word," he said kindly, "if you will accept our hospitality."

Dubroc smiled. "Thank you."

"One of you will remain with us forever," the Elder said, "then, if your word is not good, he who remains with us will suffer a painful death."

Dubroc's smile faded, but he wasn't going to give the Elder an argument. Not while nine other warriors stood about him, eyeing him as if he would be easy prey.

Kazan and the Indians carried the Eye to the North's camp at the source of the Amazon. Now fully dressed, but no less commanding than when she had stood naked and alone against Death On Two Legs, she ordered the perimeter guards to take the Eye to their hospital facility for immediate attention and demanded to see the officer in charge.

"I am Diamond," said the tall but bulky officer as he approached.

"Expensive name," commented Kazan. "I am—"

The officer didn't allow her to finish. "I know who you are. The Eye and No-one were looking for you."

"Yeah, well they found me. No-one's dead. At least, he's as good as. The Eye needs urgent medication."

"He's getting it. What about the Indians?"

"What about them?"

"They're hostile."

Kazan bridled. "They're not hostile to me."

Diamond thought this over. "All right. But you'd better keep them under control. They make my men nervous. We have few action forces here, we're mainly pioneering and administrative."

Kazan relaxed a little. "How do you keep your enemies at a distance?"

Diamond smiled. "We have some weapons grade uranium. Nanos, a dwarf who was once our leader here, made certain the Source would be well protected."

"Smart move. It's because of Nanos that I'm here."

Diamond frowned in puzzlement. "You knew him?"

"Well, in a way. It was he who first helped the Eye. Now it's my turn."

A medical orderly ran towards them. "The Eye is conscious," he said, "He's asking for Kazan."

Diamond and Kazan followed him to the small, but well equipped hospital building. Made of timber, with lead light windows, its interior was cool and antiseptic. The Eye was draped on a couch, covered with a single silk sheet. He was attached to various drips. "To prevent infection," said the orderly. "It is an honour to have the Eye here."

"Why?" Kazan queried.

The orderly looked nonplussed for a moment. "Because he is our future."

Diamond, looking stern, nonetheless nodded agreement.

"OK," Kazan said. "Maybe you're right."

The Eye whispered something. Kazan leaned very close to him, her ear to his mouth. "You must help me."

"That's what I'm trying to do."

"Only you can help me. Get rid of the others and fetch the solid case I brought with me."

"Did you hear that?" Kazan asked the others.

Diamond nodded.

"My, what big ears you've got."

Diamond sent the orderly to get the Eye's case. "I'll be in my quarters," he said. "Anything you need will be provided. We will do anything to help the Eye."

"Seems like he's going to walk the election," said Kazan lightly. "Not that he's been nominated yet."

The tall, dark and handsome warriors led Dubroc and the still-unconscious Lech – two of the men carried him with ease – through scrubland, patches of thinning forest and hardened rock formations to a plateau with breathtaking views over a desert of multicoloured sand. On the plateau were pitched a number of elaborate tents, circling a deep well. From the tents, into the blazing heat of the now fully risen Sun, emerged fifty or sixty warriors who matched the physiques of the ten already known to Dubroc. Again, there was an equal division between men and women. Dubroc noted the absence of children.

"They are hidden," said the Elder. "Far from here there is a place for them with the oldest of our tribe. If they were to remain with us, they would be prey to disease or kidnap by slave-traders."

"Slave-traders?"

"In our new world, there are those that have and those that have not. There are those who take what they want and those who cannot. The weak and unprotected make willing slaves. We are not weak and we protect our own."

"I had no idea that slavery existed in the South," he said.

"It was imported from the North," the Elder said drily.

Lech had awakened and was being tended by many women. At first he was alarmed, but soon succumbed to their charms and ministrations. He winked at Dubroc. "I could get used to this," he said happily.

"You might have to," replied Dubroc. "One of us has to remain as a kind of hostage. If the

Eye and the North invade the South, the hostage will die."

Lech looked at the beautiful women dancing attendance on him. "Not a bad way to go," he said wistfully.

Kazan listened to the Eye.

"Although I cannot see," he said, "I can hear perfectly. I will know if we are not alone."

"We are alone."

"I am the Eye."

"I kind of knew that," said Kazan.

"I mean, I am the one Eye that has seen all of the world. That has watched from the beginning of real time to the present and, with your help, will continue to see into the future."

"But you're blind."

The Eye smiled. "This human manifestation is blind. When I return to being simply The Eye, I shall see perfectly."

"How are you going to manage that?"

"You are going to manage it for me."

"Why should I?"

"Because you want a better world, now and forever."

"That's not possible."

"It's worth a try."

Kazan smiled thinly. "Convince me you're not the bad guy."

The Eye hesitated for a moment. "Parts of me

were evil, but they have been driven out of me like exorcised demons. My human manifestations have taught me the difference between right and wrong. Now I want to right all wrongs."

"You sound too good to be true."

The Eye remained silent.

"What do I have to do?" Kazan asked.

"The case I have carried to this place contains many small discs, lenses for my eyes – my human eyes. They allow me to assume a number of personalities. I realise now that some of those personalities were destructive. They, in their turn, must be destroyed. All that will remain will be myself, The Eye. You and Dubroc and others like you will be my agents in this world. You will help to bring order out of chaos, guarantee justice in all things and lead the world out of darkness and into the light."

"That's a great pitch," said Kazan. "I'd vote for you on that one."

The Eye laughed. "So, I hope, will everyone else."

There was a silence of understanding between them.

"We must begin," said the Eye at length. "You will find a plain disc among the lenses in the box. This is the original from which all the others were programmed. It is the only plain disc, the remainder being colour-tinted. You must insert it into one of my blind eyes."

"Why don't I get the orderly to do that?" Kazan said squeamishly.

"I do not wish to recruit the entire world. A few, a precious few, will be my messengers. Please, do as I ask."

Kazan opened the box and selected the plain disc from amongst the others. Very carefully, because her hands were shaking, she held the disc in forceps and transferred it to the Eye's human eye socket. She released it.

For a while, there was an intense quiet. Then the Eye began to moan and groan, as if he were about to have a seizure. After a moment or two, though, he became calm. His body began to shimmer, as if contained by a bright light. "Look for me in the ice," said a disembodied voice. The bright light faded and the Eye went with it.

Kazan, mouth agape, thought, Magic time.

The Elder accompanied Dubroc to the edge of a stand of trees. "We will look after your one-legged friend," he said solemnly. "Many of our women would have preferred it if you had been the one to remain as hostage."

Dubroc smiled modestly. "They are beautiful women."

The Elder nodded. "Yes, I prefer beauty to ugliness. It's the ugly women who are far away with the children." He began to laugh and Dubroc joined in.

The Elder became solemn again. "I hope your faith in the Eye is not misplaced," he said.

"So do I."

"You are not certain, then?"

"I'll make certain."

"Do not forget," said the Elder, a paternal smile on his face, "that we are here for you. When the time comes – if the time comes – you can call on us."

Dubroc was touched. "Thank you, I will. You don't intend to kill Lech if things go wrong then?"

"We are not barbarians," said the Elder. "He may die of kindness, nothing else."

Dubroc and the warrior clasped hands. Their goodbyes were wordless. Dubroc trotted off into the trees. The Elder sighed. He walked back to his people.

Kazan and Diamond entered the beautiful cave that contained the mountain of ice at the Amazon's source. The commanding officer had ordered everyone else to leave.

Kazan called out. Her voice echoed and re-echoed. She received no response. "I'll have to climb the mountain," she said. She shrugged. "Everyone has a mountain to climb at some time during their lives."

Armed with pitons, hook-studded gloves and magnetic boots, Kazan began to scale the ice.

Diamond stood below, watching and silently encouraging.

Kazan was nowhere near the top when she heard the Eye whispering to her, giving her directions. She moved to her left and stretched her body over the ice. The Eye gazed at her from his frozen hiding place.

"Welcome," said the Eye.

"Thank you," Kazan said breathlessly.

"I was blind and now I can see."

"Good for you."

"Good for all of us."

"Instruct me," said Kazan.

"I've heard that somewhere before," replied the Eye.

When the Elder reached his tent he discovered that Lech, already missing one leg, was the worse for drink. He was pawing and kissing two of the women. The women looked up expectantly.

"Kill him," said the Elder.

The women climbed on top of Lech and smothered him. He struggled, but could do nothing to dislodge his assailants. Within a few minutes he was dead.

"What of the other?" enquired one of the women.

"I have decided to let him live," said the Elder quietly. "He is a Navajo. We natives, original inhabitants of the Earth, must stick together.

Who knows? There might come a time when we shall need each other."

The Eye spoke to Kazan, to Diamond and to all the workers and troops at the Source. Without exception, they were impressed with his honesty, integrity and wisdom.

The Eye instructed that he should be cut out of the ice and transported to the North. There, he could be securely and safely maintained by all the assets of the North and would be able to advise the people and point the way to a better future for the world.

Diamond led the applause that greeted this request.

Kazan stood to one side. Though flattered to have been selected by the Eye as one of his agents, a tiny doubt niggled in her brain. She brushed it aside and joined in the general approbation.

Dubroc went West. He was going home. The South didn't appeal, the East was dangerous and he could very well die in the North. He determined to return to the Navajo and the Apache.

He would find Czar and live the life he was born to. One day, perhaps, he would be welcome in the North. That would depend on a lot of things. Not least, the Eye.

Kazan returned to the Goddess pool. The waters

were undisturbed. The sand was soft, smooth and golden. She stood where No-one had faded away. She stooped and picked up a miniature lens disc that was glinting in the sun.

She was struck a savage blow from behind and pitched forward onto the sand, dazed and disorientated. No-one took the tiny disc from her. He would have liked to have dallied with the stricken woman, for he was the part of the Eye that was lustful, but there was no time. He faded into the jungle darkness.

Kazan staggered to her feet. She rubbed the back of her neck, muttered a few oaths and kicked the sand in frustration. Then, this time fully clothed, she plunged into the pool. When she strode out of the water, she felt refreshed. She wondered who it was who had hit her and relieved her of the disc. If they ever met again she'd make sure he was the one who came off second best.

The cave was empty, save for the ice mountain and the Eye within it. The humans from the North were preparing for their journey home.

No-one called out to the Eye, "I have some discs, the important ones. The rest were destroyed by the humans, as you instructed. That was a clever move. To make them think that, by destroying the discs, you have removed all evil from yourself."

The Eye blushed.

"Of course," No-one went on, "we know better. Or, rather, worse." He laughed. "Strange how the woman Kazan thought I was dead. I am No-one. Therefore, I am nothing. I neither live, nor am I deceased."

The Eye was transported in a sealed cryogenic container to a state room in Ludwig's castle. There, for a time, until he decided otherwise, he could be seen by a select few.

The Eye floated in liquid preservative in a square chamber made of the clearest, strongest glass. Some who saw him found it repulsive, others considered him a work of art. Everyone acknowledged his contribution, in the past, to their stability and well-being. They had hope for the future under his guidance.

When seemingly alone, in the thick of night, the Eye, with No-one's help, could project himself as the human forms programmed into the few of Nanos's discs he had chosen to preserve. No-one would be the Eye's messenger, welcoming contestants to the game of life or, more likely, death. Always a part of and a projection of the Eye was the ultimate monstrosity, Death On Two Legs.

The Eye basked in his surroundings and the adulation of the people. Like the Trojans and their wooden horse, these same people had dragged the seed of their destruction into their midst. The Eye gained an ironic satisfaction from that. The Eye's code of rule was announced piece by piece and the people cheered him.

No-one, the Game Keeper, returned to the Dome, ready for the first contestants, the bold and the brave, who would seek, by playing his game, to uncover the still-unsuspected secrets of the Eye.

Death On Two Legs waited patiently in the wings of the world.

One day, the Eye declared to himself and his multiple personalities, Dubroc would return from the West and would prove a worthy opponent. One day, with her small doubts still swimming in her brain, Kazan too might challenge him. Could there be someone else? The Eye doubted it. Doubted there could be more than one man with the vision to attempt to close the Eye.

The beginning of the end was over. The end itself was at hand.

Epilogue

In the time of the Eye, the North flourished. Slowly, very slowly, the Eye encouraged his people to cast envious glances East, South and West. The last World War would bring the Earth to heel and then the Eye could export himself and Death until the skies fell and there came the Apocalypse.

Under the watchful Eye, the North was virtually unpolluted, the combustion engine almost extinct.

Under the Eye, there was little or no domestic crime. Only the army and its police were permitted weapons.

The children of the North received free education. Provided they followed the curriculum set down by the Eye.

The people had plenty of work. There were crops to grow and harvest, rivers to fish and livestock to breed. There were sailing ships and galleys to be built, helicopters to replace, armaments to be manufactured. There was wine, there were women, but there was no song. The North, later the whole world, would be musically silenced. The people thought it a small price to pay for prosperity. Those few who objected were forced to play the game of the Eye and invariably lost.

The Eye bulged with contentment.

Then, one fateful day, Dubroc did come back.

"If thine eye offend thee – pluck it out"
St Matthew